STILL WATERS

PHILOMEL BOOKS
Published by the Penguin Group
Penguin Group (USA) LLC
375 Hudson Street, New York, NY 10014

USA | Canada | UK | Ireland | Australia
New Zealand | India | South Africa | China
penguin.com
A Penguin Random House Company

Library of Congress Cataloging-in-Publication Data
Parsons, Ash.
Still waters / Ash Parsons. pages cm Summary: "High-schooler Jason, who
lives with a drunk, abusive father at home, hopes to earn enough money to
escape with his younger sister, Janie, by being tough at school, but the stakes
grow ever more dangerous and soon even his fists and ability to think on his
feet are not enough to keep his head above water."—Provided by publisher.
[1. Violence—Fiction. 2. Fathers and sons—Fiction. 3. Child abuse—Fiction.
4. Family violence—Fiction.] I. Title. PZ7.1.P37St 2015 [Fic]—dc23
2014020637

Printed in the United States of America.
ISBN 978-0-399-16847-5
10 9 8 7 6 5 4 3 2 1
Edited by Michael Green. Design by Semadar Megged.
Text set in 9.5/16 point Gazzet.
The publisher does not have any control over and does not assume any
responsibility for third-party websites or their content.

STILL WATERS

ASH PARSONS

PHILOMEL BOOKS
An Imprint of Penguin Group (USA)

CHAPTER ONE

Here's what you need to know when you get in a fight: You are going to get hit. It's going to happen. No matter how good you are, no matter how fast you punch or how well you block. Sometimes you just have to get hit.

What's important is how you take it.

I used to get in a lot of fights. Now the only hits I can get in are when the spontaneous fights break out in the boys' bathroom. Some bright spark came up with this lame idea: Go to the bathroom, turn out the lights, and start hitting the first body you find. You can always tell when the fights are happening because guys will come back into class breathing heavily, smiling, and sometimes with red splotches on their cheeks or favoring their stomachs a little. I swear this one guy came back with a handprint on his face.

The teacher didn't notice.

I always ask for a bathroom pass when there's a darkfight going on. Although I sort of think they know it's me when I get in. I land a few hits, and all of a sudden there's the flash of hall light as the door opens and the other guys go back to class.

I still get a few hits in, though. A few really hard hits can be enough.

I like school, and not just because of the bathroom fights. It's quiet. I can sleep, and people usually leave me alone. Every now and then a jock'll bump me in the hall, but I can handle that. And they all know I can fight—something I learned from my dad.

That sounds stupid, like some gauzy film shot in black and white and there's this father teaching little junior how to make a fist.

My dad taught me how to take a punch.

That's pretty important in a fight because, like I said, you're going to get hit and what's important is how you take it.

If my dad lands one and you take it right, showing impact but not crumpling, he'll maybe leave off, even if you take a swing back. He might shove you away. Stop at one.

With him there's no getting out of it, anyway. No putting it off or talking your way out. No running—it'll just be there for you later. He holds a grudge like a knife, blade out, pale fist bowing around the handle, ready to mark you.

It happened last month. I got home and my dad was already there, which was the first sign of trouble. The second sign? Empty bottles clustered on the battered table, an arsenal of tiny missiles.

So when he started in, how he was tired of waiting for me to make some real money, tired of me wasting my time with school, I already knew what was coming. And that there was no way out but through.

ASH PARSONS

Instead of handing over the twenty I keep for emergencies like a good little boy, I told him what a crock it was. That Uncle Sam, not my dad's sorry ass, kept Janie and me fed.

He lunged, shoving me back, fist cocked at his side. I planted my feet and leaned forward while twisting and tensing my abdomen for the strike when it came. Which it did.

It always does.

A lot of guys don't have a clue how to get hit. They aren't prepared, haven't tensed their bodies, aren't ready for the pain. And no kid I've ever fought can throw a good punch anyway—not a real one.

One time I fought this martial arts puke. He thought he was Billy Badass and was talking trash everywhere. I was fine until he brought my sister into it, and since all the other idiots thought we should fight, we did. He fought to prove himself, and I fought so everyone would leave me and Janie alone.

It only took a few hits.

This puke was blocking my test punches, and he looked good doing it. My blocks are short and tight to my body, but his arced in these graceful curves, leaving his body open. It was easy to spot when and where to hit him.

I let it play out. Even though I knew how to get him. Because I kind of wanted him to hit me. It was just one of those days—I knew it would help.

I relaxed. I dropped my arms.

He pressed his entire body forward. His fist drove at my

stomach, turning as he punched. I thought, *Here's something,* because it looked good. I tensed my stomach.

But when it landed I started laughing.

That's probably why everyone except Clay still thinks I'm psycho, because I let him hit me two more times while I just stood there laughing. Because his punches were nothing. They looked great but stopped short—a little thump, like getting hit by a paperback book.

At first I wondered why such a strong-looking punch whiffed. Then I realized that he'd never really hit anything. He was one of those guys you see in strip-mall karate places, punching at the air and pulling their punches when they face each other. His punch was like that. Robbed of its own force. I laughed and hit him so hard he doubled over. I thought about my sister, what he'd said about her, and broke his nose.

Janie wasn't happy with me, so I felt like an idiot, but it was almost worth it because everyone pretty much leaves her alone now.

It would have been totally worth it, except I was suspended for two days. The suspension was nothing, but I ended up staying out the rest of the week because of broken ribs.

They didn't come from the fight.

That was my second year in high school, and no one's fought me since. I kind of miss it. I'm not a bully or anything, but it can feel good to take care of yourself. It can feel good to have some power for a change. But I don't pick fights or mess with people. If they leave me alone, I leave them alone.

There's nothing worse than a bully.

That's what most everyone thinks I am. A lazy bully. A should-be dropout who somehow hasn't gotten a clue. Teachers are afraid of me—ever since eighth grade. Which makes sense. Or they see me sleeping in their classes and act surprised when I actually turn in some homework or do okay on the tests. Although Clay gets most of the credit for the me-doing-homework part.

Teachers don't get that I actually like it at school.

I stay as long as I can, and so I end up walking home every day. Sometimes I go to the old gym and work out, or I walk to my under-the-table job at the building supply store. But mostly I go hang at Clay's house and play video games.

I met Clay at the start of seventh grade. We were all new to the junior high, and there was some stupid hazing getting handed out, but as the new kid in town, Clay wasn't just new to the upperclassmen, he was new to us, too. That made it worse for him. For everyone else, the hazing was lame—shoving in the hall, pushing runts into lockers. Pack dynamics.

I already had a bit of a reputation, and I had begun to cement it on that first day. Punched an eighth-grader in the stomach when he got in my face, doubled him over, and walked away before a teacher saw. It was enough that un- less I flirted with the wrong girl, I was pretty much going to be left alone.

The day I first met Clay, I was in a good mood. Having a pretty great day.

Not Clay, though. He was trying to get to class and the eighth- and ninth-grade pre-dropouts were blocking his way. They wouldn't let him through to the hall. Stupid, proud fool that he was, Clay would not back down, turn, and go the long way around. And he wouldn't throw a punch, either, but I didn't know that at first.

Let me tell you, Clay shines like a new penny in a grate, and that is not a good thing.

Anyone could tell Clay had a future. That he had someone at home who cared about him. But he didn't fit in with the preps; his clothes weren't that nice. He didn't fit in with any of the groups. That was enough for most people.

That was enough for me, too. Just in a different way. I walked right up behind him. Like I needed to get through the door, too.

It went about like you'd expect.

When the leader finally stepped to me and threw a punch, you could see it coming a mile away. I slapped it aside, pivoted, and drilled a fist into his solar plexus. Gasping, eyes big like he was trying to catch his slammed-out breath through them, the bully stumbled aside. The others backed up, except for one who lunged at Clay. He chunked a lousy punch at Clay's face, mostly hitting his chin. Clay fell down and didn't get up. Just put his hands up, saying, "I won't fight you."

The second guy blinked at him, like he was trying to do fractions in his head. Then he realized his friends were moving away, and I wasn't.

He left with the rest of them.

Clay stood up, and I handed him his bag. We walked through the doors. Once we were on the other side and down the hall a ways, Clay stopped and glared at me.

"I suppose you think that makes us friends now?"

I will never forget it. A busted lip, blood dripping on his new shirt. And he was pissed off at me.

I couldn't help it. My lips twitched up, and it felt like a bit in my mouth, in a good way, like something was taking hold, steering the smile onto my face. Sticking it there. Nailing it in place. Something you couldn't even think about. Something full and inflating—filling up the empty places and under it, a laugh.

I worked really hard not to laugh. I didn't want him to think I was laughing at him.

He had that look in his eyes. Like he knew he was being stupid but was still too fired-up-proud to care. Like it was at war in him. A battle for his expression.

"Well, yeah?" I made it a question. Trying not to laugh. Because I liked this kid. Skinny and on the short side, and absolutely disregarding that fact in the face of those bullies, not backing down, even if he wouldn't fight.

How the hell do you not want to be that guy's friend?

He glared at me, but the smile was sliding in, and the laughter, too. And that's when we became friends.

To almost everyone else, Clay is practically invisible. He's still a little short, but he slouches so it's hard to tell how much. He's rail thin with shaggy hair, and he's got this narrow face. It makes him look younger than he is.

But he's dead-loyal and smart. Like I said, he's one of those weird ones that you can tell has a future, and yet somehow doesn't count in the here and now. Like someone just randomly decides this. And he has to wear that until he graduates. Apart from Nico and Spud, he's the only one

I hang out with at school. And since he doesn't count, it doesn't affect my reputation in a single solitary way that I have a real friend. People think I'm psycho. That's fine with me.

When it gets near enough to dinnertime, I usually head home, from Clay's house or from work. Because you don't want to get home after my father, or he'll notice you: ice-blue eyes tracking as you walk in, his thick, mortuary-pale fists clenched.

During the day he sleeps but is gone by the time school gets out, heading to meet his buddies. They'll go work out at a run-down gym that looks like a prison yard moved indoors and is filled with meaty juice-heads just like him.

He spends the rest of his time at the strip joint out near the airport. And I can't catalog his activities there, except I know he runs book on any fights or games going on and loans money to people stupid or desperate enough to take it. And of course sells drugs, which is how he got collared last time.

He gets the girls to bring free drinks and give free dances, his sorry racket enough to make him sugar daddy for life to the spent girls who work there.

But he's a low-level crook, ousted when it gets to the most lucrative time—night—having to hand over all but a small percent of the take to the next guy. All of which means when he heads home he's been drinking, is pissed off, and you do not want him to notice you.

So that's how it all started. Like any other day, I was walking home from Clay's, heading deep into crap land.

ASH PARSONS

Trying to ignore the screaming little kids. Trying not to think.

Which is pretty easy, actually, when you're walking into the repetitive nothing of government housing: all redbrick and flaking paint, and iron railings corralling concrete porch steps.

A long, nothing walk, long because Lincoln Green is kind of big, the whole thing dumped off this five-lane drag. The central road into Lincoln Green, named after a civil rights leader, naturally, spirals around these semi-circular pods, each facing the road with the single-level duplex units ringing the two-level townhouse units in the middle—which is where we live. I guess the single levels are on the perimeter so that their view won't get blocked. Because everyone loves to stare at traffic or a concrete drainage ditch deep enough to float a ski boat if there was ever enough rain.

Yeah, swift thinking. It gets better. Each little semicircular pod u-bends toward the street and each other, arcing around a pathetic patch of grass and dirt. Like the patch is this luxury that deserves spotlighting. Like the curve is beautiful. It's supposed to feel all spacious: *You're not trapped at all, see? You've got this* patch. *Choked with weeds and sun-bleached toys, but it's there.*

Behind the buildings is a little access road with parking spaces—so there's this double rainbow of crap: scrub yard, old AC units, laundry, cars, salvaged grills, sofas and plastic lawn chairs, busted window screens, cinder blocks, and people. Everywhere.

The best part of the crap-rainbows design is it actually

amplifies noise. Late-night fights, people screaming on their porches, girls shrieking and pulling hair, kids crying, men and women throwing down—you can hear it all.

Which is how I heard the thrum of the car engine, even over the screaming kids.

The car pulled up behind me, the crunch of tires on gravel announcing the slither to the edge. I moved onto the scrub and waited for it to prowl by.

"Hey! Jason!"

I turned and saw Michael Springfield shouting out the window of his vintage Mustang.

You wouldn't normally find guys like Michael or cars like that within one hundred yards of public housing. Prom King Jock—sandy hair flopping into dark eyes, like a movie star. Girls thought so, too, but Cyndra was his steady girlfriend.

She wasn't the obvious choice for the job, until you looked at her. She wasn't a cheerleader, she wasn't going to be in the homecoming court, she wouldn't give a damn about painting banners or shaking pom-poms. There was an edge to her, beautiful and cold, like a dagger made of ice.

She sat in the passenger seat, watching me with emerald eyes and a scythe-curved smile. The fingers of one hand toyed with the large diamond stud in her ear.

My school is kind of bizarre—it's like two schools in one: the public school and the private one. And most of the Lincoln Green kids get bused to another school—don't ask me how they pulled that. Some politician loved his alma mater too much to see it overrun, I guess. Anyway, the rich kids are all on the "advanced" diploma track—so they're usually not in the regular classes with the rest of us.

Except every now and then the regular classes are full to bursting, and so they'll pull some of us and put us in advanced curriculum classes. I've been in Advanced Lit and Honors History, and one time Botany—which, believe me, they don't push to regular diploma kids. I guess they're afraid all of us regular trackers'll grow weed in the hydroponic wheel or something. Clay wouldn't even let me joke about that. It's funny what gets under his skin sometimes.

This year it was an AP History class they put me in. They said I didn't have to take it for college credit, but that I should try anyway.

Which was maybe why Michael Springfield was talking to me, because I sit in front of him in class.

"Jason," he repeated. He gunned the engine as he popped it out of gear.

I didn't speak. Just waited.

Michael stopped smiling. I guess he isn't used to silence when he speaks to a nobody. If he stayed at the curb much longer, snot-nosed kids would steal his hubcaps while he idled.

Cyndra curled forward, clasping her hands between her knees. She has to know what that move does to her breasts.

"Listen," Michael said. "I want to talk with you about something. I'll pay you for your time." He sounded like a bad movie and looked like one as he laid a fifty on the dashboard. "Cyndra—"

She tilted her cleavage toward her boyfriend.

"Get in the back, baby. Jason's going to ride up front."

She popped on all fours and slowly climbed between the seats.

I pulled a cigarette out of my coat. I know, I know, smoking is lame. But it's not like I'm going to be an old man on a ventilator. I'll be dead long before then.

I ignored the fifty and peered in through the open window.

"What time is it?"

"Six o'clock," Cyndra said.

I let the cigarette dangle from my lip and pulled a hand through my hair. Janie won't cut it as often as I'd like—she says it looks tough longer. Personally, I think the last time I asked her to cut it she just went through the motions, but if that makes her happy, I guess I don't care.

The Mustang idled like a predatory cat, purring. I ran the time in my head. If it was only six, then there was a little more than an hour, probably, before my dad would make it home. Time to burn. Besides, I was curious. And I thought of what I could get with that fifty.

Cyndra might give me a few more glimpses, too.

I could feel the eyes of the neighborhood on me. To his credit, Michael didn't rush me.

"Fine." I took a deep drag before letting the smoke fume slowly out of my mouth. "But you bring me back here by seven fifteen at the latest. No games, no waiting."

Cyndra laughed. "What? Don't tell me you have a curfew."

What an idiot.

It must have showed on my face, because she stopped smiling and for the first time looked away.

"Sure, no problem." Michael leaned across the car and popped the door open.

I climbed in. The bucket seat molded to my back. The fifty slid into my pocket like it belonged there.

Michael peeled out, leaving twin black streaks behind us. I thought he was going to drive like an ass, but once he had his bucking bronco moment he settled down and drove cautiously.

I relaxed a little.

The Mustang carried us into the hills.

CHAPTER TWO

amn, baby. I can't concentrate," Michael said as he drove higher into the subdivisions that surround the city. He smiled into the rearview mirror.

"Well, hell." Cyndra groaned, pushing her knees into the back of my seat. "It's so boring. Don't you talk?"

I ignored her. She was one of those girls used to attention. If you're male and have a pulse, then she *expects* you to be into her. Assumes that you will be, accepts it as tribute.

Her hand brushed my earlobe. "Gimme one of those."

Even though I knew what she was doing, I shivered as the warmth of her hand hovered over my ear. My fingers fumbled for a cigarette.

"Thanks, Slick." She gave my ear a tweak.

"Don't touch me."

"Whooo," Cyndra replied, fake scared.

"What do you want?" I asked Michael as he eased past a gatehouse. A security guard waved as we passed.

"Let's just wait till we get there," he said.

"Where?"

"My house."

Cyndra's hand hovered by my ear again. "Light this for me? I won't bite. I promise."

I didn't want to twist to face her, so I flipped the visor down and stared at her in the small mirror.

"Damn, X-ray Eyes! Stop glaring." She licked her teeth. "You know, you have really blue eyes?" She made it sound like a question. "They're, like, startling. Like a dog's. You know—a wolf-y dog." Cyndra's fingers hovered by my hair.

I jerked my head away. "Don't."

She pouted. "Touchy." She waved the cigarette over my shoulder.

I lit it. The filter tasted like her lip gloss, like berries. I handed the cigarette back. Cyndra took a drag.

"Mmmm." She sighed.

She wanted me to look at her again, so I flipped the visor up.

The car prowled along the top of a baby mountain. I knew the area by reputation—rich people lived here, one mansion after another. I tried not to look at the houses. I tried not to think about things that aren't mine and never will be.

Instead, I thought about my little sister. Imagined her in our room at home, waiting for me to get there. Pretending like she's not worried when I walk in. Succeeding in not saying anything about me cutting it close for all of five seconds. Like she's going to tell me something I don't already know.

The car zigzagged along the ridgeline. Houses, huge

and commanding impressive views of the city below, competed with each other to be bigger.

"Here we are." Michael whipped a smile at me and turned into a winding driveway that led to a mansion. It looked like it had to have at least fifty rooms.

Janie and I share a room. I put up a piece of Sheetrock in between our beds, so we each would get a little privacy. But there's no hiding the fact that it's one room. I didn't even want to think about how spacious and private Michael's room was.

When we got out, Cyndra flicked her cigarette into the bushes. Mine was already rolling down the driveway.

She came and stood too close, sizing me up.

She smiled at Michael, so I couldn't tell if she really liked what she saw or if she was playing a role for him.

"C'mon," Michael said. He shielded a keypad with his body and punched a few buttons. The keypad blipped, and the door opened with a slight suction smack.

Inside, it was freezing, like a museum or a theater. We passed rooms that looked like advertisements in a magazine and ended up downstairs at a bar or den or something.

I tried not to touch anything.

"Sit down." Michael gestured to a large sofa.

"What do you want?"

Cyndra padded in with three sparkling glasses on a tray. When she walked by I could smell the rum mixed in with the Coke.

"Help yourself," she said, leaning over Michael.

He stared down her shirt, but did it cold, like he was checking an investment.

I took the drink and leaned against the wall. "So?"

Michael took a huge swig. "I need a favor. It's nothing, really, not for a guy like you. It would only be for a couple of weeks."

I waited.

Michael drained his glass.

"It's like this." He talked through his teeth like the alcohol had a bite. "I need you to hang around with my crew."

He made it sound like it was some big crime syndicate or something. I pictured his jock and prep friends, imagined them pissing themselves if they ever stood in front of my dad and his juice-head buddies.

Michael gave his glass a little shake. Cyndra left to refill.

"Why?" I asked.

He scrubbed his head and beamed a lopsided grin.

"It's stupid," he said. "Does it matter? All you need to know is I'll pay you. You'll sit with my crew in classes, if you can, join us at break and at lunch, and show up out at a few places where we hang."

"Why?"

Cyndra brushed past me again. She curled next to Michael on the sofa.

"Think of it like a bet," she said.

"Yeah, like that." Michael smiled at her. "Like I made a bet with some people. About my connections. About things I could deliver or supply."

I didn't think I let anything show on my face, but Michael stopped talking.

I put my drink on the table. "I don't deal. I can't get you anything."

Which wasn't really true.

Michael held up his hands. "I don't want anything. I mean, I can get whatever I want. I mean, just listen. Sit down, okay?"

I stayed leaning against the wall and waited.

"You don't have to do anything. It's what people *think* you can do." Michael smiled. "It's the school and the grapevine, right? The gossip. You're practically a contract killer, you know? There are all these stories. Remember that fight? The one with the black belt?"

What a stupid question.

"He wasn't a black belt."

"Whatever. The martial arts guy, right? Well, it's like that. You laughed, and that's part of it. There's a rumor you brought a gun to school. That locker check? That was all because of you. Where you live. People think you deal or your parents are in prison or something. You don't hang out, you don't talk, and in eighth grade you punched that teacher."

I guess when you're a rich man's son, you feel like you can say anything. Maybe you can. Maybe Daddy can get you all lawyered up if you go too far.

Michael held out a hand toward me. "See? Look at you! I say all this crap, and who knows what's true and what isn't, and you don't say a word. You're golden, man."

I shrugged. What's the point of explaining? Or the truth? People believe what they want to believe. You can't fight it.

Cyndra frowned at me. She twisted a piece of auburn hair around a finger and yanked it. "What's true?"

I thought about it. The laughing during the fight everyone knew about—although there were alternate versions where I spat on the idiot or had to be pulled off him.

I guess there was enough truth to all of it. Enough to make simpleminded people in need of a distraction happy. There are drug busts in Lincoln Green all the time. My dad has been to jail.

And when I punched that teacher he deserved it. And I went to juvie.

Cyndra yanked at her hair again. "Well?"

I felt my eyes go tight. My fingers curled, and I took a step forward. "Yeah, it's all true. Does that make you happy?"

"Easy, easy, killer." Michael walked over to me. He laid a hand on my shoulder. I slapped it away.

"Don't touch me."

"Sorry." Michael looked at me, and there was something strange in his eyes. Almost like he didn't know what to do. Like he, Mr. Movie Star, was uncertain, or wanted something, or was somehow . . . hungry.

It was a stupid thought. The look was gone in an instant.

"Well, what do you say?" Michael asked.

"You still haven't told me why."

"For some specific people and occasions, I need your presence to project a certain image of *me*. That we're friends."

"And?"

"All you need to know is I'll pay you fifty dollars a day. That's just for the school stuff. Extras will be another fifty, per occasion."

"That's a lot of your dad's money you're prepared to spend," I said.

His eyes narrowed as threads of muscle noose-tightened around them. His voice was low and intense. "Well, it's a good thing he gives me so much, isn't it? About the only thing he's ever done for me, in fact." He leaned back, but it wasn't relaxed, more like a performance, pretending to be casual. "Something you should know about me, Jason. There are only two things that matter: what I want. And what I have to do to get it."

I looked down. I tried not to think of the coffee can at home and its petty roll of cash. Tried not to think of The Plan—my escape with Janie—and how far we were from getting there. I tried not to think about hauling product around the building supply. I tried not to think of screaming and fists and having to sleep outside.

"All you have to do is hang around some. Try to act like you like us. You don't even have to talk. Just hang around."

I knew there was more to it. There had to be.

But I figured I could handle it. I thought maybe my part would be just what Michael described. Maybe it was some foolish jock-game, and I'd be the punch line. They'd pick a fight with me or want me to fight someone else. I thought: *good.*

And I thought that would be all it was.

"Fine." I glanced at the clock. "A couple of things, though."

"Okay, what?"

"I may have to turn down some of your extracurricular

activities. I may not make it to school every day, and you won't always know when that is. I won't stick around if there's trouble, and I won't get caught with anything illegal. In fact, if we're breaking any laws, you better clear it with me first, and the pay rate will be a hell of a lot higher."

Juvenile hall was a cakewalk, but I couldn't leave Janie again. And I couldn't forget The Plan.

"That's it?" Michael's eyes were bright. He was all but rubbing his hands together.

"Yeah. And I can quit anytime, no refunds."

"Sure, but you won't want to quit. Easy money, baby. But I don't pay you days you don't show up."

"Fine."

We shook hands. I was afraid for a moment the fool would try to throw some sequence-shake into the number. You know, some kind of I'm-cool-you're-cool shake. But I guess he had more sense.

In the car on the way back to Lincoln Green, I asked him why he had to take me to his house to tell me about all of it.

"Privacy." He pulled over to the curb. The kids were still screaming. The weight set in front of our unit was unoccupied. "And so you could see that I'm not a bad guy."

I wanted to ask him how his house was supposed to show me that.

Then I looked around and saw where I lived.

CHAPTER THREE

anie thought I should do it. It took her a while to get there, though. She just has to talk stuff out. And if it keeps her from gnawing on her cuticles for five seconds, I guess it's worth it.

So after about thirty minutes of us talking it out—otherwise known as me listening to her worry—she said okay.

She agreed there was more to it than I was being told, but she said, "You're right, probably not much more."

And we both knew the money was too good to walk away from.

She told me about something she'd read online at her school library. About this stupid pact that a bunch of girls made in some school, some junior high school, get that, that they would all get pregnant. Janie said it was proof that kids will get into stupid-ass stuff just to have some event going on. A way to pass the time. She said that Michael's "crew" had money to burn, so they needed something else.

As for us, we needed the money.

"Maybe it could be good for you," Janie said, but it was more like a question. A hope. "You should hang out with people more."

Janie and Clay both bang this drum often. The give-people-a-chance thing. Which makes me want to scream.

It's not like I'm completely antisocial. I just know the truth: Most people suck.

"You're going to have to think on your feet," Janie said. "I bet once you're not so scary, those cheer girls will climb all over you."

"Fringe benefit."

She punched my arm. For a fourteen-year-old girl, she can really wallop. She brought her finger to her teeth and started gnawing off slivers of skin. "Just keep your head down and your powder dry."

"Live to fight another day," I finished.

"Right. You have to watch out for the girls as much as the boys, you know."

As if I didn't.

She scooted around the drywall partition to her side of the room. I heard the soft creak of her bed as she lay down. We quit talking. No doubt she was reading a library book, one of those happily-ever-after stories with a couple on the cover gazing at each other intensely. The kind where any problem's solved by the last page.

Our two-story unit is in the center of Lincoln Green. One of the oldest buildings here. But since it's one of two stories, Janie and I pretty much have the upstairs to ourselves, at least at night. My dad only comes to the second bedroom upstairs to sleep when the night has passed and gray light tinges the horizon.

I stared at the permanent moisture stain on the ceiling. Sometimes I see different shapes in it—a witch's profile or something.

Tonight it just looked like a stain.

I thought about Michael's cold house and the plush furniture. Imagined Michael and Cyndra cuddled in his room, a king-sized bed for a kid with a vintage Mustang. I imagined me in that bed with Cyndra. Her hot breath in my ear and my hand down her shirt or gliding up her impossibly long leg.

I flipped on my side and tried to think of something else.

The coffee can secretly stashed away—filled with a roll of bills. I imagined the roll doubling in size and tripling in value. The future and some city where Janie and I would live. Me with a job, acting as her legal guardian. Her in school and us living in some other government crap land, but not here. Not with him.

The Plan.

Repetitive clangs of the weight bench and grating laughter sounded outside. Music blared through the unit.

"Keep your head down and your powder dry. Live to fight another day," I whispered. The mantra Janie came up with when I came back from juvie. She read it in one of her books, and neither of us understood about old-fashioned guns and gunpowder. We just liked the sound of it. Then I stopped talking to most people and started living it. I liked the idea of living to fight another day.

I imagined bloodied knuckles and the wet crunch of his breaking nose. Bending an arm behind his back until it dislocated the shoulder. A kitchen knife twisting into his muscled gut. I fantasized about buying a gun and holding it to his head while he slept. Red mist and blood pooling out of his ear like evil syrup.

The gun in my hand after. Still in my hand. Heavy and promise-filled.

After a while, I slept.

The next morning, Janie and I got dressed and out of the house. Some mornings, one of Dad's buddies might still be awake or barely conscious, watching infomercials. Today the unit was silent.

I waited with Janie for her bus.

"Remember, you're supposed to act like you're with them, so that means eye contact, Jason. Probably talking some or at least making listening sounds," she said.

"Mmmm."

"Very funny."

"I can handle it. Chill."

Janie had to stretch to push my hair out of my eyes. She smiled. "I almost feel sorry for those cheer girls. They don't have a chance."

All I can say is Janie lives in a dreamworld sometimes. But if it makes her happy to imagine me covered in girls, well, I can go along with that. It's not a bad thing to imagine, as far as things go.

After getting her on the bus to junior high, I walked to Clay's. On the way I thought about what to say to him. How to explain the job with Michael. Which felt like a betrayal, even if Clay would understand.

I got to the slumpy, concrete steps and jumped up them. Knocked softly, because maybe Clay's mom was already home sleeping.

"Okay," Clay said from inside.

After a minute the door opened. Clay nodded, slapped a quick shake, and then he was out the door, locking it and turning around in a fluid motion that was still somehow the opposite of smooth.

"Jason, you've got to read this book," he started, before I could even take a breath. "I think you'd like it. It's about survival, and it's about long odds and justice and how do you know the right thing. And how sometimes you know the right thing, but you can't do it. And there are zombies, and that's awesome. Okay, so they're not really zombies, but they really should be, because anything that's trying to eat you and is humanoid, that's a zombie, right?"

But he wasn't asking a question—he was inhaling.

"Sounds great," I said before he could continue. "I need to talk to you."

He shot a glance at me, and his steps shortened.

"I took a job," I said. "It's a secret, though."

Clay started shaking his head. The words gathered behind his teeth.

"It's not drugs," I said. "It's for Michael Springfield." I explained about all of it. Michael picking me up and taking me to his house, Cyndra's teasing, the thin-ass explanation that it was just to convey an impression to someone.

Clay wasn't walking anymore. I stopped moving, too. Every now and then a car whooshed by us.

"Fifty dollars *a day*?" he exclaimed. Disbelief that was only for the reality that Michael, or anyone, had that kind of money. "That's two hundred and fifty dollars a week, and that's only if you work during school!"

"I know."

Clay started walking again, slowly. "That's insane. He's got more money than sense."

I nodded.

"What does Jane think?"

My shoulders bounced, shifting the duffle strung across my back. "Take the money and run."

"Huh." The sound was of agreement. "Well, it's not like you can't handle yourself in a fight. If it comes to that."

It had been my first thought, as well. That Michael wanted me to fight someone.

We arrived at the crosswalk to the school. Cars were already filling the student parking lot. Somewhere over there was Michael's cherry Mustang and his sexy girlfriend. Along with the rest of his "crew" and whatever he was really going to be paying me for.

My shoulders bunched tight.

The light changed, but we didn't cross. Clay thumped my upper arm.

"Well, go make some money, Champ." Like I was a prizefighter. "If anyone deserves easy money, it's you."

Clay stepped forward to the curb.

I fought the urge to pull him back, like he would step out into traffic and get flattened.

"I guess I'll see you in the gym after school," he said. "Unless you get another assignment. In which case, go for it." Clay stepped into the street, long slouchy steps. He never looks both ways. Just trusts that the cars will all stop for him.

I slid a step ahead of him.

Once across the street, Clay slowed down. Gave me a funny look when I waited for him. "Go on, you've got a job to do. They're probably waiting already." He nodded at the student parking lot.

"Sorry." The word didn't feel big enough.

"I can take care of myself." Grit in his words. Like he knew and resented that I didn't think he could.

"Fine." I started taking longer strides. Clay paced me for a final line.

"Try not to flatten them with your charm," he said. "And remember, use protection. Cheerleaders have STDs, too."

"Asshat."

"Dick." He thumped my back like a blessing, and I walked faster, leaving him behind.

Instead of heading straight to the cafeteria, I cut into the student parking lot.

Someone shouted my name.

"Over here!" Michael and his friends were lounging around showroom-ready cars. "Gotcha breakfast." Michael held up a bag from Burger King.

If I'm supposed to be Michael's new best friend, I'd lean against his car. Girls giggled as I pushed through the crowd. Some guys glared at me. I wondered who was in on whatever game this was.

Who was the show for?

"Here you go, man." Michael handed me the bag and a drink.

"Thanks." We slapped a handshake like old friends.

I opened up the breakfast sandwich. It looked good, but I wasn't so stupid that I didn't suspect anything. I flipped through its layers and didn't see anything weird, so I took a bite.

It tasted fine. Little conversations started around me. Heavy music blared through car windows. Some of the girls kept glancing at me and smiling, and since I don't have Janie's delusions, I knew something was up. Cyndra caught my eyes and shook her head slightly.

That's when I knew for sure that there was something wrong with the food. Or the drink.

I finished them both.

When I'd swallowed the last gulp, the hyperjocks started whooping and pounding each other's shoulders. Some of them reared back, curling their hands in front of their mouths like they'd just witnessed something so funny they had to contort their bodies or they would fall to pieces. Their girls were less animated, hugging their books and giggling.

"Pay up," Michael said. He held his hand out to Dwight, one of the football studs.

"Screw that." But Dwight was laughing and digging in his wallet. He handed over a couple of twenties. A few other jocks pressed bills into Michael's hand. I'd just earned my pay for a few days.

"Hey, man, welcome to the gang, right? No hard feelings?"

Dwight held out a hand, making wet snorting sounds that reverberated in his head. He coughed the loogie into his mouth and made a face. "Anyone have a cup? I don't want to spit this monster on the ground in front of the girls."

The jocks started pounding each other again.

I handed the Burger King cup to Dwight. "Here, use this one." I waited until everyone was quiet. "Again."

The laughing stopped. Everyone held still as if a bee hovered nearby and they were all allergic.

Dwight leaned forward and let the glob of phlegm plop onto the dregs of ice in the cup.

I wanted to fight him. Not because I cared about the first loogie in the drink, but because it looked like he actually would fight me. He wouldn't be able to back down in front of all his friends.

But then I imagined the coffee can, and I thought of the fifty I'd already earned.

Dwight handed the cup back to me. I hawked and spat into it, snapped the lid back on the cup. "I wonder what we're having for lunch. You buy lunch, don't you, Dwight?"

The whole crew erupted at the look on Dwight's face.

"Burn!" Michael yelled. The jocks howled, turning on a dime from ridiculing me to laughing at their buddy. Several slapped hands with Michael.

"I told you he was cool." Michael looped an arm over my shoulder and shook me gently. "My man. Psycho Iceman."

I fought off the urge to push his arm away.

Some of the gang slapped hands with me and told me their names, as if I didn't know already. Like I was a transfer student they were meeting for the first time instead of someone they'd been ignoring all along.

More cars began to fill the lot. Stereos warred with each other.

"Sorry about that," Michael said softly when there was a lull and it seemed no one else was paying attention. "That's just, like, hazing—now you're in. You're cool."

"Whatever."

Cyndra picked up her books.

"Time to go to class," she said. "I think Jason should walk with me, since we're on the same hall."

"Sure, Cyn. We hang in the courtyard during break," Michael told me. He kissed Cyndra and grabbed her ass.

Cyndra walked away. She was moving fast, sending her red-gold hair swinging.

When we were near her classroom, she stopped and whirled. "You knew, didn't you? I thought you didn't suspect, but when you saw me shake my head, you knew."

I shrugged.

"I would never have done that," Cyndra said, and at first I thought she meant that she would never have played their stupid trick on me. "I would never have taken that."

I felt my lip curl. "Well, I'm guessing a little girl like you doesn't have to take much of anything."

She moved closer, suddenly smiling all sweet and cute, like I was Michael instead of me. "Is that what you think?"

I took a step back. "It's what I know, princess."

She was smiling before I called her princess. When I finished, you could strike sparks off her eyes.

She stomped into class. I smiled at the way her hips whipped from side to side. She sat down near two preppy girls I'd seen hovering in the parking lot that morning. They cut me glances and whispered.

I leaned in through the open doorway. "Hey, Cyndra!" I called across the room.

The class went silent. Eyes shifted to me. Even the teacher stopped puttering at her desk.

"See you at break," I said.

If looks could kill, I'd be in a drawer with a tag on my toe.

CHAPTER FOUR

sually I'd meet Clay in the hall outside the lunchroom for break. I showed up in the courtyard instead, ignored Cyndra, and made sure Dwight saw me still carrying the Burger King cup. Let him think about the putrid contents and his lunch.

But break was a nonevent. I made listening noises, looked at people, and saw what you'd expect to see: posing and stupid pranks and a bunch of bored kids. Mostly I just stood near Michael and acted like it was the most natural thing in the world for me to be transported from nobody to inner-circle darling.

Some of the girls kept walking past. I didn't mind watching them walk by, but didn't think they were doing anything special until Cyndra cussed.

"Told you," Michael said.

"Shut up." Cyndra hit him lightly, like he was being funny.

"I give it three days. No, two days." Michael glanced at me, as if expecting me to ask what the hell he was talking about.

The hip-shot parade went by again. My eyes followed.

Michael laughed, almost a high giggle. "Oh yeah. Two days for sure. Iceman."

"Only if they can get past the lasers." Cyndra widened her eyes at me. "But I guess that's part of the allure."

I was suddenly tired. I couldn't wait for break to be over so I could go to shop class. Couldn't wait to get my hands on a hammer and just start hitting things. I thought about getting up and walking away.

I thought of the coffee can and the pathetic roll of bills. A way out of this crap.

Took a deep breath.

"Michael," Cyndra's voice was deep, pitched to just above husky. "We've *got* to do something about his clothes."

"Not necessary," Michael replied.

"It's part of the whole deal," Cyndra said. "The look of it, right?"

I didn't have to glance down to see why she disapproved. I usually wore a T-shirt, washed out at best or stained at worst, and some lousy cheap jeans. If it was cold, I'd wear a Goodwill army jacket.

I glanced around at the crisp shirts and label jeans. Cyndra was right. I fit in like snot on a tiara.

I took another slow breath and watched the parade go by again. This was the longest break in Mercer High's history. I wondered if Clay was hanging out in the library.

"If you think it's important, then you take care of it," Michael said.

Cyndra clapped her hands lightly. "Perfect! We'll go to the mall."

I frowned at her. "I get paid for extra time."

"What does that make you?" Cyndra asked. Like I was supposed to feel trashy or something.

"An employee."

I reminded myself that I didn't care what they thought. "Besides," I added, "if you're short of cash, make another bet. I'll eat whatever crap you feed me."

I stood up before the bell went off. Was down the hall before it stopped.

The hammer didn't help. Not when it slammed the nail, not when I banged the joints of a drawer. Nails and boards don't grunt when you hit them.

I asked Mr. Hernandez for a bathroom pass.

Inside the bathroom there were a couple of freshmen trying to plug up the sinks. My face must have shown how I felt, because they dashed out of there.

I flipped the switch off and leaned against the wall. My hands curled, waiting for someone to come in.

Usually I just like to get in a few hits—to feel a solid whump or even a glancing blow because you've misjudged in the dark. Usually it's about blowing off some steam or taking something back.

Today it was those things and something more.

The door cracked open. It closed again immediately.

I pushed away from the wall and went back out into the hall.

A freshman was hotfooting it away from the bathrooms. He glanced around and got a little smile on his stupid face, like he'd been so smart. Like he'd made the right call.

Back in class I banged a few more things with the hammer. It was like there was a rumbling volcano in my chest.

Maybe I could get in a fight at lunch.

In Speech I put my head down on my desk. The coach who teaches it couldn't care less about anyone sleeping.

I tried to figure out why I was so pissed off. This money would get us there. Then it was just a matter of hanging on to it until my birthday. Then poof. We'd be gone. And then there was the second part of The Plan—the one Janie didn't know about. The part where she's grown and I come back.

Live to fight another day.

I thought about the money. Cyndra's mind games. The Mustang and the castle-house, and a group of kids who lay twenty-dollar bets before their day even begins.

And me. Going through their scraps. Trying to avoid my dad and his corpse-pale fists. Watching with one eye for him, always there. Watching for that look. The grooves that arc over his mouth when he comes after you, upper lip curled onto his teeth. The twin lines blooming into the skin between his lips and nose, slashing down at his barred teeth—like his teeth are fangs. Like the skin will split to let them out.

I tried to sleep.

At lunch Clay was already sitting with Nico and Spud at our usual table. I stopped there, thinking I'd just check in quickly. But Clay's eyes slid past me as Michael walked up.

"Come on, Iceman," Michael said.

In the food line people swirled around us but didn't push or complain.

"What's with the Iceman bit?"

Michael smiled. "Look, everyone loves a nickname, right? Some of the gang had started calling you Ice because of your eyes and because you're cold, man. It's good. And this morning you played it true. So you're the Iceman."

We started walking again.

"What's your nick?"

Michael shrugged. "It's stupid. Most people don't use it anymore." He looked down and away.

"It's not Pretty Boy, is it?" I asked. The corner of my lips tugged up.

Michael laughed for our audience, then clapped me on the shoulder. I stepped away. Michael just laughed again. People in line around us turned and smiled. It was like there was a gushy ooze of hero worship going on. The girls sighed, and the guys nodded like they were in on a joke with the main man.

"It's Face."

I grabbed the tray the lunch lady shoved at me. "Well, that fits, I guess."

"It's stupid. Came up in junior high. Some kid saw episodes of *The A-Team* on the retro channel and thought Face was a great nick for me."

"Well, it could be worse," I said. Michael steered us past the cashier and propelled us to the outdoor tables.

"Yeah?"

"It could be Ass-Face."

Michael laughed, for real this time, and I felt that slight moment—that I'd made him laugh. Mr. Popular Super Jock. Man, he sure had some charisma to make everyone want to be part of his cool flame.

"Listen"—Michael leaned in—"not for nothing, but I'm not paying you to hang out with your loser friends."

"Actually you haven't paid me anything yet," I replied. Michael grinned and stepped off like he hadn't said anything.

We were the first ones to get outside. Michael popped open his backpack and pulled out a big container with noodles in it.

I put the Burger King cup on the table and started wolfing my chiquitos.

"What's Cyndra's nickname?" I asked around a mouthful.

"Cyn. As in a body for. It's not too original."

"Still works."

Dwight and some of the other jocks pushed through the swinging door and clomped down the ramp. When they reached the tables they slammed their trays down and straddled the benches like they were too manly to be able to throw both legs over.

Except for Dwight, who stood at my back like he was waiting for me to move.

I ignored him.

"That's my spot," he said.

"Not from where I'm sitting, asshole," I said.

Michael and the other jocks laughed. Dwight stood for

a moment longer, and I understood why he was the one who'd spit in my drink that morning. Because he didn't want me there. Who knew if the others felt that way or not, but Dwight hated it. I was in his spot.

He walked around to sit across from us, making a cheer-girl move so he could at least get in front of Michael's face, if not at his right hand.

He glared at me. I made sure he saw me look at the Burger King cup, and then I smiled and glanced at his nachos.

He took it as a dare and started eating, shoving food into his mouth. When he was five nachos in, I held up a hand.

"Relax, man. Relax. It's empty." I showed him the empty cup. Some of the other jocks started laughing.

"Yeah, fool. It's empty."

"Iceman already took care of it, see?"

They started making hawking noises.

Dwight shook his head. He studied his nachos. "Screw that. I watched them put the cheese on. I've watched it the whole time."

"You know Big Mack?" I asked, pretending to be surprised. The lunchroom worker was part cafeteria worker, part security, all legend. "Did you know that he was in county lockup with my dad?"

A total lie. And if they thought for two seconds, they'd realize it, since Big Mack was a school employee.

But they didn't think. And given what they assumed about me, of course they went for it.

Still Waters

39

A few of the jocks started repeating, "In county with his *dad*," like it was the best part.

Dwight had to choose between looking pissed and playing along. You could see he was pissed. But he forced himself to laugh and ate six more nachos.

"Tasty," he said.

His friends howled.

"No hard feelings, right?" I said. Throwing it back at him, just like he'd done in the parking lot.

Michael lifted his chin at Dwight. "Good play, man." Like the team had just made a touchdown or something. Dwight relaxed.

That's the kind of power Michael had. Three little words and the whole thing was over, because Michael said *good boy.*

Terrell slapped my hand and straddled the bench next to me. Everyone called him **T-Man,** partly because of his first name, but mostly because he was the go-to receiver on the football team and so scored more than anyone else.

"County, huh? What'd he go in for?"

LaShonda scooped her arms around his neck. They were looking at me like junior gangsters, even though I knew that T-Man's dad was a dentist and LaShonda was president of Future Business Leaders of America.

"Drugs." I decided it didn't matter. Anyone with halfway decent computer skills could probably look it up anyway.

Which made me wonder if Michael had.

T-Man and LaShonda nodded like they knew firsthand what I was talking about.

I managed to keep a straight face.

By the end of lunch I'd learned a few more nicknames. Reagan (Ray-ray) was a cute girl who seemed smarter than her boyfriend, Mike-Lite, who was apparently so called because he used to want to be just like Michael. His real name was Ethan.

Beast, who everyone in school recognized on sight, was perhaps the biggest high schooler I'd ever seen. He didn't look like he should be able to stand, much less play football, but he must manage somehow.

Cyndra's cheerleader friends from first block were Samantha (Sammy) and Monique (Mona)—also the same two who had kept walking by during break.

Cyndra brushed her hair and didn't eat anything, laughing with her friends and flirting with everyone.

Michael didn't mind. It was like he got a charge out of it.

Cyndra and her girls made me feel like a bug under a magnifying glass. They kept laughing, talking between themselves, and looking at me—letting me see it.

I resisted the urge to check myself. Just looked away, waiting for the bell and wondering how long Michael would want to pay me for this nothing act. If I would ever get what the point was.

When the bell rang, T-Man slapped my hand, slid it into another clasp, and bumped shoulders. I tried to look like I knew the move. A couple other jocks held little one-potato fists over my arm and waited for me to make one—then they dropped a quick bounce on mine, one after the other.

Michael and I sat, watching everyone file indoors.

"That was fun, wasn't it?" he said, when they all moved away. "Power. It's the ultimate."

I guessed he was talking about my little game with Dwight.

"You would know," I said.

He smiled. "Yeah, I would."

Chapter Five

lay was gone when I walked back through the cafeteria with Michael. We dumped our trays and headed upstairs.

Mr. Stewart's AP History class is the only one that I never want to sleep through. He goes into such great detail, it's like you know the people he's talking about. You almost hate that they lived centuries before you. He was the only teacher I had this year who really seemed to care about the subject he taught and wanted to make sure you understood it. Like he was imparting some important, life-changing secrets and not just information about people who died a long time ago.

We were doing a section on ancient Greece and Rome. And the more Mr. Stewart kept talking about those Romans, the more I thought it sounded like something I could learn from. It's stupid, I guess, but the way I was thinking about it was Michael was a Roman general or something, and I was a Barbarian—a Germanic tribesman. And we were fighting, only the Romans all knew battle plans and formations and had better technology, while my side had nothing but pure strength. It, of course, was a pre-done deal. I was a goner and would never understand what had felled me. And once it was over, would I want to become Roman myself? Or would I die fighting?

When the bell rang I stuffed my notes in my coat. There was only one class left—and since it was a study hall, I could get some sleep and avoid Michael's gang.

"Hey, Jason"—Michael walked with me out the door—"after school I have football practice. Meet me in the parking lot after. Cyndra wants to get you some clothes."

"As long as I get paid."

"Everyone has their price."

I shrugged and walked away.

In study hall I put my head down and slept. After school sometimes I go to the building supply store and lug around product for contractors who come in. The library's open for thirty minutes after school, so I sometimes go in there and get on a computer or look at magazines, sleep, or watch Ms. Knickerbocker shelve books. Everyone calls her Ms. Knickers, which helps explain why watching her shelving books is a spectator sport.

But most days I end up in the old gym. Like most schools, Mercer has busted out all over the place as more students come in. A while back they built a new gym. It's been here as long as I have, but still everyone calls it the new gym. Like it's the jewel in the crown of the campus.

So the old gym is pretty much neglected. The special ed students go there for PE mostly, and sometimes if the weather is bad or there's testing in the new gym, PE will meet there. They set up random events in there like the science fair and health screenings, but usually it's completely empty.

Just the way I like it.

Most days Clay will hang out, too, waiting while I work out. I used to try to get him to spar or to let me show him a few things about fighting. But he won't. Says that violence is never the answer, that you can't solve anything with fists.

Usually, if someone said that, I'd think they were a coward. But Clay, he won't ever back down. To him, the just cause is the one that doesn't need a fist behind it. He says that in a confrontation, a witness or voice is what's needed. That it's not the same thing as fighting. He says violence doesn't change the world; resistance to violence does.

He's into Gandhi. And the Civil Rights Movement. And hippies and stuff. Obviously he's completely naïve. But he's a true believer in that crap. And since we're friends, we leave it alone. I think he's learning a few pointers just hanging out with me, though.

I still felt like hitting something, so I headed straight for the corner farthest from the door.

There used to be a boxing team at Mercer. That just totally sucks—the one sport I would try out for, and it doesn't exist anymore. But there's a couple heavy punching bags left, a speed bag, one of those bags on a bungee cord that you're supposed to set swinging and dodge around and hit, and jump ropes, and free weights.

When I got in the corner, I pulled a couple of ratty gymnastic mats off the floor and stacked them behind the heavy bag to help minimize the swaying. When I first found this place there was a decent pair of boxing gloves in one of the old lockers, and I got some tape off the PE teacher's cart once when he wasn't looking.

I took off my shirt and started taping my hands. I like to punch the bag with the gloves; it feels more disciplined, like a ritual, like warfare. But I tape my hands anyway because some days the gloves feel too cushioned. It feels like you're not really hitting things, and I miss the ache in my hands and the scrape of the bag against my knuckles. So sometimes I take the gloves off and finish with my taped hands.

I already knew it was one of those days.

I pulled on the gloves, using my teeth to close the Velcro. Before I could start punching, the door banged and a familiar shuffle-lope crossed the floor.

"How'd it go?" Clay asked.

"Fine." I dropped a shoulder and sunk a punch into the bag. Then I followed it with a combination jab and hook.

"Yeah," Clay drawled out the word, sarcastic. "You seem fine."

"It sucked, but nothing I can't handle."

Clay dumped his backpack on the floor and leaned against the flat wall of bleachers. "So tell me. What sucked the most? He's got you pretty short-chained."

I fired another combination into the bag, not surprised that Clay saw it, the thing I hated most. That I was Michael's dog. "I have another job after their practice." I tipped my head at the whistles and yelling coming from behind the gym.

"What is it?"

"Going to the mall. To get clothes." My fist slammed the canvas bag.

"Wait"—Clay stepped behind the bag, moving the mats—"they're buying you clothes? *And* paying you?"

"Yeah. Cyndra's idea. She says my look isn't right."

Clay shook his head. "Then this is more than fighting someone. It's bigger than that."

"Maybe."

"Cyndra. Damn."

"She's Michael's girlfriend." I had to state the obvious, since he had a stupid-ass grin plastered across his mouth.

"Playing dress up with *you*," Clay retorted. "You realize to play dress up, you've got to get naked, right?" He whistled low and shook his head again. "Cyndra Taylor. Fine as fine print."

He said it like poetry. Like it wasn't supposed to make sense except on a gut level. Or lower.

"Tool," I said.

"Douche."

He held the bag for me for a few minutes while I punched.

"Will you come by after she's done with you?" he asked when I stopped. That stupid smile tugged at his lips.

I felt a matching smile pull at the corner of my mouth. "Boy, if she even starts, you won't see us for a week."

Clay smiled and slapped my glove. He somehow hoisted his overstuffed backpack without tipping over.

"See you in the morning."

The smile was still on my face when I faced the bag

again. Without the rumbling volcano in my chest, I was able to focus on pure technique, slow and measured.

The feeling of a clean punch sailing straight and driving into the bag with my shoulder behind it. I switched legs and arms, aiming punches higher and lower on the bag, now punching through my shoulders and my hips, now rocking forward on the balls of my feet. Techniques I'd picked up from the library computers, watching those cage-fight clips and reading tip-a-day blogs.

I took a break and started working the speed bag. I'm not very good at it, but every now and then I can get it to make that repetitive *ba-da-pa ba-da-pa* patter that sounds like a ball dribbling superfast.

I got some water and went back to the heavy bag. I shored up the mats and started punching again. This time I focused on sequences, on combinations and rhythm. Rocking around the bag, I started hearing a beat. I accelerated, pushing out triple punches and jabs. Moved in closer, hugging my elbows tight to my sides and shooting punches and jabs and drop-shoulder uppercuts into the bag.

And then it happened. It always does. I started to feel great. I started to feel like I could do anything, fight anyone, punch until the heavy bag's chain broke. I lowered my head and started to imagine the bag was something else. Someone else.

I took off the gloves and kicked them aside. With each punch, a hiss eked out from between my teeth. The hisses became grunts, and I hit harder and faster. I lost track of time and stopped when the joy passed, stopped when I couldn't hit anymore and could barely lift my arms.

I leaned against the mats and panted, tilting my head back against the canvas.

"Damn." It was drawn out in two syllables—*day-um*—like a southern hillbilly.

A couple of girls stood in the doorway. They were back-lit, the light gleaming through the insides of their thighs, shining along the curves of their waists. I couldn't see who they were and hoped that they could see me as indistinctly. I dragged an arm across my face and stood up.

"Woo, baby," one of them said. It didn't sound like Cyndra, but they were here because of her or because of Michael.

I picked up my shirt and threw it on. Grabbed the gloves and retreated into the locker room. Hopefully it didn't look like a retreat.

My bag was already stashed back there, so I flipped on the shower, locked the door, stripped off my clothes, and stood under the pelting water. I let the water run into my eyes.

I was so tired I didn't want to think about the girls waiting outside. I had felt good at last, punching until I couldn't lift my arms anymore. I didn't want to think about how long they had been standing there. Or if they planned to make a habit out of showing up.

I draped my towel over the window and got dressed again. My bag banged against my back as I walked across the gym floor and climbed the steps. I thought they were gone until I stepped outside.

The football jocks and their girls lounged against their cars.

"Hello, Slick," Cyndra said.

Monique, her small cheer bag dangling on her back, glided forward and squeezed my arm. "Woo, y'all. Ice is *ripped.*"

I twitched my arm out of her grip. Of course. The southern girl.

Michael walked over and slapped my hand. "So this is what you do after school? Boxing?"

"Sometimes," I said. Michael grabbed my bag and tossed it into his car.

"Let me tell you, he was going after that punching bag like it had a name," the other cheerleader, Samantha, said.

Monique fanned herself and leaned close to Cyndra. "All I can tell you is he looked good doing it."

She didn't mean it. It was just some flirt game designed to make me feel self-conscious or make some of the other guys start posing.

"Mmm-hmm," the other girl agreed. "Like a statue or an underwear ad."

I raked hair off my face and glared at them.

"Zap-zap." Cyndra squinted at me.

I glared at her, too.

Dwight moved forward. He lifted his shirt over his head, still keeping the sleeves on his arms.

"What, like this? Right?" He flexed his pecs. Some of the other guys joined in, popping their shirts over their heads and striking muscle-man poses.

Michael leaned against his car, laughing. He kept his shirt on. It was one of those tight, athlete shirts, so you could tell that he could join in the posing if he wanted to.

He didn't feel the need.

I walked over and leaned against the car next to him.

"Nice try. Yes, very nice. That's a very admirable muscle you have there." Monique was poking various arms, butts, and abs. "But sorry, fellas, it just doesn't cut it. Right, Sammy?"

The other cheerleader popped her gum, nodding.

"Sorry, boys. Maybe you should take up boxing."

"Or drink less beer," Cyndra added. She smiled at me. "Come on, Slick. Let's see the gold standard. Take off your shirt."

I snorted.

Cyndra frowned. Monique sidled in. "Yeah," she drawled. "Show the boys we're not being too harsh."

"Not happening." I turned to Michael. "We're going somewhere, right?"

"Sure, but hold on a sec." Michael had a strange look in his eyes.

There was silence as everyone watched. I was suddenly not so tired anymore.

"I think that this is something you should do," Michael said. "Go on. It'll only be for a second. I think you *owe* us that."

He didn't have to stress the word. I already knew he had decided this was a condition of our deal.

I'd seen that look in his eyes before.

It was power—wanting something, setting your mind to get it. Control over someone else.

Something he was used to.

I lifted my head and narrowed my eyes.

"No."

"Jason . . ." His voice trailed off, almost like a warning teachers give you before they learn better.

Did he just want me to do it because he could see I didn't want to? Did he want to show everyone his control over me? Did he want to check out the competition?

I didn't care.

I grabbed my bag out of the car and walked away. I'd wasted the whole day playing his damn game and hadn't thought to get the cash up front. So I probably never would.

Still felt good to leave them behind.

I cut across the soccer field and trotted out along the street, heading to Clay's house.

I heard the rumble of the engine as it glided up beside me. Michael leaned over, glancing at the road sporadically.

"Jason," he called. "Listen, it's okay. Never mind. I thought you'd like the opportunity to show off without looking like a conceited poser. I didn't mean to make you mad."

I didn't believe him.

"Yeah, we didn't mean to make you mad," Cyndra echoed.

"Yeah," Monique agreed from the backseat. Another car purred over to the curb behind Jason's Mustang. I glanced back and saw Dwight, T-Man, and some of the others crowded into a Lexus.

"C'mon." Cyndra popped open the door. "Let me make it up to you. We'll buy you dinner." She climbed out and

ASH PARSONS

leaned over to flip the seat forward. Monique and Samantha scooted over so Cyndra could squeeze in next to them.

Michael pushed the seat back. "Okay, Iceman?"

I walked over and climbed in. I was thinking I'd get the
dinner and the day's pay. I was thinking I would quit after
that.

As if it was that easy.

Chapter Six

he girls in the back murmured, but Michael kept quiet until we reached the interstate. We were going to the swank mall, not the closer one. I shouldn't have been surprised.

"Man, you're a strange one," Michael said. As if he wasn't. "I mean, you have some good-looking girls practically begging to see your muscles, and you act like it's embarrassing or something."

I didn't say anything.

"Yeah, I just wanted a better look, that's all. I mean, I saw enough to get me all . . ." Monique moaned.

The girls laughed.

"But it *was* dark in there," Samantha said.

"And I didn't get to see at all," Cyndra whined.

Our exit was coming up.

"Yeah, so. Again. I have to wonder why a guy doesn't want to take advantage of all that attention." Michael downshifted and pulled onto the access road.

I didn't say anything.

"You got an embarrassing tattoo? Tweety Bird or something?"

I waited until he parked. Then I pushed him back in the seat and twisted the keys out of the ignition.

"What the—" Michael said

I held up a finger in front of his nose. "Stay."

I jumped out of the seat and popped it forward. My eyes narrowed at the girls. "Get out."

They filed out without a word. I climbed back into the front seat and slammed the door.

"What the—" Michael began again.

"Pay me. Fifty for today at school. An extra fifty for this crap."

His lips curled up, like he wasn't surprised. Like he understood everything now. He dug into his wallet and handed over the money.

I stuffed it into my pocket.

"Okay. Now listen."

Michael raised his eyebrows, still smiling that superior grin.

The rest of the gang lingered outside. T-Man thumped on the rear window. A few impatient whistles echoed around us.

"If you keep dicking around, I will not only quit, I'll tell your whole gang about our deal."

He stopped smiling.

"And then I'll beat the crap out of you. I'm not your dog, I'm not your friend, I'm not one of your little sycophants, either. So stop messing with me and stop trying to manipulate your 'crew' into doing it for you."

You had to hand it to him. He kept cool. He just smiled

that smile and nodded. Like there was a secret ace he held. Like he still had all the control.

"Fine," he said. "But you shouldn't be mad at us, or me, Iceman. But fine. Noted. In the future, avoid all body references. Anything else going to make you fly off the handle?"

I shrugged. "Wait and see. Don't act like you couldn't tell you were pushing it."

"Oh no, I'd never act like that. It might piss you off." His voice was cool with mockery.

I shook my head and stared out the window. Thought about getting out and walking to the nearest bus stop, wherever that was. Quitting like I had told myself I would.

My thumb brushed the bills in my pocket.

"Here's what I know," I told him. "The only reason you'd hire me for some vague 'impression' I can give is because you're scared about something. And after today, I know that it sure as hell isn't anyone at school."

Michael's eyes jumped to my face, like I'd surprised him.

"And if someone's got you that scared, maybe you should tell me what exactly is going on."

It wasn't quite a resignation.

Michael changed before my eyes. The assured king-of-the-school front dropped. His eyebrows drew into a tense line.

"You're right." He scrubbed his palms on his thighs. "Hell."

Dwight thumped the trunk. Monique sidled beside my window. Leaned back against it, sliding slowly from side to side.

"I can't tell you. I can't. You're right. I . . . am scared," Michael said. "It's not good. But Saturday night, there's a party. I need you to come. Maybe after that, we can be done. Maybe after that, it won't be so bad."

I wasn't the one he was trying to convince.

"Sorry about the shirt." His eyebrows quirked up in self-conscious apology. Like he was new to all this, too. "It won't happen again. Truth." His head bobbed once on the promise. His eyes met mine. Held.

"Fine. For now." The keys chinked as I handed them over.

We got out of the car. Michael walked over to Cyndra and mumbled something in her ear. She nodded and corralled Monique and Samantha.

I guessed he had told them to lay off.

We walked inside.

A security guard eyed my stained shirt and crappy army jacket. He let me go on, probably because I was with the right people.

I'd never been in this mall, for obvious reasons. It was crazy—all sparkling glass and tile, chrome and high-end product ranging in every window. There were designer label shops and not a Sears or JCPenney to be found. Not a fingerprint, not a smear, not a scratch, or a speck of dirt anywhere. It took me a while to notice it, but there were no kiosks, either—you know, little stalls selling those silver skull rings and crosses, or phone covers and designer sunglasses.

When we got to the food court, I tried not to gape. There was a two-story glass water wall with water flowing down and trickling into a trough. Like even the waterfall had to be hushed in the presence of so much money. Fat clear tubes arched overhead and connected two giant aquariums. Fish lazily swam through the tubes and into the aquariums.

Like I said, I tried not to gape. I stood in front of the larger aquarium and watched the fish chase each other. You could tell they were tropical because of how bright they were.

There was an orange-and-white fish like the one in that kids' movie and a fat, big-lipped fish with neon speckles across its entire body. Fish darted through rocks and plants, over sand and behind a bubble jet.

"So you do smile." Cyndra leaned against the table next to me. Behind us, the rest of the group had taken over several tables in the middle of the court.

"I smile all the time."

"No, you don't. Not like that." She twirled hair around a finger and took a little step closer.

"How do I smile, then?"

Cyndra glanced over her shoulder at Michael. "Like him."

"Mr. Movie Star? Bullshit."

Cyndra laughed and bumped against me like I'd just said something bad. Her breast brushed against my arm. "No, not like his smile *looks*—just like his in that it's not sincere usually. His smiles aren't real smiles, and neither are yours."

"Okay."

"It's true. His smiles are fake—they look great, but you watch his eyes. Usually there's something else going on."

"Like what?"

"Well, that's the question, isn't it?" She frowned up at me. "Your smiles aren't that mysterious."

"Oh yeah?"

"Yeah. They're really not smiles at all."

"What are they, then?"

Her eyes narrowed. "Anger."

I snorted. "Angry smiles? Listen to yourself."

Cyndra shook her head. "And there one is."

The line of my mouth went flat. I went back to watching the fish.

After a moment, Cyndra murmured, "Sorry I said anything."

I shrugged, thinking she was going to walk away. She pulled out a chair instead. I sat down next to her and propped my elbows on the table. We stared at the tank.

"You like the fish, huh?" she asked.

"I've never—" I stopped myself from saying that I'd never seen anything like it. Thought of how that might sound to someone like her.

"I've never really looked at them," I said instead.

"They're pretty cool," she said, and somehow I didn't feel so stupid for staring at them.

I imagined Janie sitting before the tank, the small frown-crease on her forehead disappearing as she watched neon colors dart around. Her gnawed fingertips resting on the table, still.

"What are you thinking?" Cyndra asked.

I shrugged. "My sister, Janie. She would love this."

Cyndra leaned forward and brushed her hand down my arm. "We'll bring her next time, then."

My cheeks burned. Why was she trying to make me feel like we could be something?

I pulled my arm away. "Forget about it. She wouldn't want to come here."

Cyndra's eyes tightened and she glanced away. She crossed her arms. It was like she was saying, *Fine. If that's the way you want it.*

"I'm sorry, Cyndra. I didn't mean—" I stopped myself. The orange-and-white fish darted into a swaying plant. "It's just . . . why act like we're going to be friends? This isn't about that."

She crossed her legs away from me and stared at a tube overhead. "Right. It's about the cash." Her voice was flint.

My chair scraped as I shoved it away from the table. I leaned back, stretching my legs out and crossing my arms and ankles.

I watched the fish.

We sat silently. Finally, Michael walked over, depositing Chinese noodle plates in front of us.

"Dinner, as promised." He stroked Cyndra's hair. "If you're going to get any shopping done, you'd better get a move on, babe. Don't forget Iceman's curfew."

Cyndra sat up, straight as a razor. Her silver chopsticks clinked against the china plate as she ate.

The food smelled wonderful. My stomach rumbled as I glanced at the chopsticks laid across my plate. The corners of my mouth twitched up, and I returned to watching the fish.

ASH PARSONS

After a while, I didn't even smell the food. Mostly. There was a large white-and-black fish with trailing fins that was real tough. Anytime another fish happened by, no matter how big or how small, man, that white-and-black fish just charged at it. That fish had a whole corner to itself. It just sat there, charging at any other fish that maybe got a little too close.

Cyndra got up and carried her plate away.

I was not looking forward to the shopping.

Cyndra sat back down with a scrap of paper and a pen.

"What size shirt do you wear?" she asked.

I shrugged and fingered the T-shirt I was wearing. "This is a large."

She wrote down *M or L.*

"What size jeans do you wear?"

I pulled on the leg of my thrift-store jeans. "How should I know?"

She shook her head. "Would you mind standing and holding up your shirt so I can see the waist, please?" She sounded like a waitress or an operator.

I pushed my chair back and stood, hitching up my pants before lifting my T-shirt.

"Well, those are clearly too big," Cyndra said, eyeing me. "Would you come here, please?" She stopped writing and twisted sideways in her chair.

I stepped forward. Her hot hands grabbed my waist and pulled me a half step closer. Laughter from the other table rang over us. She was face level with my stomach and only a dip away from my crotch.

My head felt light as I stared down at the top of her

head. She messed with my T-shirt, instructing me to hold it a little higher. She lifted my jeans and pinched the sides until her fingers lay flat against my sides.

I glanced at the others. Dwight circled his thumb and fingers and brought them to his mouth. He tongued the inside of his cheek rhythmically.

I looked away.

Cyndra let go of me, and I sat down before I embarrassed myself. Curled over the table, hands clenched on my legs.

She wrote something on the paper.

She smiled. "Well, from what little I saw of your abs, Monique was right."

I stared at the fish.

"Shy, huh? You've got nothing to be ashamed of."

I stared at the fish.

She sighed and drummed red-tipped fingers on the table. "Sorry. I shouldn't talk sometimes. Here." She handed me a fork and walked away.

I ate the noodles.

CHAPTER SEVEN

I t should have made me happy that Cyndra thought I had nice abs, but it just pissed me off. I didn't really know why, though. Maybe because of Dwight's gesture, maybe because I wasn't really part of their circle. I was bought and paid for.

And because it all brought me back to the shirt thing.

Which had to do with control—and what they didn't know about my life at home. My dad may be crazy, but he's not stupid. Usually. And so it's fists and you keep your head together and it's over and you're okay. Live to fight another day. No real marks and you can pretend it never happened or that it's going to stop—like my mom used to.

But once it was a broken bottle. Something had gone wrong, some buddy narc'd. Something. And I did my part, because I knew he was going to go off, and sometimes it's better to get it over with. But I didn't know how much he'd already drunk. I thought it would be like a pot on the stove, and he could just boil over a bit. Take the pressure off. And then it would be done.

It didn't work out that way. He exploded. Broke the bottle

he'd been drinking from against the table and came at me with the neck curled in his fist like a roll of quarters and the jagged end hanging out past his thumb and forefinger. It started out just fists but ended up a slashing arc across my back with me curled away from it. Which just made the gash worse.

Afterward, Janie patched me up. I lay out a bit, and it was like it never happened. Except for the scar. And I'll be damned before I parade it in front of a bunch of cheerleaders.

I finished the noodles and thought about The Plan. I imagined putting the money I'd earned today into the coffee can, imagined buying Janie a little stuffed animal or necklace before going home. She'd probably rather put all the money in the coffee can, like a responsible little adult, but I liked the idea of surprising her.

I was about to get up and go find something for her when Michael sat down next to me.

"Shouldn't take too much longer. Don't worry. Cyn's got good taste."

Behind us, the others were scattering into the mall. Dwight humped a pillar, making the others laugh.

Before I could stop myself, I asked the question. "Why'd you let him do that to her?" Thinking of the suck gesture, thinking of how Cyndra hadn't noticed.

"Oh, so it's like that, huh?"

Cyndra was right; his eyes didn't smile when his mouth did.

"Like what?"

Michael held up a hand, like he was trying to keep me from interrupting, when I'd only said two words. "No, no. It's a good thing. Knight in shining armor. I just never would have thought you'd be that way."

"You're full of it." I turned back to the aquarium.

Michael crossed his arms and leaned back. "You don't like that I let Dwight act up toward her. You think it's wrong or disrespectful."

I shrugged. But he stayed quiet, and quiet long enough that I felt the silence standing over me.

"I'm just saying," I began, "that if I had a girlfriend, I wouldn't let anyone treat her like that."

I watched the black-and-white fish chase the others away.

"You don't know jack about women, Iceman." Michael stood up and grabbed my shoulders. I knocked his hands away.

"They *like* being treated that way. Especially her, man. Watch her. You'll see. It's a little game."

Cyndra walked toward us, a big bag dangling from her skinny wrist. Her full lips pursed like she was on a runway and everyone was watching her go by.

Everyone was.

"Something you should learn about the world, Ice." Michael's voice was a reverential murmur conveying a profound truth. "There are two types of people: users and the used. The secret is to know which one you are and which one everyone else is. Which one *she* is."

Michael's lips curved as she hip-swayed closer.

I stood up.

Michael wrapped an arm around Cyndra, nuzzling into her neck. She leaned into it.

"We done?" I asked.

Michael turned his smile to me, just a curve of the mouth. "Almost. Gotta get you a cell phone."

"Why?"

The scared kid ghost-flitted in his eyes. "Everyone should have a phone, Iceman. How will I let you know what's going on without one?"

While he and the others went into the cell phone store, I darted into a gift shop and bought Janie a little stuffed poodle. It was black and growling, wearing a dippy rhinestone collar below a stupidly big head, and I thought it would make her laugh. Michael raised his eyebrows at the bag when I found them in the cell store.

He opened the phone box right there. Handed the phone to me, along with the booklet in four languages. Michael turned to the older man behind the counter.

"The problem with you people is you give too much crap," he said, shoving the papers, the plastic wrap and shells, the empty box at him. The box thunked off the counter. The papers fell with the plastic.

The older man didn't blink. Just stood in the wash of packaging and paper. "I couldn't agree more." Smooth, like he didn't mind the piss raining on his head.

If I was him, I'd deck the little punk.

Dwight laughed. T-Man slapped his palm.

Cyndra winced at the salesman, then grabbed my arm. "Let's go." She led the way out the store.

In the mall, walking toward the exit, Michael sped up to catch us.

"See, Ice? What type of person was he?"

I ignored him.

"You'll see," he said.

At the Mustang, Cyndra climbed into the backseat. Once we were on the road, she pushed the department store bag over my shoulder.

"Okay, Ice, here's the deal."

I flipped down the visor. Cyndra waved a finger at me in the mirror.

"I got you a pair of jeans and two shirts, a hoodie, and that's it. Wear the new stuff tomorrow. I think it'll fit, but you need more, so just plan on coming out again Saturday. Bring Janie."

I nodded like that was going to happen.

"Aren't you getting a bit ahead of yourselves?" I asked.

Cyndra's eyes narrowed in the mirror. "What do you mean?"

"I mean, what if I call it quits tomorrow? What if you decide you don't need me anymore? What about all this money you're prepared to spend on clothes, then?"

Cyndra shrugged. "You're cute when you're obtuse." Her eyes locked on mine in the mirror. "Zap-zap!"

I looked away.

"Don't worry about it." Michael downshifted, taking the exit ramp too fast. "One: Cyndra's stepdad doesn't even blink at her credit card bills. Two: If it's a big deal, we can take some clothes back. Three: I have to state the obvious—your clothes suck. So just take it, and if it keeps going, it keeps going."

I shook my head, staring out the window as the buildings of downtown zipped past.

"What?" Michael asked.

I didn't say anything because I knew that what I was thinking would sound pathetic.

Users and the used.

Money.

How it didn't matter to any of them, but it mattered so much to me that I was selling little pieces of myself in order to get it.

I didn't want to say all that. Didn't want to say how I wished I had so much money that I didn't need to worry about where it was coming from or going to.

And when the Mustang stopped in Lincoln Green, I thought if they had a brain between them, they'd be able to guess what I was thinking anyway.

I pulled the clothes out of the store bag and shoved them in my duffel along with the stuffed poodle. "See you tomorrow," I said, popping the door open.

"Tomorrow," Michael echoed as I closed the door. The Mustang idled next to the curb for a moment as I crossed the litter-strewn dirt to our unit. I didn't hear any noise from inside, so I slid my key into the lock and let myself in.

I crossed to the stairs, avoiding looking at the piled plates crusted with rotting food, stained clothes in heaps, and drug accessories. I usually try to hold my breath until I close the bedroom door behind me. Rancid food and body odor—you don't get used to the stink.

"Jason?" Janie's voice called from the other side of the drywall partition. She stuck her head around the wall.

My sister has the most beautiful eyes—almost obsidian in a porcelain-pale doll's face. I wish I had eyes like hers instead of my dad's.

"How'd it go?" She clambered onto my bed, bouncing a little.

I dug the money out of my pocket and handed it to her. Janie squealed and clapped her hands, like a six-year-old instead of a junior-high schooler. She disappeared back around her side, and I heard her rummaging in the ceiling vent for our hidden coffee can. She brought it out, showed me the pathetic roll, counted it. After she put the money back in and stowed the can, she came back to my side.

"My hero," she said, giving me a squeeze. She let go quickly, but I was okay with her hug. I handed her the growling poodle. She smiled and shook her head. She liked it, though.

Chapter Eight

n the morning, I checked the cell phone and tucked it back under the bed. Put on the new clothes. It felt weird wearing them. They looked good—dark jeans, a navy T-shirt, and a black-and-red hoodie— but they felt weird. Not mine.

The jeans were so new, the ink so rich and dark, I expected it to rub off on my skin. Cyndra had cut the price tags off, or the salesperson had. I couldn't decide if it was a nice gesture or if it pissed me off.

"Wow," Janie said when I came downstairs.

I glared at her.

"What? They look nice. You look sharp."

"I feel like a jerk." My hands tightened. I didn't know why wearing new clothes should make me feel ashamed.

"Don't. They're not dorky—they've still got your"—she waved her hand—"look."

Like I had a look.

Janie twirled her fingers. "Take the hoodie off and turn around."

I felt stupid, but it made her happy.

When I was done I held out my hands like *Enough?*

"They really fit, too," she said.

I rolled my shoulders forward and felt the fabric tighten. "Nah, they're small."

Janie shook her head and smiled. "That's called fitting, Jason. You look . . . great." She sounded surprised. Like I was a whole other person.

"They're just clothes, Janie."

She handed me my bag. We headed to her bus stop.

After she was on her bus, I walked to Clay's house. Clay's mom opened the door.

"Good morning, Jason."

She turned slowly, ruffling her son's hair as he slouched to the door. "Have a good day, honey."

"You, too," Clay said. His eyes flitted over my new clothes.

As we closed the door behind us, Clay's mom was shuffling up the short hall. Slow, like all the tired had pooled into her ankles.

There was a slight bite to the morning air. I zipped up the hoodie.

"Cyndra's Ken doll." Clay smirked.

We walked up the street. Our breaths puffed on the air.

"Not sure why I hate this so much."

"Because you know it's not real. And you can't explain any of it."

"Yeah, and people look at me different."

Even him.

"You *are* different. It makes you different." His hand waved in the direction of the high school. "People may not know why. But it's there, wearing you. Not the other way around."

Vintage Clay. Pinpointing the problem with laser accuracy. Like Michael had said, users and the used.

Clay was watching me as we walked. Gauging it. And that made me feel better than anything else. Knowing he had my back, to keep me honest. Keep me true.

"There's a party tomorrow night," I said. "Do you think you could get your mom's car?"

"God. Me at a high school party. Perish the thought."

"I just need another set of eyes there. I'll be working." Thinking of how observant he was, and the fact that there was something deeper going on.

Clay glanced up, brushing hair out of his eyes. "Okay. Sure."

And that made me feel confident, like a weight had shifted. "Thanks. I'll text you when I find out where."

"Ooh, a cell phone, too! Oh, text me. We can send texts. Like BFFs."

"Fuck off."

Clay laughed and jumped up, throwing an arm around my neck. Trying to pull me into a headlock.

I let him.

Until I grabbed his backpack and yanked down. He fell back, but I caught him, blocking his stumble with my foot as I looped the backpack off his shoulder.

"Hey!" Clay yelled as I took off. On my back, Clay's pack and my duffle clobbered each other as I ran to the corner.

I waited at the lights for Clay to catch up. He lightly popped a hand across the back of my head.

"Hey!" I rubbed my head like it had hurt. "I thought violence never solved anything." I handed him his bag.

"That wasn't violence. That was justice."

The lights changed, and Clay stepped out without looking. I slipped ahead of him, glaring at the driver of a beat-up green truck that was still zooming up to the crosswalk. On the other side of the street, Clay slowed down and stuck out a hand. I slid a shake.

"Go do this," Clay said. "Take that bastard's money and don't let it get to you."

"Thanks, coach. I won't let you down."

I crossed through the senior parking lot, but Michael's cherry Mustang wasn't there yet. I headed into the cafeteria for breakfast and told myself it wasn't cowardly to feel relieved.

Hunched over my biscuit and OJ, I nodded off so quick it was like sinking into something more than real. More than true. Darkness and fangs, fists and ripping. Threats and something clawing you.

"Jason." A hand gripped my arm.

I lunged away, yanking my arm up and back.

Cyndra's perfect mouth fell open into an O of surprise.

"Michael send you to get me?" I pretended my reaction had been normal. "Where to?"

"It's—uh—different from yesterday." She hugged her books to her chest. Her eyes flicked to the coaches: Protectors of the Cafeteria.

"Sorry," I said, trying to relax my gritted teeth. "I didn't mean to scare you."

"It's not that." She shook her head, swift and tight. "I was jumpy already."

She was jumpy?

"We have to ditch. Come on." She didn't wait for me to ask what was happening and didn't offer an explanation.

Leaving my tray on the table, I followed her.

"Hey!" called one of the coaches, a former juice-head now running to fat. He pointed at my tray.

I met his eyes. Felt my blood pressure drop as my breathing and heart rate slowed.

He broke the gaze first. Slid his eyes to the tray behind me. "You!" He shouted to someone else. "Pick that tray up."

"But it's not mine!"

"Shut up and do it." The coach put his hands on his wide hips and watched the other guy take it. Acted like he'd never even been talking to me.

Cyndra huffed a soft laugh, puffing a lock of red-gold hair with her breath. I didn't mind everyone watching as she led me out.

We walked out to her silver Mercedes and got in. She threw the car into gear and sped out of the lot.

"Where are we going?"

"Michael's waiting for us just a few minutes from here." She drove away from the school, weaving through modest residential streets.

Eventually, we pulled into a pharmacy parking lot. Michael's Mustang was parked by the door.

"He called me," Cyndra said. "Told me to get you and bring you here. Why didn't you answer your phone?"

"Don't have it. We're not supposed to have them at school, remember? Michael called me?"

"Yeah." She parked next to his car. "No one pays attention

to that rule." Cyndra opened her door. "Just make sure the ringer's off."

I got out and followed her around to the passenger side of the Mustang. I couldn't see Michael through the tinted glass.

Cyndra tapped on the window before cracking the door open. "We're here. I'll go inside and get the stuff." She turned to me and gestured to the car seat. "I'll be right back."

I climbed into the car as Cyndra walked into the pharmacy.

"Should've answered your damn phone." Michael's voice was muffled. He was pressing a gym shirt to his mouth.

His bruised eye was swollen almost shut. Ugly purple streaks spread over his cheekbone and up to his eye socket. Closest to his eye, the bruising turned a vivid red. Just above his cheekbone, near the temple, was a cut that had already clotted.

"Nice look, Face," I said.

Michael coughed a laugh, groaned, and clutched his stomach. He eased forward and spat a glob of blood into a McDonald's cup.

"What happened?"

"You were right. Yesterday." He gasped as he fell back in the seat. "I'll tell you. I don't know what else to do."

"Who did this?"

His good eye went wide. Even in the safety of his car, he glanced around before answering.

"Lonzo Cesare," he breathed in fear, like he was naming Satan.

I watched him, waiting for more.

"Wait. You don't know him?" He rubbed the back of his neck and shook his head slowly, like he couldn't decide if he should laugh or sob.

"He's a drug dealer. And a bookie. More than that, I don't want to know." His fingers continued to knead the muscles in his neck. "I lost some bets."

Like they were inconsequential things.

"So pay him. Instead of me."

"It's more than I have right now. Way more. I need time." He let go of his neck to wave the hand at his face. "This is what he did when I told him that."

"How much time did it buy you?" I asked.

"A week." Michael closed his eyes and leaned his head back. "I'll fix it. I can get ahead of this."

Something about the tone of his voice and what he said. The bets laid before school and the power-lust glint in his eyes clicked with images of my mom before she overdosed. The way she would come into our room, shake us awake, and promise that she was going to change. Just so she could hear the lie spoken aloud.

Everything was going to get better.

"I'll take care of it. But I need you to help show him I'm not helpless. And to come when I call, damnit. So I *won't be* helpless. He's got kids that deal for him at Mercer. Don't think for one second he doesn't. With you hanging around, he'll think twice about coming after me again."

"I'm not *that* scary."

"Your dad is." His eyes shone on my face like a police-man's light. "Everyone knows your dad's a badass." Then he muttered, "I bet *he* knows who Lonzo Cesare is."

So *that's* what this was about? I was a stand-in for my dad? Like my dad is some underworld kingpin. Instead of a low-level thug.

"Whatever," I said. Maybe *badass* and *kingpin* are relative propositions, especially to the ignorant.

Cyndra walked out, a bag in her hand. Michael put his window down and took the bag. "Go ahead to school. I'll be fine now."

Cyndra frowned, chewed on her lower lip, and shifted her weight. She stared at her boyfriend's bruised face.

"Go, I said."

He put the window back up.

She went to her car and got in. Slammed the door and laid tire marks as she pulled out of the parking lot.

"She doesn't know all this," Michael explained. "She knows I'm in trouble, not how much."

"She knows now."

Michael laughed, then groaned. He fumbled through the bag, fished out some painkillers, and took two.

"How'd you meet this guy?" I asked.

Michael pulled out a chemical cooling pack. Twisted and folded it until it got cold, leaned back, and put it over his swollen eye.

"I went to a bar with my stepbrother. A dive. We'd just dropped off Cyndra and her mom for their trip to Paris last

---

Still Waters

summer. Mark was on break from college. He said, 'Let's light this town up.' This was a couple weeks before school started back." He sighed, shifted in the bucket seat and hissed in pain. "Damnit. I'm not used to this."

He shifted again. "Mark and I, we drove to this dive he'd heard about. And there were these trashy girls there. We picked them up. And the next thing, we're drinking, and there's drugs. And this girl says, 'Two high rollers like you, you should meet Alonzo.' Just like in a movie."

A tiny blue car parked next to us. An old lady got out, glaring at the Mustang parked so close to the door.

"So we say, 'Who's that?' And of course she gets him. He says call him Cesare. And he's got more drugs. And he's getting the girls to come over. Then we go to the back, this private party room, like. Gambling there. Card games. Track bets on a big screen. And we start playing. We won. We won everything. It was like we were unbeatable."

His busted lip stretched into a smile at the memory. "And that was it. Mark went back to college, and I went back to the bar. Kept gambling. It seemed so easy. I was a dumbass."

He didn't have to finish the story. I already knew how it ended.

The house always wins—especially after they lure you in.

So that was it. What put Michael, and now me, in danger. A spike of adrenaline dumped in my veins as I cut my eyes around the parking lot.

"I thought I was smarter than him. I thought, you know, I could keep ahead of it. I could get it back. Instead I kept getting deeper and deeper in debt. More money. So much money." Michael's busted lip stretched in a tortured smile. He leaned forward and spit into the cup again. Shifted the cool pack from his eye to his lip.

"This morning he was waiting for me. Said he wanted to talk. I didn't think he'd get violent, though." He sighed and repositioned the pack. "But it's gonna be okay. I've got a week. And I've got you. And a plan."

"I won't be able to protect you from him. Even if I wanted to. I'm not much of an insurance policy. And neither is my dad, especially when it's not for him."

"That's why we're going to get a gun."

My eyes tightened and my mouth went flat. I reached for the door.

Michael grabbed my arm with clawed fingers. "Wait!"

"I won't shoot anyone for you. And I don't want to hear any more of your plan." I wrenched my arm out of his desperate vise. Michael gasped at the jostling movement, hugged his arm across his stomach.

"I don't want you to kill anyone! The gun is for protection. It's like me hiring you. A message. He thinks I'm a punk-ass kid he can just bully. He won't stop until I show him I'm not. The gun will buy me safety for just a little while longer. Not one week, two. That's all I'll need."

"You shouldn't even be paying me, then. You need every cent you can get, right?"

"You idiot." His eyes cut with his tone. "You work for dimes. I owe him an entire bank. Let me worry about how I'm going to get his money."

He sighed and leaned back. His curling lip shifted to a pressure-flat line. "Lonzo Cesare is a vicious, evil bastard. But he's not more than that. I can beat him."

Moments ago he sounded like the name was demonic. Now he stroked his own ego to fight back. The football player needing the pep squad.

"I'm smarter than him," Michael said. "I can beat him."

"Good luck with that."

"I'll still pay you. Nothing has changed. I just need you to hang out with me. Act like we're friends. Come to the party tomorrow."

"What's going to happen there?"

An acid-edged laugh cut out of Michael's chest. "It's a party. You've heard of them, right?"

He reached for the steering wheel, squeezed like it was a throat. "I don't have to tell you jack, Ice. I didn't have to tell you any of this. You either want the money, or not. So are you in or out?"

Maybe even he didn't know if he was bluffing or not.

I didn't answer. Imagined Lonzo Cesare, a violent but small-time gangster milking a high schooler for his daddy's cash.

I remembered giving the money to Janie last night. Her little claps and how she counted the pathetic roll of bills before hiding the can again.

"Fine," I said.

Chapter Nine

On the way back to school, Michael said he'd explain his face to the others by saying he and I had decided to ditch and go to a convenience store that would sell us beer. But when we got there, some kids I knew from Lincoln Green picked a fight. They'd jumped Michael while I was inside, but then I came out in hero mode, and kicked their asses.

The secretary in the office heard a similar story, except we hadn't decided to ditch, we were running late, and we weren't after beer, but soda.

She gave us tardy slips and told us to wait for the bell, which was only a few minutes away.

"Why even show up? We should have ditched the whole day," I mumbled.

Michael gingerly sank into a seat by the plate glass. "And miss the chance to show off this shiner and brag about the fight? Never."

We waited. I stood next to him, trying to enjoy the jumpy eyes of office staff and student aides. Trying to ignore the appraising glances at both my clothes and Michael's face.

The bell finally rang, and we headed into the throng of students. Muffled exclamations greeted Michael's face. He smiled and walked on like their gossip would be nothing but pure adoration.

He turned at the courtyard door and stretched an arm out to me, making sure everyone saw as he flaunted my presence along with his face.

We pushed through the double doors and walked into the prep throng. It wasn't like the talking stopped completely, but it sure got quieter.

"Holy . . ." T-Man walked over. "What happened, man?" His eyes took in Michael's face.

I stopped next to Michael and stared out at the rest of the group.

Michael spun the story quickly and effortlessly. He shot a knowing grin at me, the only concession that his story wasn't entirely true.

T-Man and Dwight cursed and started talking about vengeance. Michael shook his head slightly, and they stopped. There was a lull as their eyes shifted from Michael's face to my clothes. Next subject of conversation. So much gossip to get through before the bell.

I felt like a bug under a magnifying glass.

Cyndra lifted a side of the zip-front hoodie, smiling expectantly. "Looking good, Ice." A compliment to her taste in clothes more than my look.

She tugged the shoulders of the hoodie off my back.

I knocked her hands away.

"Relax. It's warm. You don't need it."

I shook my head.

Cyndra sighed and the corner of her mouth twisted. "What, you think I'm going to jump you or something? Get over yourself. I just want to see how the clothes fit."

People eyeing me, wanting something. Laying hands on me. Throwing their influence like punches.

Me—taking it.

Something twisted in my gut.

Cyndra gave me a quick, secret smile. It was warm, not sexy, just real. Like the smile was saying *Please?*

I took off the hoodie.

"Thank you," she mouthed. Heaven forbid anyone actually heard her say the words.

"Perfect," she said aloud. "Perfect fit."

Monique slid over, squinting and half-smiling. She looked like a little girl playing sexy—and not actually succeeding.

"Day-um." Her finger ran down my arm.

I pushed her hand away.

Cyndra laughed at her. Monique acted like it hadn't happened. She stuck out a hip and propped a hand there.

"Nice threads, Cyn. Great shirt." She blew a kiss at me. "Flex for me, Ice."

"Screw you."

Cyndra smiled. "It's okay, Ice. Stop being so prickly. No one's going to attack you."

When she looked at me like that, I would do whatever she asked of me.

Michael laughed and clapped my shoulder. Loving it.

I glared at him.

He backed down, let go. Grabbed Cyndra and led her and the others a few steps away.

I blew out air and sat down on the bench.

Fifty dollars. Fifty dollars. Fifty dollars.

Michael murmured into Cyndra's ear. She frowned at him before glancing back at me. She came back and sat on the bench next to me.

I didn't say anything and tried not to look at her.

"Don't do that, Jason." Her voice was soft.

My eyebrows lifted.

"Don't be mad," she explained.

I let a burst of air out my nose and looked away again.

"You can look so scary sometimes," she said. Like I should immediately smile at her and try to make her feel all safe.

"What do you want, Cyndra?" I looked at her finally.

"Don't be mad."

"Fine." I smiled the smile she didn't like. "Why should I be mad?" Wanted to ask if she understood. And why she cared.

Cyndra shook her head. Red-gold hair spilled over her shoulders. Then she shifted, sitting back and lifting her ankles onto my lap. She gave me a manufactured smile.

"Okay, Ice, you're right. You shouldn't be mad. Certainly not at me." She edged her feet higher. I tensed, ready to push them away, but couldn't take my eyes off her tiny toenails, polished like perfect candy apples.

"You like me, right? So don't be mad."

I told myself to brush her feet off my thighs. Stand up and walk away.

The whole thing was a display. Far from intimate or real. Or anything other than power and use.

I shoved her feet off my lap.

Before I could get up, she pressed me back and straddled my thighs.

My head was on fire. My eyes narrowed as my breathing all but stopped.

It was like that moment when you see his fist coming. Scarred, bone-ridge knuckles loading on you like a freight train, and you know it's going to connect. And you know it's going to hurt like hell.

What's important is how you react.

I lashed her hips to my legs with one arm and wound my other hand in her hair, pulling her ear down to my lips.

"Stop playing games."

Cyndra gasped and pushed against me feebly. "You're hurting me."

I wanted to see the tears. I wanted her vision blurry from trying to blink them back. I wanted her to cry, from being pushed and pulled. Wanted her to understand.

Users and the used. Which one was she?

I let go of her hair and shoved her off my lap.

She glared at me like it was the biggest insult in the world.

I stood and grabbed my books from the bench. Tried to look like I always look.

Uninvolved. Unemotional. Distanced.

T-Man and LaShonda backed away from me. Michael forced a smile.

"Your face looks like a doormat," I said.

The smile disappeared.

When you can't change the news, change the news cycle. His face was going to get plenty of play. I slammed through the double doors as the bell rang.

CHAPTER TEN

t lunch it was like nothing had happened. Maybe nothing had.

Michael talked about football practice and the team they would play for next week's game. He talked like I knew all about it already, like I cared. Cyndra held court and didn't look at me once. T-Man and Dwight hassled Beast about some lame remark he'd made in English. Beast was laughing like their taunts were fun, but if you checked his eyes, you could see the laughter didn't reach all the way up.

For the rest of the classes that day, I pretended to be somewhere else or slept. After school I decided to skip the punching bag. Hoisting product at the building supply store and getting honest money (well, mostly honest money) would do as much for me as pounding a canvas bag would. Plus, nobody would show up there. Besides, Clay and his mom always took her paycheck and got groceries for the week on Friday afternoons, so he wouldn't be home for a while.

Cyndra chased me down as I crossed the athletic field.

"Hey." She stopped short from actually grabbing my arm. She handed me a fifty. "From Michael."

I took it and waited.

She squinted at the press of kids hustling across the parking lot, all trying to be the first to get off campus.

"Sorry about today." She glanced in my eyes and glanced away again.

I put my bag down and shook out a cigarette.

"Can I have one of those?" Cyndra asked, then held it to the flame of my lighter.

We smoked in silence for a moment.

"I can't read you," she said when our cigarettes were halfway done. "I didn't mean to piss you off."

Her lips closed on the filter.

"You're not like the other guys," she said, exhaling. It sounded like a line. She shifted her weight.

"Thanks," I said, smiling in spite of myself, smiling at the way she looked so nervous and sexy all at once.

A relaxed smile crept across her face like a sunrise. The open expression of a kid who's gotten away with something.

I pitched my stub into the grass. "Besides, I think I've got it figured out."

Cyndra took a final drag and raised her eyebrows.

"He told you to. Another bet, right?" I asked. "A dare. You're all betting who jumps me first."

Another moneymaking proposition. Another way for me to earn my keep.

Users and the used.

She jammed her hands into her jeans and shifted her weight again. "That's what you think of me?"

I shrugged. "It's what I think of him. Doesn't matter to me, but it explains that crap today and Monique and the ass parade yesterday. I've been in school with all of you since middle school, and suddenly I'm the stud."

Cyndra shook her head. "Or there's another possibility."

I snorted.

"Maybe we like you."

We.

Cyndra took a deep breath and watched a plane overhead. "Anyway, I just wanted to say I'm sorry."

"Is it true?"

"Yeah, I'm sorry."

"No, is it true about betting who jumps me first?"

She glared into my eyes. "Yeah, it's true."

"Then it may as well be you, princess." I stepped closer. "If your boyfriend really doesn't mind."

Cyndra watched me like an exterminator watches a cockroach.

I stroked her arm. "I'm sure we can work out a price. A cut for me."

This time, it was Cyndra who slapped my hand away. "You're disgusting."

"I'm a pragmatist. And I'm for sale, right? Just like anything. That's what was going on at break." The sneer crept into my voice.

"It wasn't like that, I just—"

I waited.

"I just don't know how else to be." She rubbed her arm like I'd burned her. "I don't know how to act around people."

The T-shirt stretched as I shrugged. "Whatever. I'm sure you planned to give your winnings to charity."

She actually laughed—a shout, boisterous and unaffected. "Yeah. Something worthwhile. The Schnauzer Rescue Fund."

I couldn't help it. I smiled.

"The real deal," Cyndra said, glancing at my mouth. "Now I know I'm forgiven."

I picked up my pack.

"I'll pick you up tomorrow?" she asked. "Five o'clock?"

"The party doesn't start that early, does it?"

"Nah, but we have to go back to the mall, remember? I've got to finish shopping for your accoutrements." She pronounced the last word with a little French accent, not trying to be seductive, just saying it the right way. Which made it sexy as hell.

"And before you ask, yes, I'll pay you for the mall trip, and Michael will pay you for the party."

I felt the corners of my mouth flatten. "Deal."

"Then meet me here at five." Cyndra turned and walked toward the senior parking lot. "Bring your sister," she called. "We'll show her the fish."

Like hell.

I wanted to watch her walk away, wanted to watch the way her hair and her hips slung from side to side. I even wanted to watch her give Michael his kiss and his hug and get into his car.

I turned and finished crossing the field.

At the building supply store, Jonesy set me to lugging bags of cement mix onto a flatbed truck. After that I got a load of cinder blocks and Sheetrock. After an hour or two, my arms were like noodles, and my hair was wet with sweat. Jonesy paid me in cash and gave me two coupons for the fast-food chain nearest home.

"What the hell, it's Friday," he said. "Live large."

What can you say when an overweight, middle-aged man with a smoker's cough tells you to live large?

On the way home, I traded in the coupons and some money for two chicken combos and then weaved through Lincoln Green's double-crap rainbows to our unit in the middle.

Janie was already in our room. She made a mock crowd-goes-wild cheer when she saw the bag from the fast-food joint.

"And my contribution," she said, presenting a DVD with a little flourish. It was some recent zombie movie, boot-legged. I couldn't give a damn about zombie movies.

"Wow, is that a new release?" I asked.

Janie smiled and wobbled her head a little, like the goose that laid the golden egg. "Boy, that crap's still in the damn theater." She drew her head back a little on her shoulders, showing off the statement.

It was hard not to smile at her. "Don't cuss."

She swatted my arm.

We got the laptop out of the hidey-hole and set it up on my bed. Janie says a friend gave the laptop to her when the

---

friend got a new one. I act like I believe this story. Sometimes you've got to take what you can get.

We sat on the floor and ate. Before long the zombie apocalypse had struck, and the citizens were fighting for survival. Janie cuddled closer, although I don't know if she was aware that she was doing it.

"Eww," she whispered. "Gross!" She lifted a lock of hair to her mouth and began chewing.

I tried to feel scared of the zombies and even remotely interested in the fate of the humans. All I could think was, *How cool would that be? How cool would it be to be able to take over a warehouse store and live there? How cool would it be to shoot or decapitate the thing that was trying to eat you whole?*

I fell asleep before the final showdown.

I woke to Janie shaking me. The credits to an animated princess movie were playing. Janie loves this movie, where the princess falls in love with the monster and frees him from a curse. I will never understand girls.

"Bedtime, huh?" I mumbled, rubbing my eyes.

"Yeah." Janie closed the laptop and gave me a hug. "Thanks."

I hugged her back, inhaling the smell of oranges that wafted up from her hair.

Downstairs there was a crash, raucous laughter, and the sound of furniture being dragged across the floor.

"For what?" I asked when the hug was over.

"Two hundred dollars. I know it wasn't easy."

I told her about the party and mall trip tomorrow.

ASH PARSONS

Janie nodded, understanding without needing me to spell it out. "I'll spend the night at Clay's."

Clay's mom was used to us showing up. Clay told her it was the pressure valve we needed, downplaying how bad it really was. Telling his mom not to call anyone about it because Janie and I didn't want to be separated in foster care.

"What about you?" she asked.

"I'll be partying all night."

Janie nodded like it was the truth. "Just as long as you don't come home until morning."

"I know the drill."

Janie stood and picked up the laptop. "Night." Her mattress springs groaned as she lay down.

I pushed my bed against the closed door of our room. As the night went by, the noises downstairs grew louder. The front door slammed repeatedly. Men shouted at each other. A woman, crying and yelling. It got quieter, except for the television's gunfire and action music. Every now and then, I could hear Janie's light, whiffling snore from the other side of the partition. I imagined decapitating monsters and waited for daylight.

ate the next morning, the cell chirped. I came awake with a start and fumbled for it under the bed. Flipped it over and read the message. Cursed.

"What is it?" Janie poked her head around the partition. Her hair was rumpled from the pillow.

I grabbed the hoodie off the floor.

"Cyndra's waiting for me outside." I cursed again, feeling my stomach knot. It was bad enough that Michael had prowled his sleek Mustang around the neighborhood after school the other day. But at least then, no one was home. Unlike now.

Janie popped around the drywall and shoved her feet into her sneakers. "It's okay. Maybe he's already gone or asleep." She grabbed some clothes and the stuffed poodle, shoving them into her backpack. She hoisted it onto her shoulder.

I cracked the door open, listening. There were no noises from downstairs.

We crept into the hall and down the creaking stairs. The couch was empty.

A heavy hand pulled me back by the hood.

"Where you going, boy?"

It amazes me how someone so big can move so silently.

I turned and faced my father. Cold eyes glared into mine—blue so pale it was almost transparent. Deep-set eyes with a blade of brow ridge lowered in a don't-fuck-with-me glare.

"Go," I ordered Janie. She could get to Clay's on her own.

The screen door banged as Janie lit out.

Good girl.

"Where you think you're going?" my father asked again, giving me a little shake.

"The mall."

"Smartass."

I feel slow around him. I can never think clearly, and I always say stupid things. I knew enough to stay quiet when I could.

His upper lip curled on his teeth. The fang-grooves appeared in the skin over his canines. He dragged me to the window. "I want to show you something." He pushed the smoke-scented blanket aside.

"See that car? Now, what's a choice car like that doing driving up and down the street for the last five minutes? That for you?"

Sometimes he'll ask something like that—and I have no idea. Maybe he's just looking for a reason to blow. Or he's being extra paranoid—it was that way when he came back from county, seeing a narc around every corner. But this time it's real, and I know who's driving the silver Mercedes with the tinted windows.

"I don't know," I said.

He dropped the hood and grabbed my hair. My cheek ground against the metal window frame.

"Try again. You holding out on me, boy?"

I dropped my weight and spun. My hair twisted in his grasp, and my chin jutted up, but not before I landed an uppercut into his solar plexus. It was like hitting a bag of sand at the building supply store: full, heavy, and so dense that you can't even make a dent.

He drove a fist into my stomach. I hadn't seen it coming, hadn't been able to tense up enough. I fell to my knees. He let go of my hair and cocked his fist again. Came at me, his massive form gliding. Improbably graceful—wide neck broadening into heavy shoulders, almost like his whole body sloped outward in one thick, muscular flare. I tried to uncurl, tried to dodge as the punch flew toward my eye. I succeeded a little, able to rise up enough so that the punch landed on my jaw instead.

When you see a real fight, it's not loud like it is in the movies. You don't have these resounding *whump*s that echo around a room like a biology book hitting a desk.

It's more like punching a piece of meat.

Unless you're the one getting hit—then it rings in your head like a sledgehammer hitting concrete, and you're shocked no one is running to see the demolition.

He seized the front of my shirt and pulled me to my feet. Did it without effort, like he was curling a weight instead of lifting a person off the floor. He shoved me against the wall. My knee shot up, but he saw it coming and knocked it aside.

I imagined the canvas heavy bag and slung a punch into his stomach.

He smiled until I sent the second one.

A fist drove at my side. I pushed into it. Sometimes that's the only thing you can do, blunt the force by stopping it short.

Grabbing the thumb around my neck, I twisted and with my free hand slung a sloppy punch at the underside of his jutting elbow.

It must have jangled some nerve endings, because he let go of my neck and swore. I ran for the door and threw myself outside and down the porch steps.

I fell against Janie, who was waiting to see if I was going to be okay.

"Go, go!" I shoved her, hard. She sobbed and ran across the scrub yard. Disappeared around the next duplex.

The Mercedes was parked right outside. I rushed to the passenger door before glancing back.

My father stood in the doorway, rubbing his elbow and smiling. He stretched, planting a hand on the door frame above him and leaning forward, opening out his chest muscles like a promise.

I opened the door and collapsed in the seat.

Cyndra squinted at the unit.

"Is that your dad? He's huge."

I slammed the door. The Mercedes started down the street.

My jaw throbbed and felt wet. I passed a light hand over it—no blood. The wet feeling was the bone bruise forming.

I hugged my ribs and caught my breath carefully, so it wouldn't hurt as much.

"Why the hell did you come here? We were supposed to meet at school." My voice was harsh. "Goddamn it!"

"Michael told me to pick you up early. To take you to lunch." Her eyes flitted between me and the road.

I leaned against the door. Rage warring with the shaking in my chest.

Cyndra kept glancing at me. She steered us onto the highway and headed toward the swank mall.

She didn't speak again until we were winding onto the access road. "I'm sorry. I'm sorry."

My eyes closed. My head rested against the leather. "Sure."

She parked. The Mercedes gave an excited rev as she turned it off. Her hand brushed my arm.

"You came out of there like your tail was on fire."

I turned to face her, and she released a slight gasp. My jaw.

"Are you okay?" Concern lit her eyes and made her voice sound different.

I nodded, because what else do you do? "Just don't pick me up at my house. Ever."

She nodded, like it was her fault. The corner of my mouth twitched up.

"I should have told you yesterday."

But Michael had already known. He'd sure as hell answer for it when I saw him.

We got out of the car and went into the store.

I was on autopilot, still feeling shaky from adrenaline and the fight, just following her gentle tugs on my arm. But what I really wanted was to sit down.

Cyndra steered me through the store, down an escalator, and led me to the same chair I'd sat in before. I let out a pent-up breath and watched the black-and-white fish defend his corner.

"Be right back."

She came back with a tray piled with food. She also had some ice wrapped in a cloth napkin. She eased a chair close and hesitantly held the napkin up toward my face, like she was afraid of me or afraid it would hurt.

"It's okay." I must have looked pretty vacant for her to be moving so carefully.

She smiled and touched the cloth to my jaw. My arms were lying on the table, and she had to reach over them to hold the napkin in place. Almost like she was reaching out to hug me or like I could lift the arm off the table and drape it around her.

We sat like that for a while, her holding the ice-filled napkin on my jaw, me watching the fish and imagining holding her. When the napkin got too wet, she put it down.

"Thanks," I said.

We ate and talked about stupid things like the fish or movies. I told her about the zombie movie Janie and I had watched.

"I don't really get zombie flicks," she said. "The others sure do seem to like them, though."

The way she said *the others* made it seem like she wasn't part of the scene.

She pushed her chair back and patted her stomach. "Ugh. I'm going to look fat tonight."

"The hell you say," I told her, taking another bite of the

gourmet burger. I had to chew slowly and on only one side of my mouth.

"Why, Jason, I do believe that's the nicest thing you've ever said to me." She leaned into me a little, for just a moment, seeming happy.

"Then you weren't listening, princess."

She smiled and leaned into my shoulder again, as I had hoped she would.

I finished the burger and tried to banish thoughts about Cyndra that went beyond the food.

"My stepdad's got a personal shopper here," Cyndra said, after we'd finished eating. We stood and started walking. She steered me into the guts of a plush department store. "I had her pull us some stuff to save time."

A thin woman in a form-fitting skirt glided over to us. "Cyndra, my dear." They clasped hands. The woman brushed a kiss above each of Cyndra's cheeks.

She turned to me. Her eyes flicked to my jaw and widened slightly. It only lasted a moment before she drew herself up and looked back at Cyndra. "So this is the young man?"

I tried not to look behind me for anyone else.

The woman led us to a dressing room and indicated a rack of clothes. She and Cyndra exited, waiting in plush chairs right outside.

I eased off the hoodie and T-shirt, taking a moment to check out my jaw and side in the full-length mirror. The jaw was already red-gray and heading to black-and-purple, with a crusted welt to one side from his ring. My side wasn't bruised yet, but it would show up later.

I tried on the clothes and some shoes, not stopping to look at the price tags, not trying to keep track of which ones Cyndra had said yes to and which ones she had said "weren't me." How she knew, I had no idea. But I had to admit that she had good taste. When we finished, Cyndra signed something and handed me the bags.

She led me back through the mall. We walked toward the exit.

"Do you like them?" she asked as we went past the aquarium and the water wall.

"The fish?"

"The clothes, Slick." Her voice took on that mocking tone so quickly. I wondered if I'd hurt her feelings.

"Yeah, they're nice," I said. "I like them fine."

Cyndra shook her head and pushed through the mall door.

Chapter Twelve

I stared out the window as Cyndra drove us into the hills surrounding the city.

We stopped at a security gate, and a guard offered a salute as we entered.

"I'm taking you to my house," Cyndra said. "It's too early for the party yet. Besides, we've got to change."

It sounded like a mandate: *We've got to change.*

She glanced at me.

"That's okay, right? I figure you'd rather hang with me than go home or whatever."

I tried on a smile, telling myself the fact that she'd seen it wasn't her fault.

"Yeah. Fine."

She flashed that magnetic smile, like she knew the power it had and wasn't afraid to use it. "Good."

"Where's the party, anyway?" I asked as the car climbed up a hill.

"Highland Terrace," she said. Like that meant something to me.

I would text it to Clay later, when Cyndra wasn't sitting right there.

We pulled onto a private drive. The road snaked through

trees and over a rise before the house appeared like magic. The driveway curved in front of massive double doors. A fountain splashed to one side.

Something else Janie would love to see—the fountain, cascading water over a mermaid and dolphin.

Cyndra handed me the department-store bags and led the way inside. The door hadn't even been locked.

I guess when you have a security gate, you don't have to worry about door locks so much.

"Come on, we'll go to my room."

"Cyndra? Is that you?" a woman's voice called.

Cyndra whispered a curse. Her shoulders slumped for only a moment before she straightened and turned an empty smile at me. She didn't say anything, so I followed her through a series of rooms toward the voice.

"Cyndra?" the woman called again.

We entered a room where a wall of glass looked out at the setting sun and over the city below. Talking heads jabbered in mute from a giant TV mounted over a massive fireplace.

The woman was on a stair-climber, the setting so fast that if it was real steps, she'd be at the top of the Empire State Building in no time.

She was gorgeous, not quite as much as her daughter, but clearly someone who spent a lot of time trying not to look like anyone's mom.

When she saw me, she came to a sudden stop. The platforms she stood on sunk slowly, finally resting at the bottoms of their arcs.

"Oh, honey, I didn't know we had company." She flashed

a dazzling smile at me and climbed off the machine. She walked forward with a hand outstretched. "Hello, I'm Tiff."

I shook her hand and glanced at Cyndra.

"Jason. Nice to meet you."

"Cyndra. Where have you been?" A man was reclining on a large sofa in front of the TV, a smirk flashing on his lips.

Cyndra crossed her arms.

"The mall," she said, an edge to her voice.

Cyndra's stepfather didn't look at me, his eyes peculiar and intense on her instead. Like she was holding a secret in her mouth, dark and vaporous.

Suddenly things started clicking, but my brain was too slow to make sense of it at first. Something about Cyndra, the way she'd been at break yesterday, the way she now wore her pose like a shield.

The way her stepfather watched her mouth, then let his eyes slide down her chest.

Tiff tinkled a laugh and mounted her stair-climber again. The steps accelerated as Cyndra's mom leaned over the arm rails of her machine, running those steps like if she could only get high enough, fast enough, she would be in time to stop some horrible event from happening.

I moved forward next to Cyndra and wrapped my arm around her.

Her stepfather barely glanced at me. "Party tonight?" he asked, flipping channels. He stopped at a scene of bikinis bouncing on the beach.

"Yes," I answered.

"Is Michael going to be there?" Tiff panted the question. An oblique way of asking just who the hell I was, again?

"We're meeting him there. Ice, let's go to my room," Cyndra said, both answering her mother's question and planting a new one. Like she wanted them to imagine exactly what we were going to do. She led me from the room.

We climbed a curved staircase, then walked down a long hall. Cyndra pushed the door closed behind us.

A huge bed dominated the center of the room. A recliner, television, and stereo filled various nooks and walls. A deep, double-door closet gaped, clothes spilling out and across the floor. Another door opened into a large bathroom.

Cyndra took the bags and tossed them into the recliner. She sighed, pulling fingers through her hair.

I leaned against the door. "I think we picked the wrong house, after all."

Her smile was brittle. "I don't get it." She knocked a stuffed elephant onto the floor and sat on the bed.

The clock ticked. Outside, the burnt sunset faded.

Cyndra pushed all the other stuffed toys onto the floor with the elephant and clicked on the TV. She got off the bed.

"I'm taking a shower." She waved at the TV. "Watch whatever you want."

She closed the bathroom door behind her.

I stretched out on her bed and texted Clay.

`Highland Terrace 9pm? I'll send the address when we get there.`

Some cooking show was on TV. I flicked the remote, amazed as always at all the crap channels.

The phone buzzed. K

I flipped the channels around to a music channel, thinking about Cyndra and her home. And mine. My eighth-grade girlfriend, Celia. And the teacher I'd punched.

I remembered the wet snap of his breaking nose.

Imagined the gun I'd buy at some pawnshop. Two bullets, each with a name.

I closed my eyes and dreamt.

Chapter Thirteen

he shifting bedsprings woke me. I opened my eyes.

Cyndra sat next to me, her hair falling in a fluffy wave. She leaned over just a little, not on top of me, but so close I could smell the flowery scent of her hair and feel the warmth of her hip next to mine.

"You frown even when you're asleep."

Every heartbeat struck an anvil behind my eyes. "I have a headache."

She traced a feathery finger around my jaw. "I'm not surprised." She lay down, propping her chin on a hand.

Her bathrobe opened a little. She curled her finger around a strand of my hair. "I could give you something to make you feel better."

She leaned forward, lips parted.

I turned my head toward her. She tasted like strawberries.

She pulled my shirt up, snaking a hand underneath. The kiss got deeper.

She climbed on top of me.

I pushed the robe off her shoulders and we kissed some more. I used the robe to trap her elbows and rolled over on top of her.

The room was dark except for the flickering light from the music channel. I worked a hand under the robe and pulled it open.

She was perfect.

She lifted my shirt. We stopped kissing long enough for me to pull it over my head. Her hands roamed my back and found the ridge of tissue there, but she didn't stop and didn't say anything.

I think I loved her.

She slid a hand into my jeans.

I kissed her mouth, her neck, moved lower.

"Stop."

I pushed up, head on fire.

Cyndra scooted over and pulled a condom packet out of her bedside drawer.

We had sex. Because she was prepared. Because she acted like it was no big deal. Because I was stupid enough to think that it wouldn't change anything.

When we were done, she rested her head on my shoulder, her hand across my stomach. It was nice, holding her, smelling her hair, not thinking about anything, just watching some singer scream a song about love as buildings exploded around him.

Her hand rubbed up and down my stomach. "Monique is going to be so jealous."

The bet.

It was all I could do to hold still. All I could do to keep from shoving her off me and onto the floor. Because of course, it was never about her actually liking me. The constant teasing, trying to get under my skin, none of it for me.

But for her. Using me, taking what she wanted, not to feel good for a moment, but just to win the fucking bet.

"Mmm." She nuzzled my ear. "I could lie here all night, but we've got to go to the party."

She got off the bed and walked to her closet. Her perfect skin gleamed in the light from the TV. She slipped a short, shimmery dress over her head and pulled on high heels. She didn't put on underwear.

"Wear this," she said, digging a light blue shirt and dark jeans out of the department store bag. She went into the bathroom.

I pulled on the jeans and walked over to the full-length mirror. If Michael looked into these pale eyes, would they give anything away? A dark bruise spread across my jaw. Another shadowed my side.

I pulled on the shirt before sitting in the recliner in front of the TV. Put on the black work-style boots, so new they creaked.

After a while, Cyndra came back from the bathroom. Her hair was fluffier, and dramatic makeup made her look like a model.

I stood as she picked up a tiny purse and jingled her keys. "Before I forget." She held out a folded bill. "For your"—her voice trailed off until I met her eyes—"time."

My face burned. I took the fifty, crumpling it into my pocket. Made myself meet her eyes.

"Just kidding." Cyndra's voice was singsongy, like we're so close now she can say anything and it won't be misunderstood. Like that was just a joke: *Don't get mad, I was just playing.*

We left her house and drove to the party. It didn't take long, which was good, because each time the Mercedes came to a stop, I nearly jumped out. Because when her slender legs worked the pedals and her hand gripped the stick shift, it reminded me of how competently she'd controlled me.

We parked and walked to the front of another mansion. This one was white, with gaslights flickering along a path and on either side of the door. It looked like an old house, but you could tell it wasn't. Music blasted inside. I slowed my steps, falling behind Cyndra as I texted the address to Clay.

At the door, Cyndra ran a hand into her hair. "Why are you dragging?" she asked, waving me forward.

"I just wanted to get a picture of the view." I leered at her as I slid the cell back in my pocket.

Cyndra giggled and brushed the front of my new shirt like it had something on it.

"All right, then. Showtime."

Her bright eyes made me dread the moment when she told the others that she'd won the bet.

I told myself I didn't care.

It wasn't like I loved her or anything pointless like that.

My head thumped in time with the music.

I followed her inside, past throngs of people and outside toward the back of the house, where more kids stood around a crystalline pool. There were kids I didn't recognize and some I did.

Beast, Dwight, and T-Man were by a keg, clutching plastic cups, standing with their legs as far apart as possible without looking completely ridiculous. Michael leaned against a low wall, his arm around Monique. His black eye was darker, but less swollen, and did nothing to mar his looks. His eyes widened momentarily at my jaw, but he didn't mention it.

"Cyn. Ice. You've arrived," he said instead.

"Hey, Ice." Monique waved her eyelashes in my direction but didn't budge from Michael's side. She licked her lips, and for a moment I actually looked forward to when Cyndra told her the bet had been won.

"Jason." Michael lifted his arm off Monique and held out his hand. I shook it and he dislodged Cyndra long enough to give me a one-armed hug.

"We need to talk." I spoke through gritted teeth. Remembering my father in the doorway.

"How'd you get that shiner?" Monique asked me. "I thought you were invincible."

Crossing my arms, I leaned against the wall. Felt Cyndra's heat next to me.

"Shut up, Mona." Michael stepped away from the girls. "Come on, Ice. Let's get you set up."

I followed him back into the house and over to a bar. Some girls had climbed on top and were dancing. One waved her shirt as she tossed her head around.

I grabbed Michael's shoulder. "Wait."

He turned, moved back against the wall.

"Why the hell did you send Cyndra to my house?" I shoved him. A controlled threat. "I should blacken your other eye."

Michael's eyes tracked down to my jaw. The muscles around his eyes eased.

If he turned that pity-filled gaze up, I *would* punch him.

He kept looking at my jaw. "Your dad." His voice was soft. More confirmation than accusation. "I'm sorry. I didn't know."

"Bullshit."

He shifted his wounded gaze up. "I mean I didn't know he'd react like that. To her picking you up. I mean, that's crazy. I'm sorry."

My fists squeezed. Eased.

"I really didn't think." His gaze was open and steady. A slight furrow to his eyebrows. "It won't happen again."

I dropped my arms. Nodded.

A clean smile, wide and easy, shined from his face. He squeezed a quick hand on my upper arm. It felt brotherly.

I stifled the surge of pleasure it gave me. Stepped back from his grip.

"We've got to meet someone, but he won't be here for a little while. Let's get you that drink while we wait, all right?" Michael walked to the bar and poured two drinks. Jerked his chin for me to follow. We weaved our way through the party, back outside where the others waited.

"Having fun?" Cyndra asked me.

"Sure." I leaned against the wall.

"You don't look it."

Michael draped his arms over her. She leaned back against him.

"That's his having-fun face," he told her. "You've seen it, right?"

I didn't know if his words were supposed to mean something. If he was saying he knew we'd had sex, testing her or me to see what we'd do.

I ignored him.

Dwight and T-Man started shoving each other. It got out of hand fast, Dwight tweaking T-Man's ear and T-Man yelling curses as they grappled.

People from another school shouted as T-Man and Dwight crashed into their group.

Michael took his arms off Cyndra and pushed between T-Man and Dwight, making them stop. "I've got a better idea." He glanced back at me. "Let's play One Hit."

Cyndra perched on the wall next to me.

"How do you play?" Dwight cracked his knuckles as he glanced back at me.

"It's easy," Michael said. "Two guys stand about this distance apart." He moved up to Dwight, squaring off. "You plant your feet like this." He moved his feet into a narrow stance. "And then you each throw a punch. Only to the stomach. One hit each. And you can't block. Try not to stumble. Don't move your feet at all."

T-Man stopped jumping and twitched his head from side to side like he was limbering up. "How do you know who wins?"

Michael smiled. "You'll know."

"Yeah, baby." T-Man laughed.

A cup was pressed into my hand. Cyndra smiled and tipped her own beer up to her lips.

The beer was warm, but I was thirsty, so I didn't mind.

"I'll go first. Who wants me?" Michael waggled his eyebrows.

Mike-Lite stepped out. "I've got it."

T-Man and Dwight looked disappointed.

I felt the heat of Cyndra's leg next to mine. LaShonda whispered into T-Man's ear. T-Man snickered and glanced at Dwight, like he was going to call him out next.

Mike-Lite and Michael squared off in the middle of the patio. Some girls I didn't recognize walked by, trying to get to the keg and ignoring us, until Michael took his shirt off.

"Anywhere you wanna go, gorgeous," one of the girls said, stopping on a dime.

"Taken, bitch. Keep walking," Cyndra called.

The girl laughed. Her friend pulled her away.

Mike-Lite took his shirt off. They didn't look like an even match, standing across from each other. Mike-Lite was burly and half a head taller. Michael's muscles were more defined, but he also clearly weighed less.

I still felt sorry for Mike-Lite.

Michael shrugged. "You wanna go first?"

"Okay." Mike-Lite dropped a shoulder and drove a fist at Michael's stomach. The hit sounded like a dull clap. Michael let out a grunt and leaned forward a bit.

Mike-Lite shook out his hand. He looked pleased with himself.

"That looked like it hurt," Cyndra murmured beside me.

I shook my head. "It was nothing."

Michael rubbed his stomach, like it actually was sore. He stood up. "Whew. My turn." Without any other warning, he slammed a fist into Mike-Lite's stomach.

Mike-Lite doubled over, gasping. He stumbled.

"Woooo!" T-Man shouted.

Michael threw an arm around Mike-Lite. The generous victor.

It wasn't surprising that Michael knew how to throw a punch, or that he wasn't afraid to follow it all the way through.

T-Man jumped up and down on the patio. "Who wants me?"

Beast smiled and ambled out. He took off his shirt and looked less like a person than a flesh-colored mountain. T-Man wasn't daunted in the least.

Beast smiled and took up the stance. T-Man jogged in place, fists up like a boxer warming up. A crowd started to gather, people drifting out from the house, thinking a fight was going to start.

T-Man held out his arms and turned in a circle. Beast popped his knuckles and waved a paw in a you-go-first gesture when T-Man was done posing.

T-Man punched Beast in the gut. It looked good, but Beast just shrugged it off.

"Aw, shit," T-Man said, but he looked eager.

Beast slung a fist at T-Man's abdomen. Beast's fist didn't turn over, smacking into T-Man's stomach vertically, and driving him back so hard he fell over.

The crowd hooted and clapped. Beast helped T-Man up.

Michael jogged back into the middle of the patio. "Me again."

Dwight took off his shirt and joined him. More people gathered, music and beers forgotten for the moment.

Dwight punched, driving his shoulder behind his fist like someone'd given him a few pointers. Michael stumbled and nearly fell. Michael's return fist was faster and hit deeper. Dwight coughed and stumbled.

It looked like a draw to most watchers.

Suddenly guys from other schools were joining in. Squaring off in little groups scattered around the patio and pool, shirts off, taking turns punching each other in the gut. Sometimes there were two, or even three pairs going at once. Guys who didn't go to the same school matched up. Michael partnered with a golden boy—someone from another school who almost looked like his equal in looks and popularity.

Michael's punch drove him to the ground.

Mike-Lite and Dwight punched. Dwight toasted him. Beast was unstoppable, and soon people stopped calling him out. He put on his shirt and came back to lean against the low wall.

"Good job," Cyndra told him. Beast smiled like she'd kissed him.

I felt my ribs, because part of me wanted to go take a few shots. Because I felt like shit for all of it. For being Michael's friend or muscle for hire. For sleeping with Cyndra, who just wanted to win a bet. For being someone who felt out of place here unless punches were being thrown.

But I didn't go out. Mostly because I guessed it was what Michael wanted. And it'd look like boasting, which only shows people that you've got something to prove.

And I didn't have to prove a goddamn thing to anyone here.

The music got louder. Guys who'd been hitting each other a moment before were smiling, arms draped over shoulders. They stood around with their shirts off for the girls, and fewer and fewer went out to play the game.

I guess they'd had enough.

I exhaled and leaned over, elbows on my knees. It was probably a good thing no one had remembered me or decided to try their luck, because I wasn't sure I would be able to stop with just one hit.

"Don't breathe a sigh of relief yet," Cyndra murmured. "Dwight's burning you up."

I glanced at him. He rolled meaty shoulders forward, crunching his pecs. He glared at me, gum snapping in his jaw.

Air huffed through my nose. "He's gonna have to do more than glare."

It was like he heard me, because he pushed through a small clump of people and stood across from my perch.

"Let's dance," he grunted.

I couldn't help it. I laughed, because he sounded so lame—like a pretend mob boss.

The crowd, mostly kids from Mercer, got quiet fast.

I guess hanging with the in-crowd only went so far. To them, maybe I'd always be a psycho.

Good.

"Promise not to step on my toes, honey?" I spat a swig of beer on the ground by his feet.

His eyes got smaller.

"One Hit," he said, like I didn't understand. "You and me."

I shook my head. "Oh, I don't think I'll be able to limit myself."

Michael cleared people off the center of the patio, making a larger space for the contest. "Come on, Jason."

I gave my beer to Cyndra and slid off the wall. Some Mercer kids were murmuring to kids from other schools standing near them. Giving them the backstory.

Dwight took up a narrow stance. I stood across from him, putting my uninjured ribs in front.

"Who goes first?" he asked.

"I don't care."

"Fine. I'll go first."

I tensed up my abdomen. But he didn't move. Just stood there.

"What's the holdup, dick?"

His eyes got so small, I thought they'd disappear.

"I'm waiting for you to take off your shirt, asshole."

"Oh, so that's what this is all about. You got a crush?"

His fist dodged out an inch or two before he stopped himself.

Damn.

"No." He shook his head like a giant struggling with a thought. "You have to take your shirt off, otherwise you have an unfair advantage."

"Yeah. Because this T-shirt is made of Kevlar and is really gonna pad the force of your punch."

He just shook his head again, and I knew that he didn't just want to punch me, he wanted to make me do it—make me take off the shirt, too, because he'd been there. He knew I didn't want to. And I couldn't walk away. Or if I did, where would I go? Walk myself down this mountain? Past the security guards?

A switch flipped inside me. This incandescent anger burning in every socket just winked out, leaving me cold, hard. Like a blade. I didn't care about any of it anymore. I began to pull at the neck of my shirt, bunching it to drag over my head.

"Wait," Michael said. "Put your shirt back on, Dwight. Just do it that way."

Dwight cut resentful eyes at Michael, but did as he was told. Then we squared off.

Dwight's fist plummeted toward me. I held my arms down and let it come, tensing up just in time. It slammed into my stomach, but skittered toward my hip, almost like he'd tried to reposition after sending it out. It looked okay, made a nice chunking sound, even made me rock to the side a bit. But it was nothing.

I didn't make any noise and didn't move. Just waited for him to stand back and drop his hands.

"Here it comes," someone said.

Sometimes it's like time slows down. I glanced at Dwight's face and saw hatred there. Remembered all the times Michael had waved Dwight away to make room for me: in class, at lunch, during break, at the party.

I'd taken his place. Which I didn't even want.

I dropped my eyes to his abdomen—imagined all the things I hated positioned there.

My fist pumped out straight, turning and driving at his stomach.

He blocked. This was no longer a game.

Dwight's fist followed the block, driving high at my injured ribs.

I pivoted inside his punch and swept my arm around his block, trapping his arm at his side and squeezing the elbow locked.

I rabbit-punched him, hard and fast, digging up with each strike to his abdomen.

He grunted and tried to bear-hug me, clawing his free arm over me and rolling out of the armlock.

I dropped, shot a hand on his throat, and lunged beside him, pivoting his head and weight over his heel. My inside foot swept behind his heel. I slammed him to the ground. Punched him in the face.

Stood up.

Lunged down and punched him in the face again.

Dwight groaned and rolled on his side, blood gushing out of his nose, eye swelling already.

Michael stepped into the circle and looked down on Dwight. "If you're not going to play by the rules, then you should at least win."

Then Michael turned to me. "We're done here. Come and get a beer."

I waited. Caught Dwight's eyes and held them until he looked away.

"Come on, Ice. This way," Michael said.

I let him lead me away, loving the adrenaline spike. A buzz of power, raw and strong. I didn't care—if it was right or if my eyes had the same addict's gleam that Michael got when he used people.

It occurred to me later, once I was sitting back on the wall, the beer a hot weight in my stomach, that the whole thing had played out pretty good for Michael: putting the leash back on me after everyone had seen the psycho bitch-slapping Michael's lead disciple. The whole thing had probably been Michael's idea.

Which made me feel twenty different kinds of stupid.

I let my eyes drift over the faces around me. Kids I didn't know were flowing past, some glancing at me like maybe they wanted a shot.

Others darted their eyes away when they saw me looking.

T-Man slapped his hand into mine. "Man, that was some shit. You handed Dwight his *ass!*"

Everyone laughed.

The music got louder. Plastic cups crunched on the patio as more people arrived at the party. I saw Clay once, hanging back, just inside the double doors. He was holding a cup and listening in on a conversation between two girls.

I was glad he was there, although it was starting to seem like nothing was going to happen.

Until Michael jerked his head at me to follow.

We walked back inside, farther into the house this time, past groups clustered around drugs. Pills, pipes, and powders. Michael hadn't been lying when he said he could get anything. There were enough drugs here to get a kid from my neighborhood bounced for dealing.

Must be different here, because no one seemed anxious about being caught holding.

Who was the supplier? One of Cesare's dealers?

Michael stopped so we could get fresh drinks at the bar, and then he pushed through a heavy oak door. The dim, green-shaded lights of a game room cast little spotlights across the pool table. A form in the darkness behind the table stood as Michael closed the door behind us.

A burly older guy stepped into the light. His hair was starting to recede, but his little-kid pug nose made it hard to guess his age.

I drained my glass, trying to ignore the needles in my side.

"This one's for you," Michael said, handing the guy his drink.

He put it down and glared at me.

"So, this's him, huh?"

Michael nodded. He started rolling a pool ball around the table. "Jason, this is Trent. Trent, Jason."

I leaned against the wall and waited.

"Jason Roberts." Trent smiled at me like it was a reunion.

I shrugged.

"You don't remember me, do you?" Trent smiled.

I tried to remember every fight I'd ever been in. I tried to picture every face, every person I'd ever thrown a punch at, or shoved, or walked away from (the short list). I tried to remember my father's friends, their kids, their mules.

"Sorry," I said. Hoping I wouldn't be.

Trent barreled forward, carrying his weight like a fighter: on the balls of his feet, ready to spring in any direction.

I tightened my grip on the glass.

Trent smiled like he understood. He held up a hand. "It's okay. We only met once, and you pretty much only had eyes for my sister."

My stomach dropped.

"She said you were the best boyfriend she ever had."

Celia. My eighth-grade girlfriend.

"Trent?" I said. Celia's brother hadn't been a "Trent."

"I like it better than Terrence." Trent shrugged. He held out his hand.

I took it.

"I told him," he said, nodding at Michael, "that if he wanted to do this thing, he'd have to get someone with real street smarts. You know, someone with balls."

I shrugged like I knew what he was talking about. Michael gave a cat-eats-mouse grin.

"And I want you to know, man," Trent continued, "that whatever happens—if we do this deal or not—I respect you. And thanks—for clocking that teacher. If I'd known, I would've killed him."

Talk is cheap.

"Yeah," I mumbled, wondering what Celia had to do with anything. "Where's Celia now?" I couldn't stop myself from asking, remembering green eyes and streaked brown hair, too much makeup and a too-knowing smile.

Trent frowned. "Who knows? She took off. She'll be all right, though. She's got smarts."

We didn't know the same girl. The Celia I'd known had been desperate for someone to take care of her, to love her, to do right. So desperate, she'd latch on to anyone who'd hold her, no matter who they were.

Even me. Or a teacher old enough to be her father.

Trent shook his head and smiled at Michael. "I guess you're serious, huh?"

Michael nodded, eager, like a little kid incinerating ants with a magnifying glass.

Trent squinted at me. He scratched his gut. "You're the buy-in for little man to even sit at the table," he told me.

Michael still smiled, but it didn't reach his eyes.

Trent shook his head with a kids-these-days expression. Even though he was only a few years older, you could see he liked pretending to be an authority. A petty Caesar.

"All right, all right," Trent chanted. "To the first order of business."

He reached into his back waistband. Brought out a gun. A 9mm semiautomatic, gleaming and dark. It pulled my eyes like a black hole.

"I heard about your troubles," Trent said to Michael. He ejected the clip. Popped the slide back. Pulled the trigger, clicking it back in place. Handed the gun over.

Michael sighted down the barrel. "What troubles?"

Trent snorted. "Right. 'Whatever the problem, bullets are the answer.'" He nodded at the gun in Michael's hand.

"It's clean. Well, not clean. Probably been used in some shootings. But clean to you."

Michael smiled and reached for the clip. He slapped it in with the heel of his hand, thumbed the safety, and tucked the gun in the waistband under his shirt. He fished into a pocket. Pressed a wad of bills into Trent's hand.

Michael shot a little-kid grin at me. "I need some time to talk to Trent, Ice." He tipped his head toward the door. "Enjoy the party."

Trent watched me go.

I stepped back out into the thudding music and strip-teasers.

CHAPTER FOURTEEN

he sounds of the party pounded in my head. I closed my eyes and rubbed my temples. Opened them again and didn't see anyone I knew. Fished the cell out and saw that Clay had texted, What a swell party this is. Knowing Clay, it was probably a quote or something. I could hear him saying it, dry, with just the right kill-me-now inflection.

I snorted.

It felt stupid, standing in front of a closed door with the party going on all around me, so I pushed through the crowd, heading back to the pool where the others were. I looked for Clay. Not that I would be talking to him, but just to see where he was.

I didn't see him on the way out.

No one else from Michael's group was there. So I found an empty lounge chair and stretched out. A few kids played around by the pool and some ended up in it. I draped my arm over my eyes and ignored the others. And couldn't decide if I wanted to see Cyndra or not. I pictured her shiny dress, remembered watching her put it on, and what she wasn't wearing underneath. The way her head had felt, resting on my shoulder. She'd recognized that I didn't know how to use chopsticks that time at the mall and had brought me the fork. Sat me in front of the aquarium and held ice on my jaw.

She'd given me money for my "time." Won the bet.

I pictured her telling the others about it. What would she say? I imagined them laughing, the girls congratulating, Cyndra collecting the money. Maybe Michael would congratulate her, too, before taking his cut.

"All by yourself, huh?" Monique stood over me, holding two plastic cups.

I put my arm back over my eyes. "Yeah."

"Now, we can't have that." The cushion shifted as she sat down next to my legs. "I saw you over here, lonely as a cloud, and so I brought you this." She knocked the plastic cup against my free hand.

I sat up, taking the cup. Monique looked at me, that same, overly seductive smile hovering on her lips. The fact that she'd searched me out, with a drink, told me something, I just didn't know what. Either Cyndra had told everyone and it didn't matter to Monique, or Cyndra hadn't told yet. And if not, what did that mean?

I drank, two big gulps. Monique smiled and inched closer. She brushed her fingers through her hair and squinted at the kids splashing in the pool. "That's lame," she said when two girls started fighting in the shallow end.

We watched for a little while, until some guys pulled them apart and lifted them out of the pool.

"Thanks for this," I said, holding out the cup.

"You're not finished."

"Yeah, I am." I stood up, thinking I'd go find Cyndra or Michael, or the hell with it, maybe even Clay, and get a ride out of there.

I stumbled against a table, knocked over a few drinks.

Monique was under my arm in an instant. "Easy, Ice. Here, come with me."

My head felt like an aquarium full of circle-swimming fish. An aquarium with an obnoxious kid knocking on the glass. I was feeling so sick that I didn't suspect anything until Monique piloted us to an empty bedroom. Then it clicked together.

I braced my arms against the doorway. "The drink."

Monique giggled. "Oh, don't be like that. It's just us. Let's party." She yanked at the front of my shirt.

I pulled away and stumbled down the hall. Monique followed, laughing. I found an empty couch and fell on it. Two girls danced and kissed on the coffee table in front of the sofa. A martial arts movie ran silently on the screen hanging on the wall.

Monique sat next to me, pressing into my side and snaking a hand under my shirt. She popped up on her knees and started kissing me, shoving her tongue into my mouth.

I felt like lead. Like the water in the aquarium was getting cold, like the fish weren't swimming around, even the black-and-white one drifting slowly to the bottom.

"Do you mind? I'm trying to watch two girls kissing. It's sort of a fantasy, and your roofie rape scene is ruining it."

"Clay." His name was hard to say. My head rolled to the

side. He stood in the doorway. Despite his words, he didn't spare a glance for the two girls on the coffee table.

"Who the hell are you?" Monique didn't shift her weight off my chest.

Clay didn't answer her. Instead, he slapped my cheeks as Monique slid off me.

"Are you okay, Jason?" His face elongated and tilted. The room spun—starting at my chin and arcing through the top of my skull.

"No," I mumbled. Closed my eyes again.

"He's fine. He's just had a lot to drink." Mona's voice receded slightly as she stood.

"Right. Whiskey with a side of GHB."

I fought to keep my eyes open. The room tunneled closer. Clay stood over me, an improbable protector as Monique walked out. My eyes kept rolling up.

"Ladies, you delight me, but maybe you could take your party outside? Here. On me." Clay held out something in the palm of his hand.

"Sure, whatever," one of the girls said. She took a white pill out of Clay's hand and handed the other to her friend. They swallowed the pills and left.

Clay closed the door after them and sat on the sofa. My head lolled over toward his shoulder. "Thanks," I managed through the rocks in my mouth.

Clay shook his head. "I thought only girls had to worry about that crap. I guess it's good you asked me to be here, after all."

I wanted to nod, but couldn't muster the energy.

"What were those pills?" I mumbled.

"Just caffeine. I wasn't about to come here empty-handed."

A laugh clogged my throat, gurgling.

"Laugh it up, Fuzzball." Clay picked up the remote. "We'll wait here for a while." He surfed through some channels, stopped on a lame reality show. I closed my eyes and felt stupid.

After a second episode, I could hold my head up without the room spinning too fast. Thinking was still an effort, but moving was getting easier.

"Guess you didn't drink much," Clay said.

"Half," I said. I rubbed my eyes.

"Good. Only a little longer and we can get out of here."

He watched the show. I closed my eyes. The party grew louder. As it got easier to think, it got easier to talk. I filled Clay in on the scene at school yesterday morning: Cyndra coming to get me in the cafeteria, Michael's bruised face and his gambling debts to Cesare. And what Janie had already told him: how Cyndra's coming to my house early had set off my dad.

Clay absorbed it all, nodding. "So did Michael get the gun?" he asked, holding a hand out to the party on the other side of the door.

"Yeah."

Clay whistled low. "This is getting intense."

"I know. But I need to keep it going a little longer." Thinking not only of the money now, but of Cyndra. Holding her on the canopied bed in her room. Red-gold hair sliding across my skin.

"Just don't take any more drinks from anyone, okay, Champ?" Clay said, as I stood.

"You got that right," I answered, feeling a bit light-headed and trying not to show it.

"You good?" Clay watched me closely.

I nodded. My head felt like it was packed with gauze.

"What now? You're not going home." His eyes snagged on the bruises on my face.

A sudden image of my father, hulking in the doorway and watching me get into a car I had claimed to know nothing about.

"No." I pushed my hands into my hair, wanting to scrub off the fatigue.

"Well, I'm parked down the street. It sounds crazy enough out there, we could probably just slip out."

"I was kind of hoping to go home with Cyndra." For some reason, saying it made me feel even stupider than getting roofied had. Stupid because I figured I knew how she really felt about me. And because of how she had made me feel after we'd had sex. Stupid all the way to the bottom of my stupid heart—because I wanted to be with her again, in spite of it all.

"Oh." Clay's voice held a world of understanding. "I was right about that, huh?"

But it wasn't a question. I met his eyes. And it was like looking into the eyes of a concerned teacher—this slight frown pinching his eyebrows and a small smile, edged with worry.

I shrugged, feeling the new clothes tight across my shoulders. One more thing that I pretended: that they *fit* me.

"Yeah." I wanted to say more, but couldn't find my way

to the words through the blaring noise of the party and the pounding in my head.

The worry on Clay's face stamped itself deeper.

"It's okay," I told him. *It is what it is,* I told myself. As I opened the door, the roar of the party pounded into my throbbing skull.

I turned and held out a hand. "Thanks for the save."

Clay slid a shake. I pulled him into a quick, one-armed hug and then let go. He looked up at me with that calculation working behind his eyes.

"Don't forget who they are." What he didn't say, but I heard under the words: *Don't forget who you are.*

"I'll see you tomorrow. Tell Janie where I'll be. Tell her I'm fine."

"Yeah."

I walked out into the noise and got better with every step. Went back outside by the pool, more to get away from the relentless music than hoping to find any of Michael's crew there.

"Ice!" Cyndra ran up like she'd been looking for me. I sat heavily on the low wall.

"What's wrong? You look like hell," she said.

"Monique spiked my drink," I answered, surprising myself.

Cyndra's eyes bored into mine. "That bitch."

"I'm fine. She didn't get what she wanted."

"She'll do anything to get there first, I guess," she said.

I knew what it meant—but not what to make of it. Was our having sex supposed to be a secret because of Michael?

Could it be that she didn't care about bragging rights or the bet? That she actually cared about me?

My head throbbed all over again. Yet I somehow felt good at the same time.

Cyndra ran her hand down my arm. "You feel okay?"

I shook my head. Wished I hadn't.

"I'll kill her." Usually if someone sexy like Cyndra said something like that, it'd make me laugh or smile. But she looked serious.

"It's okay. I can handle it," I told her.

"Fine. I'll hold her down and you kill her."

I had to laugh. It made my side sting.

Cyndra tucked herself under my arm. "Let's go find Michael. Then we can get out of here."

"Or we could just go."

"Yeah, but I want to go to his house. I'm not too anxious to go home tonight. You?"

Michael's house. Seemed better than the old gym.

We wandered through the party and found the group sitting around the kitchen table: Michael, Beast, Mike-Lite, T-Man, and the others.

A distinct, burning smell punctuated the haze of cigarettes.

"Hang on," Cyndra murmured. "Wait here."

I leaned in the doorway as she walked around the table and whispered in Michael's ear. He fished in his pocket and spiraled a key off the key ring. He grabbed Cyndra's elbow and pulled her close, murmuring in her ear.

Then he shoved her away.

Cyndra stumbled, caught her balance. Her eyes darted around. She lifted her chin.

"See you there later," Michael said. He nodded at me like it was important I see him. To see that he was dismissing me. That he was still in control, had finished with me after getting what he'd wanted. What had he wanted more—the fight or the gun?

CHAPTER FIFTEEN

On the way out, I stood by the door, waiting for Cyndra to finish her good-byes. Part-iers eddied around me, yelling boasts and knocking plastic cups together in toasts.

Someone stumbled into me.

"Oh. Sorry," Nico slurred, then smiled when he saw who it was he'd fallen against. "Jason! The man we're looking for!"

He turned and waved Spud over. We clasped hands briefly. I wanted to ask my stoner friends if they were in the habit of attending King-of-the-Mountain parties.

They seemed comfortable enough.

Nico tipped his head. We eased back toward the door. He leaned in close, dropping his voice.

"We want some. For later. You holding?"

Anger match-struck in my chest. It flared out fast, though. They were wasted, and it wasn't like we were re-ally close to begin with.

I thought they knew me better than that, though.

At least they knew me well enough not to mention, or perhaps even notice, my jaw.

"You're barking up the wrong tree, Nico."

Nico leaned back. Squinted up at me. Shifted the knitted beanie he wore with a quizzical scratch.

Spud gave him an assist. "Dude, it's cool. We've got money." He fumbled in a pocket.

"Listen to me." My eyes speared their attention. Spud quit digging for the money. "I don't have any of that crap."

"Dude," Spud breathed. He could give the word a hundred different meanings. This time it was filled with not-cool betrayal.

Nico shook his head, still scratching at his beanie. "Then what the hell are you doing here?"

It fell in my mind like a missing puzzle piece. And then I really did feel stupid.

Of course it would look to all the world that I was dealing drugs to the rich kids. The new clothes. The mysterious and sudden elevation to their social strata.

And Michael had to know it. Had to want that puzzle taking shape.

So if *I* wasn't dealing to them . . . who was?

"It's not me." I looked between them.

Nico nodded.

"Dude." Spud held out a fist. I bumped it.

"I need a favor," I told them. Spud crossed his arms and took a wide stance, like a badass bouncer, ready for anything the crowd could throw at him. Nico nodded and fiddled with his beanie again.

"When you find out who it is, tell me."

Nico nodded.

"Ready to go?" Cyndra asked. She curled a hand around my bicep.

Spud's eyes slid over her spangled dress. Pinballed between her legs and chest. I slapped hands with Nico and Spud. Cyndra and I left.

In the car, I leaned my throbbing head against the seat. Let my thoughts slow. It didn't matter what anyone thought. Including Michael. It didn't matter who was dealing drugs or that Michael wanted everyone to think it was me.

I'd worry about it later. I'd figure it out.

Back at Michael's house, Cyndra led me to the downstairs bar, where Michael had first hired me.

Hard to believe it was only three days ago.

"Guess Michael's parents are at a party, too, right?" I asked. It was obvious no one was home. "Wonder if they'll play One Hit?"

Cyndra laughed. "Who knows. Travel and work, that's them. They're never home. I swear, I think they only have a house because it's what people do."

I looked around the empty room, trying to imagine what kind of problems come from being alone in so much space.

I couldn't think of any.

"Have a drink?" Cyndra was already fixing herself one.

My head throbbed. I still felt a little fuzzy—like everything was happening apart from me.

"No thanks." I sat down.

"Not here. Follow me." Cyndra turned and carried her drink into another room. She disappeared, and a light switched on. She came back and stood in the doorway. The dim light glinted off her short dress.

"In here." Her fingers toyed with the edge of the dress.

I walked to her. "I feel like hell. Do you know where an aspirin or something is?"

Cyndra stuck out her lip. "Poor Jason." Her fingers brushed the hair off my face. My hand twitched—wanting to knock her hand away, or catch it and pull her closer.

"Seriously," I said. "Do you have something?"

Cyndra took a step closer. So close I could feel her breath. She turned around, brushing against me.

The dress lifted.

"'No fun tonight, dear,'" she singsonged, "'I have a headache.'"

My pulse anviled in my temples. My jaw felt swollen and wet.

Anger burst like a flare. I caught her arm and twisted it behind her back. She gasped as I propelled her into the room and pushed her down onto the giant bed.

She arched back into me.

My head splintered. Part of me wanted to give her what she wanted.

The other part hated her.

I let go and stood. "It was a mistake coming here." I made it to the door before she caught up.

"Jason, stop."

My arm whipped out of her grasp. "I. Feel. Like. Hell." Each word gritted in my teeth.

"I'm sorry!" Her hands opened. "I'm so sorry. I didn't mean—I mean—I thought you'd like—" She held up a hand.

"Wait. Okay? Wait. I know where some medicine is." She turned and went to a bathroom attached to the bedroom. The sounds of opening drawers and cabinets crashed in my ears.

"Don't go, okay? I didn't mean to make you mad." She came back—holding out a red-capped bottle. "See? Extra strength." Her eyes were wide, glistening in the dim light. A wisp of hair dangled near her mouth and puffed with her breath.

I grabbed the bottle.

"I'll get you some water," she said.

I popped open the cap and shook a couple of capsules into my hand. "Don't bother." I tipped my head and dry swallowed them.

I felt the heat of her arm as she moved to stand by my side again. Her hand slid into mine, a butterfly landing on a cactus.

"Why don't you lie down?" she asked.

I opened my eyes, not trusting her for a second.

"Just lie down. That's all."

I looked at her, studying. The sexy pose was gone, just a believe-me look in her eyes.

The bed was huge—covered in a black puffy comforter. Cyndra pushed the covers back. I took off my shoes and lay down in the middle. The bed was bigger than my side of the room I shared with Janie.

Cyndra lay down with her head on my shoulder. She carefully draped her arm over my stomach, rather than have it press against my side. I kissed the top of her head.

"Sorry," she breathed.

Still Waters

"Me too."

We fell asleep.

The house was so quiet it woke me up about an hour or so later. Cyndra's head was a warm weight. Her quiet breathing and the soft shush of the air-conditioning were the only sounds.

From the dim light of the adjoining bathroom, I took my first real look around the room. It was stark and impersonal. The walls were a sandy color, and thick carpet covered the floor. There was a TV and stereo—but no DVDs or music or books anywhere. No posters, no knickknacks, nothing lying around. A room that no one lived in, empty like a shell and less homey-feeling than a motel room.

There was a single picture, a large painting—it looked old. In it, some fruit, some cheese, a bowl, and a dead dove were draped and painted with meticulous detail. The dove's still eye, glistening but vacant, shone into the room. Its sinuous, limp neck dangled off the table. A blood-matted cluster of feathers pressed up against the firm curve of an apple.

I looked away.

A practically empty room. A guest room rarely used— in a house full of rooms. All rooms and no people.

I could get used to this.

My fingers brushed over Cyndra's hair. Was Michael upstairs in his room, or was he still at the party?

I rolled a lock of silky hair between my thumb and forefinger, rubbing gently, feeling the strands cling to and slide over each other.

We should get out of this bed. I should wake her up.

I remembered the robe coming off. Her tan skin—her body, soft under me. The taste of strawberry lip gloss.

My arms closed back around her.

. . .

Someone was shaking my shoulder.

A splintering headache stabbed behind my right ear. I groaned and opened my eyes.

Michael stood beside the bed. He let go of my shoulder, and the corners of his mouth twitched up.

"You make yourself right at home, don't you?"

My hand reached out before I could stop it. The sheets were still warm, but Cyndra was gone.

I sat up and immediately regretted it. Nausea coiled in my stomach. I leaned back against the headboard.

"Didn't think you'd mind," I said. My jaw ached.

Michael sat in a leather chair. "I don't mind. I'm just surprised."

I cautiously tented my fingers over my side and probed. It wasn't that tender, so no broken or cracked ribs, at least.

I glanced around—trying to hide the search for my shirt. Michael picked it off the floor and threw it to me.

"And now you're ready once again to shroud the fabled abs. Poor Monique. Too bad she isn't here."

I slid the shirt on.

"And no embarrassing chest tattoo. So, still a mystery why all the modesty."

I changed the subject. "You knew I was crashing here. Why the surprise?"

Michael's eyes glowed with that weird light—a power-mad glint. The look that told you something was wrong, and he was happy about it. It felt predatory. It made me think of my father right before a blowup.

My fists clenched. Tensed shoulders dropped and squared. I stayed leaning against the headboard.

"It's surprising, that's all." He leaned his elbows on his knees and rolled his head, like his neck was stiff. "Surprising, the way you make free with my things."

I froze. Of course he knew about Cyndra.

Had he walked in and found us? Watched us sleeping? Where was she?

At least my pants weren't on the floor by the bed.

But he wasn't stupid. Even so, pretense was maybe the best defense.

"What do you mean?" I asked.

Michael laughed—the eerie look intensified. If he were my dad, I'd be running.

Or dead.

He relaxed, suddenly throwing out a hand like he was a game-show host showing off a car. "Look at you. In my bed! All the places to sleep in this house, and Iceman picks my room, my bed. Please tell me you're not commando under my sheets."

His smile wasn't real.

Neither was my laugh. "You're safe."

He sighed and mimed wiping sweat off his brow.

Was he gaming me? This empty room was his? Why had Cyndra brought me to *this* bed?

I remembered Michael, murmuring in her ear at the party. Shoving her away.

"There you both are." Cyndra leaned in the doorway.

The black comforter puffed as I threw back the covers and planted my feet on the carpet. I leaned over, shoved my feet into my boots, and worked the stiff laces. My head pounded so hard I thought blood might pool in my ears if I didn't sit up soon.

Cyndra padded over and sat on Michael's lap. She kissed him.

I ignored her. This wasn't the girl who'd spent the night with me.

Don't feel it.

I told myself I wasn't stupid.

Michael grabbed Cyndra by the back of the neck. "Give us a kiss."

For a second it looked like she'd refuse. For a moment, I thought, *Here it comes. Let it come.*

She kissed him. He pressed his face so hard against hers, she whimpered. It didn't sound sexy.

I walked out.

"All right, let's go." He stood in the doorway behind me. Cyndra bit her lip. Michael waved a hand. "Let's go, Ice."

We walked outside to his car. I could see Cyndra standing by the pool when Michael started the engine. The sunrise was bruise-purple. Low clouds glinted like gunmetal.

Cyndra stared out at the horizon, hugging herself.

ichael stopped and got us breakfast at a drive-through. He drove to a lookout and handed over the bag.

"What are we doing here?" I asked.

"Just a talk," he said. "Why, you wanna make out?" He got out of the car. He jogged over to the other car parked at the lookout and thumped on the window.

"Screw you!" The man inside yelled.

"Cops are coming. Passed them on the way up. Trying to help." He walked away with his hands out like *kill a guy for trying.*

After a moment, the car started and pulled out.

"Sucka."

We walked toward the wall at the lookout point. The sun edged farther into the sky. I ate.

"So here it is. Advice for you," Michael said. "Don't trust her."

"Who are we talking about?"

Michael's lips twitched, and he glanced away from me, squinting out over the city. "We're talking about Cyn, Ice.

Little Miss Temptation." He glared into my eyes, that small smile hovering around his lips. "Temp-ta-tion," he sang. "Temp-ta-tion, I can't resist."

I took another bite.

"She'll use you. I've seen it happen. Use her first. Put her in her place."

"Whatever."

"Listen, cut the bull." Michael caught my eyes with his. "I know. You know I know. So let's just talk."

"Then talk." The food was a lump in my stomach.

"I don't care, okay? Cyn and I—we're open."

I couldn't tell if it was true or if he had another goal he wanted more than her. "You're lying. You care."

"No, that's you. Not me."

"That scene in your room. You care."

"Not about that."

"She's your girlfriend. You control her," I said.

"That's like controlling the tide, Iceman. You don't control it. You use it."

"Okay." I squinted at the rising sun, hanging low like a stranger at a party.

"You don't get it. It's cool. You'll see." He threw a rock over the wall.

"Listen, you don't have to worry about me," I said. This was maybe the most surreal conversation I'd ever had— reassuring a guy that I was fine after sleeping with his girl-friend. "Just keep the money coming, all right?"

"It's a business thing."

"Right." I shrugged.

"And screwing Cyndra, that's just perks."

I kept my mouth shut. If he wanted to convince me he really didn't care, he'd have to stop laying traps like that.

Michael whistled and shook his hand like he'd just punched something and it hurt.

"Wooo. She's got you. My girl has gone and got you!" He jumped off the wall and started pacing. "Stay cold, Ice. Don't let her melt you away."

I just watched him and didn't say anything.

Michael got serious. "Listen, I only want to give you the key. The lever that will move her little world. Do what you want with her, but don't go getting any delusions."

"You're trying to protect me?" It was so ridiculous I couldn't stop a real smile from coming. "I don't have any delusions, believe me."

"Yes, you do."

"All right, Prom King, what am I deluded about?"

"About her. True love. Knight in shining armor. Saving the damsel in distress," Michael said.

"Saving her from what?"

A faint smile hovered on his lips. "Come on. You know. She took you home, didn't she? Let you watch the creep show live and in person? Don't let her play that tired old card."

My stomach felt like I was in a dropping elevator. I kept my mouth shut and watched as the streetlights in the valley below us started winking out.

He chuckled. "She's good. Got to give her that."

"What are you saying?"

"Given your background"—he waved a hand—"you reached certain . . . conclusions."

My mouth snapped shut so fast my teeth clicked. My eyes dared him to say it.

"She's got him right where she wants him."

My jaw ached with the words I held back. Typical abuser justification. Excuses. She-wanted-it rationale.

Michael kept talking. I imagined breaking his nose.

"It's what she gets off on. Power. It's how she gets everything she wants. I'm telling you so you can stay in control. You work for me—not her. If you want out, just say so. But don't expect any freebies, from either of us."

My head hurt.

"You can't blame her," he said. "For setting you up to 'save' her. It's her favorite game."

I stood—fighting the urge to argue.

"So tell me now. You want to quit?" Michael asked.

My heart pounded, but I was still on the outside.

"Didn't think so," he said. He was back in control, and he knew it. "Let's go."

We walked back to the car. He opened his door, grinning. "I'm glad we had this little talk, son."

On the drive down, he drummed the wheel and took the corners so fast I thought we'd go up on two wheels.

"Where to?" he asked.

"The school."

He didn't ask why, just took me there and cut the engine once we were in the deserted lot.

"Postponing the inevitable, huh?" he asked.

I was tired of trying to understand him. I stared blankly.

He gestured at my jaw. "You're in no rush to go home."

I made an effort not to look away.

"It's not a mystery, you know," he said. "Once you start paying attention, it all comes together."

I shook out a cigarette. "You got my money?"

It was his turn to ignore me. "For example—all the fights. The legend of the ass-kicker. What better way to learn to kick ass than to have yours handed to you at home?"

I blew smoke in the car.

"And punching that teacher. That was for your little girl-friend, but she was trash. So what was that really about?"

I unlocked the door and held out my hand.

"Your sister. Janie, right?"

"Keep her name out of your mouth unless you want it wired shut." Inside my head there was a buzz-saw whine and the calm that comes before I start throwing fists.

He fished in his pocket and brought out a fat roll of cash. "You know you had twenty-five absences last year?"

"Are you going to pay me, or do I grind this out on your dashboard?"

He handed over a twenty.

"That business with the shirt. That's about your back. What was it, a belt buckle? Extension cord?"

He peeled off another twenty.

"You know what gets me?" he asked, handing the sec-ond bill over. "According to your file"—waving the wad of bills toward the school—"your home has been reported to

DHR three times since you've been at Mercer. That means it's been investigated, and you're having to lie to them. You're having to *work* to stay where you are."

I felt like a fish in the open air.

"My file?" I'd never even thought of one—at least, not one that reported more than my absences and discipline referrals.

Michael smiled. "I got LaShonda to make a few copies. She's an office aide. Future Business Leader of America, my ass. I told her to think of it as corporate espionage. Then she went for it. Sick, right?"

He handed over another twenty.

"Yeah. *Congratulations.* You're real good at manipulating people."

"It's a gift."

He unrolled the wad of cash and fanned it.

"What I can't figure out, and no file will ever tell me, is why you're still there." He held out a bill, a lure to talk.

I took it. "Foster care is worse. Group homes, too."

"Not for you, though. For her." Walking the line. He peeled off another bill. "Okay, no foster care. And also no running away. Janie again. I get it."

My hands clenched.

He held out the bill. "Why don't you just kill him?"

The air went out of my lungs. I imagined my plan—a few years from now—the barrel of the gun pressed into his temple or jammed into his mouth.

Pulling the trigger.

"It's not that easy."

Michael pulled the bill away. "If that's your answer . . ."

I scrubbed my hands on my legs. Hating him. Wanting the money.

"Look, so I kill him. Then what? He's dead. I go to prison. Janie—"

My mouth snapped shut.

Michael slid off another bill and held it out.

"Who said anything about getting caught?"

I took the money. "He's strong. And he's not stupid. He's paranoid. I'd have to shoot him. My record? They'd put me away."

"Make it self-defense."

"How exactly do I do that?"

"Well, shoot him, like you said—"

I interrupted him. "With what?"

"His gun."

I shook my head. "Impossible. He keeps it on him."

"You could use mine."

My head spun. "Okay—so I use *your* gun. How is it self-defense?"

"The DHR referrals. Your record."

"My record shows a kid who got sent to juvie for decking a teacher. Among other things."

"Make it airtight. Make him go for you. In front of witnesses. And then, shoot him."

"What if a judge thinks I need counseling or a residential care center or a group home? You can't just shoot somebody and get away with it."

"I could."

ASH PARSONS

He changed like a fast-moving storm, intensity lighting his eyes. I laughed but felt like running.

"Sure, Prom King." I put my hand on the door.

He handed me another twenty. "I did it, officer. It was me." His voice shook with nerves and adrenaline. "I was worried about my friend. You know his dad beat him? Damn useless social workers. I was getting worried. It was escalating. I tried to get him and his little sister to run away." His voice was panicked. A good kid caught in a bad situation. "They finally agreed. I went over to get them—was gonna take them to the bus station. I walked right into it. It was the worst thing I've ever seen."

I sat, transfixed.

A tear slid down his cheek.

"I didn't know what to do!" His voice broke. "His dad was *killing* him. I found the gun—"

"What gun?"

He dropped the act. "The one you had."

"Mine?"

"Weren't you listening? I gave you mine. We don't say that, though."

I shook my head. "What are we talking about here? You're going to kill him?"

"I could get away with it."

He could, too. And I could stay out of juvie and maybe even get appointed as Janie's legal guardian.

"You'd have to get the crap kicked out of you, but that's no big deal. Is it?"

He talked about it so easily.

"Sorry," he said. "I just mean that's happening already, right?"

"Why would *you* do it?" Not asking about his alibi—asking the real question.

He shrugged. His lips pursed. "I've never killed anybody."

He said it like it was an experience he should have. Something on a bucket list. He didn't give a damn about me. My situation was his opportunity. Nothing more. Chills marched over my skin.

"It's too risky," I said. "It wouldn't go down like that."

"You're wrong. It's perfect."

"It's messed up." What I was thinking: that he's never watched someone getting killed, either. That he might go for the double header. Watch me get killed, then shoot him after.

"You don't trust me."

Which was so obvious it didn't warrant a response.

"My dad's not stupid. He might smell it and not go for it. And that'd leave me worse off than before."

"The same."

"Worse."

He put his window down and propped an arm there. "You don't trust me." Repeated, like he could fix it.

"I don't trust anybody."

He sighed. "Maybe there's another way we could do it. Some way you'd trust." He made it sound like we were a team.

"Sure," I said, but my tone was fat-fucking-chance. I

opened the door. "You have your own problems to worry about."

Michael smiled. "Don't you see? This would help with that. It's perfect. Cesare would leave me alone for sure once he heard I'd killed someone and gotten away with it."

I shook my head, put my foot out.

He held out a bill. "What's going to happen when you get home?"

I ignored the bill and stood. "I'm not going home." I slammed the door and waited for him to drive away.

He got out and leaned on the roof. He waved the money. "How much would it take to get you to try it?"

"More than you have."

"All right, give me something else, then." He counted out a hundred. Held it out to me. "You can have this if you let me see your back."

My blood turned to ice. "Go to hell."

He added another bill to the stack. "Now?"

I stood.

He added another. "Now?"

I couldn't take my eyes off the money.

He put another twenty on top. "Now?"

I watched him. Would he keep going? What would I do when he stopped?

He must have sensed me waiting, driving the price up. He pocketed the rest of the bills, leaving the big stack fanned in his hand.

"And that's my final offer." He dragged the bills under his nose. "Don't you love the smell of it?"

A hundred and sixty dollars, and all I had to do was turn around and show my back.

My hand twitched. I walked around the car and stood next to him. He smiled, that pedophile-on-a-church-picnic look in his eyes.

A coil of nausea burned in my stomach and threaded up into my throat. I told myself the money was compensation, because who paid to see a scar?

It didn't mean anything.

It was just too much money to walk away from.

I took off my shirt. Turned around. Accepted the use.

I stared at cigarette butts flattened on the pavement and thought about Janie.

I put my shirt back on and faced him.

Michael handed the money over. "Interesting. Not quite what I'd expected." A doctor at the freak show.

I glared at him. My voice wouldn't come. I didn't look for it.

"See you tomorrow," he said, getting into his car.

I watched him peel out, feeling the lump of cash in my hand. The parking lot was empty. A gang of crows wheeled overhead—diving and falling, chasing a lone outcast across the sky.

Chapter Seventeen

ometimes you can feel yourself sinking. Black water sucking at your heels, and it gets harder to move, harder to fight.

I felt it starting when I took the money— hate sucking at my heels, self-destruction not far behind.

And underneath that, the knowledge that it didn't matter when I finally went home. Now or tomorrow or the next day. My dad would be waiting.

At least if I got it over with now, Janie wouldn't be there.

I went to the old gym. Lifted the window and climbed through. Stood in the dank shower room.

Felt the wad of cash coal-hard in my pocket.

The black water settled in my chest. I pulled the money out and spread it on a bench. Two hundred and eighty dollars.

Tore through my locker, and brought out a boxing glove. Wadded up the money and shoved it inside the glove before putting it back. My dad would be waiting, and I wasn't about to hand over the cash after all the crap I'd gone through.

I turned back to the window. My reflection in the clouded mirrors, wild-eyed. I climbed out, closing the window behind me.

On the walk home, I had to stop myself from breaking into a run. Black tissue spread through my chest, tumorous fingers squeezing my heart. I took the porch steps two at a time.

The sound of the slamming door brought him out.

I felt myself smiling. The blackness buzzed in my ears, whispered, screamed. So I cursed him.

He came at me, lips curled onto his teeth. Fang-groove creases arrowing down over his mouth.

The black tide covered me, bubbled up in my chest like laughter. His fist drove at my face in a straight line, rolling as it came—perfect and true. Beautiful.

I stepped in, dodging his first punch before the second one caught me. Lightning flashed in my skull. My legs gave out and I was falling. The black water rushed over my head before I landed.

. . .

"Jason?" A little voice, mouse-gnawing on the sparking wires in my brain. A hand shook my shoulder.

"Jason, sit up."

I realized my eyes were open, although one was nearly swollen shut.

Janie's cheeks were wet. She helped me stand. The floor tilted like a ship.

"You provoked him. And you told Clay you weren't coming here." An accusation. Janie wedged herself under my arm, too tight against my ribs.

I hissed.

"Sorry," she breathed. "But you probably deserve that. Jerk."

"Don't be mad." My voice was slurry and cotton-packed. "Honest pay for honest work." I laughed.

We stumbled up the stairs. In the room, she helped me fall onto my bed.

I felt full and light, a balloon swelling to pop.

"Okay, what's two plus two?" Janie asked. "What did you eat for breakfast?"

"Four. Knuckles." A giggle fizzed in my chest. Nothing hurt. "It's fine, Janie. It's better this way."

"Yeah. You look better."

"Bitch."

"Shitbird." She sighed and pulled her hair into a ponytail. Planted hands on narrow hips, skinny elbows daggering the air by my head. Her eyes scoured my face. My laugh bubbled out again. Endorphins and relief and low tide.

"See"—I shook a finger at her—"never forget the evil bastard is a sadist. If you seek it out, he pulls his punches."

Her eyebrow rose. "Well, that's abundantly clear."

The laugh came out a cough. It was like unstopping a can of soda that's been knocked down the stairs. I started laughing and couldn't stop. I laughed because I wouldn't be going to school tomorrow or the day after that, and that might screw up Michael's plans. I laughed because Cyndra had pills that were extra strength. I laughed because she wasn't mine, and Michael was the future prom king. Laughed because the new clothes finally felt right.

Chapter Eighteen

anie took care of me. Changed out bags of frozen peas on my eye. Propped my head on her pillow and mine. Popped migraine medicine down my throat at regular intervals. The caffeine, cold, and elevation were her attempts to reduce bruising and swelling.

I checked out. Let my brain buzz like an amp turned up but not playing any notes. Let time pass. Didn't talk. Didn't think.

A day passed. I stared at the wall or slept. Janie skipped school, too. She read some teen-romance novel, card-shuffling the pages over her fingertips like the book was a puppy and she was rubbing its ears. She got us food and sodas, started movies or played music on the laptop, kept me company.

The dark waters receded, but under them were jagged rocks and creatures with sharp pincers.

Another morning, and now the frozen peas were changed to a hot pad, resting across my eyes, the plastic a hot body bag zipped over my face. A plate clinked on the floor next to the bed. She took my hand and closed it around the bread.

The door clicked as she left.

I ate the sandwich carefully. Automatically. Time passed. I took off the hot pad and got up. Went to the bathroom. Avoided looking in the mirror over the sink.

I slowly made my way downstairs, got some water and some plastic-wrapped muffins. There was broken glass and spilled food on the floor. I made a halfhearted attempt at cleaning up until the headache came back.

Back in the room I fished my cell out of the pocket of my hoodie.

Where are you? A text from Michael.

Are you okay? From Cyndra.

I'm coming over after school. From Clay, sent this morning. I smiled until it pulled at my face too much.

I went back downstairs and cleaned some more, taking it slowly. When it wasn't quite a wreck, I stopped. Then I climbed the steps and went into the shower. The hot water made me feel stronger and scooped out simultaneously.

I kicked the dirty clothes under my bed and got dressed in an old T-shirt and battered jeans.

Janie came home from school. "You're looking better."

"Yeah, thanks."

"I'm going to go to the store, then. Need anything? I thought some sport drinks or something?"

"Okay. Clay's coming over."

"Good." She leaned over, planting a gentle kiss on my forehead, like a blessing.

I went downstairs and out onto the porch. Shook out

a cigarette and waited for Clay as I sat on the stoop. The cigarette made me feel sick instead of calmed. I pinched off the cherry and tucked it back into the pack.

A few minutes of waiting, watching little kids chasing each other around the duplexes. Then Clay appeared, his shuffle-lope quicker than normal as he came up the street.

I shook my hair into my face but held up a hand in greeting.

Clay waved back and crossed the scrub. I stood stiffly and shook his hand. "Hey."

"Hey." He studied me.

I held his gaze and took out the cigarette again to give my hands something to do. Put it back in the box. "You want to come inside?" I gestured at the door.

"Okay."

Clay sat in the sprung recliner. I collapsed on the sofa.

"How many more days you gonna be out?" he asked.

"One more, I think. I'm sleeping a lot, is all."

He gave me that wise-eyed once-over twice. "That's probably because you have a concussion or something."

I shrugged.

A short burst of air pushed past Clay's teeth. Staccato, making a faint click, like he didn't intend to do it, but was moved by anger or disgust.

My eyes jumped to his face.

Clay's head was shaking slightly. His eyes, narrow and sharp. And shining. "You should have told me you were headed here. Hell, you should have told Janie. Or better yet, you shouldn't have come home at all."

"No point putting it off. Either way, it would have happened. Waiting would have only made it worse."

"Maybe. But you still should have told us."

"Right. Then you *wouldn't* have worried."

"Screw you."

"Get in line."

But there was no venom in my voice, and none in Clay's, either. Just stress, and fatigue, and the sparks that are thrown off when you care about someone. The way a real family interacts around hurt feelings or disappointment. Like how me and Janie do. Or Clay and his mom.

Just expression and clearing the air, like brothers.

I sat up, pushing hair off my face.

"Sorry." I met his eyes. "I guess I thought I'd call you when it was over."

Clay smiled, a social cue of forgiveness, not humor. "Well, I know you didn't want Janie to find you."

"I didn't want to be KO'd." A real smile tugged at my face.

"See how all that violence-preparedness doesn't work?" Clay asked.

"You're right. Pacifism would work so much better."

"Say what you want. Gandhi was badass."

I flexed a hand and then squeezed it into a fist. "I could take him."

Clay laughed and fell back in the chair. I sketched a short jab. "A quick pop on the nose." I punched the air again. "How's that for passive resistance, bitch?" I brought my elbow up slowly. "I call this one the No-More-Hunger

Strike." Pretended to grab a head, brought it in slow motion onto the elbow. Hissing a cheesy martial arts yell as I did.

Clay laughed so hard he started coughing. I was laughing too as I continued to pretend-beat-up Gandhi, adding more and more ridiculous moves and combinations, just to see Clay laughing like that.

After a while we were both laughing hard enough to gasp. Clay was holding his stomach, and I was holding my ribs. I had to dry my eyes.

I stood and went into the kitchen. Came back with sodas and held one out to Clay.

"Thanks. But I should probably get going." Clay stood.

I followed him out onto the stoop. Handed him the soda again. "We'll have it out here."

We sat on the top step. Clay shoved me, hard. "What kind of dillweed beats up Gandhi?"

I held up my can in a mock toast to myself.

"Well, answer this burning question, Charm School," Clay said, smiling. "Did Cyndra take you home or not? Because today she was hovering around your locker like she could make you appear by just standing there."

My heart gave a stupid jump. "Yeah?"

"True."

I couldn't stop the smile that tugged at my mouth at the thought. I told Clay about it—about going to Michael's house and being with her. How I wasn't sure how she felt about me, but I sure as hell knew how she made *me* feel.

And I told him about Michael coming home. Confronting me, and the things he said about Cyndra. Then the parking lot and his obsession with me showing him my scar, paying me all that money. About Michael wanting to kill my dad.

And Clay, being Clay, saw something I didn't. Put his finger on it and pressed, like a doctor diagnosing a dislocation. Or a break.

"He wanted you to go home. Michael did that to get you pissed off. To get you to that place where you would go home and face your dad."

It fit. Like a jigsaw piece but where you can't see the final image. The way Michael liked to pull people's strings. LaShonda getting my file, Dwight and the bet and the fight. Cyndra . . .

"Okay," I said, to show that I agreed with the idea. "But why?"

Clay shook his head. "Who knows? To get you to agree to kill your dad? Or something with Cesare? So Michael can tell some story about how you and Michael fought together somewhere. Or just because. To mess with you."

"He does that, but that's not what this is." Calling it on instinct, not knowledge.

Down the street, Janie walked toward us. Walking with a boy. They play-shoved each other. The way he was turning toward her, carrying her bags, like he was performing for her. Wheedling. Like he was saying *Baby, please* with every move.

Janie was smiling. And she looked her age, for once. Not younger, like I usually see her. Not older, like she acted around me lately.

"Something else," I said to Clay. "I think Michael wants everyone to think I'm dealing." I explained about Nico and Spud and the realization of how my new clothes made me look.

"Maybe he's trying to get this Cesare guy to come after you," Clay said.

I shrugged. We fell quiet as Janie and her friend crossed the yard.

"This is Hunter," Janie explained. "From school." A little breathless and not quite looking at me.

"Hunter," I said.

"Hey. I'm Clay, that's Jason." Trying to hide his smile at the way I was glaring at the kid.

"Hey." Hunter nodded at us and had the good sense not to stare at my face or into my eyes. "Want me to take these inside for you, Jane?" He gave her that all-teeth grin.

"Okay," Janie said, smiling and, honest to God, batting her eyelashes.

They eased past us on the steps.

"Stay downstairs," I cautioned as the screen door creaked open.

Janie rolled her eyes at me before they disappeared inside.

Clay smiled. "Leave them alone, man. You've got enough to deal with."

"My thoughts exactly. Which is why I'm not leaving them alone."

Clay laughed and went down the steps. The fading sun was stealing its light from the sky.

I followed Clay to the edge of the scrub.

"Thanks for coming by," I said. Threw a one-armed hug on him quick, before he could react or squeeze me back.

"One more day, then I'm expecting you on the walk to school. I was late yesterday," he said, doing a good job of pretending nonchalance at my gesture.

"Get a clock, genius."

"You're my clock."

I laughed as he walked away. Inside the unit, I interrupted Janie and Hunter saying good-bye by the back door. I pretended not to see them as I got another muffin.

Janie came back into the front room smiling a little, and she looked so happy I made myself smile back and not say anything I was thinking. Except for "Be careful."

"I like him," she said, shining like a spotlight.

We went upstairs. She told me about Hunter, and how he'd been flirting with her at school. And I told her a little about Cyndra, and about everything that had happened with Michael after the party. Why I had come home.

She frowned and said it was time to quit the job. I told her the same thing I told Clay, that I could ride it out a little longer.

She nodded, and I could feel it—how she knew I was trying to treat her like an adult about Hunter, so she was trying not to worry about what I said I could handle. I lay back on my bed and went to sleep as Janie messed around on the laptop.

The next morning, after Janie left, I went around the partition and turned on the light on her dresser. In the mirror,

---

Still Waters

165

my face glared out. Janie's treatment had worked wonders, yet the eye still looked bad. But not the worst. Not undo-able.

Around noon, I heard the phone ring downstairs. Heavy feet made the stairs creak. My dad didn't knock, just pushed the door open.

"You're going to school tomorrow, or we'll be reported to the truant officer or that bitch social worker." His frozen eyes surveyed my face. "Write a note. Tell them you fell out of a pickup truck. I'll sign it."

I didn't say anything. He walked into the room, kicked my bed. "Hear me?"

"Yes." I tried to sink into the mattress.

He grunted and started tossing the room. My teeth clenched as he opened drawers, turned out the pockets of clothes, flipped pillows, and shook out books.

He found the twenty I kept stashed in the room as a de-coy, and pocketed it. But he didn't find the coffee can, and he didn't find the laptop, either.

He left.

I started to think—to worry about the money I'd left in the old gym, and also worry that one day our luck would run out and he'd find the coffee can.

Eventually I sat up. Tore a page out of a notebook and wrote the note. "To Whom it May Concern: Jason Roberts was absent because he fell out of the back of a pickup." I carried the note downstairs. Handed a pencil to my father.

He took it and slashed his signature at the bottom. Shoved it back at me.

I went back upstairs. Lay down and felt my stomach

grumble. Started thinking again—wondering if Cyndra was still missing me or thinking about me at all. The image of her, standing against the rising sun by Michael's pool, her hair a red-gold. Or waiting for me by my locker, like Clay had said. A dream, a fantasy.

Sitting downstairs in Michael's house a week ago. Talking to Michael, who wanted to know about the rumors—which ones were true. What I'd really done. But he'd known. Known Trent. Known about Celia. Told LaShonda to copy my file.

His week was almost up. But now he had the gun and had met with Trent about something else. What did they have in common and what were they planning?

The use he had for me. Offering to kill my father or help me do it. Everyone thinking I was dealing drugs.

Cyndra's stepfather. Was it what Michael said it was?

Questions knotted like tangled coils of razor wire.

Janie got home. "Cyndra was waiting for me at the bus stop after school. She sure looks like trouble."

I sighed. "Trouble looks pretty good, then."

Janie held out a note.

I was reaching for it before I could think, wondering if it would smell like her perfume.

It contained only one sentence:

Jason, I can explain myself.—C.

A lipstick print was underneath.

One of Cyndra's unconsciously deep pronouncements: *I can explain myself.*

Like she actually could. Like there was anything she

could say that would explain sleeping with me in her boy-friend's bed, and then pretending like it hadn't happened after telling me he wouldn't care.

I crumpled the note and tossed it at the trash. Janie picked it up and smoothed it out.

What had I expected? Concern? "Are you all right?" or "When are you coming back to school?" or "I miss you." Little love heart doodles and gushy pronouncements.

I silently cursed myself for the fool I was.

Janie studied the lipstick print like it was an artist's brushstrokes. She pursed her lips before stopping and gnawing on a finger instead.

I faced the wall and closed my eyes.

CHAPTER NINETEEN

n the morning, I got up early and showered. There's not much you can do for a cracked or broken rib, but I have a back brace from the supply store that straps around my side, and so I tried it on. It actually helped, so I left it on.

Back in the room I put on my own, old clothes. I didn't have the ones Cyndra had bought, and the ones I'd worn home were bloody and stank of smoke and stale sweat. Besides, all I had to do was get through the day and get home again. I felt like my nerves were lying exposed on the top of my skin.

Janie and I walked to the bus.

"What happened to you?" a kid blurted out.

I cocked a fist. "Wanna find out?"

He shut up and scooted onto the other side of the street.

I shook my hair over my face and turned up the collar of my army jacket.

"It doesn't look that bad," Janie whispered.

In the bathroom that morning the steam-fogged mirror reflected bruises like rotting fruit.

Like I said before, my dad may be crazy but he's not

stupid—so I don't usually have to wear it on my face for everyone to see.

And the note was supposed to cover it.

Janie got on the bus, and I walked to Clay's house. The tightness in my chest unwound slightly as we walked into school together. Since I hadn't heard anything from Michael after that first text, I figured nothing was urgent and so I'd take the day off.

We went into the cafeteria through the field-side entrance, keeping the building between us and the parking lot.

Just get through the day.

I ate breakfast and listened to Clay ramble on about the zombie book "that was also art." When the bell rang, we parted. Him to class and me to the office to turn in the note.

The lady behind the counter read the note and frowned at my face.

"That was stupid," she said. And I couldn't tell if she was talking about the excuse or my supposed ride in the back of a truck. I shrugged.

She made a copy of the note and put it in a stack. Was it for my file? Suddenly I felt like a bug in a jar—everyone tapping on it and turning it around, squinting and trying to get a closer look.

She gave me the original note, stapled to a slip.

I skipped the courtyard at break. Found Clay instead. During lunch I waited awhile before going to the cafeteria. I was one of the last ones to get my tray. I took it and sat with Clay, Nico, and Spud.

Nico and Spud didn't say anything about my face or the fact that just last week I'd been sitting outside with the royalty of the school. Instead they did all the talking while I ate. They were still trying to find whoever was dealing at Mercer. They usually bought from another kid they knew, but had taken my favor as a sacred quest.

When the bell rang, I stayed seated and watched the crew parade in from outside. None of them even spared a glance for the burnout corner. Maybe they didn't realize I was sitting there.

It was more likely they didn't care.

Dwight was riding Beast like a jockey—whooping, knees high on his sides. His eye was still black, almost as much as mine. The sight made a dark satisfaction spike in my chest. Michael had a hand tucked into the back of Cyndra's waistband.

They crossed the cafeteria. Michael kept Cyndra close to his side, maneuvering her where she couldn't glance at my table across the room, even if she thought of it. His own black eye was faded, almost a smudge.

Cesare couldn't punch worth a damn.

"Don't worry, she'll find you," Clay said, even though I hadn't said anything about her not seeing me.

"Maybe." I tried to keep the hope out of my voice.

They walked out. I waited before I went to AP History. If I timed it right, I'd get to my desk before Mr. Stewart walked in, but not be in there long enough to have to talk to anyone—especially Michael.

I got to my desk before Mr. Stewart, as planned. Michael was talking to the person on the next aisle as I sat down in front of him.

"Holy crap, Jason," he said in a voice that carried over

the pre-class conversation hum. "What'd you do? Stop a fist with your face?"

The room went so quiet I could hear the blood in my ears.

"Mind your own damn business." The venom in my voice would etch glass.

Michael clapped my shoulder like we were the best of friends and I'd just ranked him.

Something stopped me from knocking his hand away. Maybe because if it looked like we were playing, then my face wasn't a big deal and they would stop noticing.

Or at least stop talking about it.

Mr. Stewart walked in sipping a soda. He went behind his podium and squinted out at us. "You're all being quiet today." He smiled. Then his eyes snagged on me. "Okay, everyone, your work is on the board. Get going."

Papers shuffled as people began writing their answers.

I closed my eyes.

"Jason. Good to see you back. Do you have an excuse?"

He was the first teacher to ask.

I walked up to the podium, pretending I didn't feel the eyes of every damn person following me. I handed over the note, stapled to the office slip. Went back to my desk and watched him through my hair.

He made a few marks in his attendance book and then read the note. He sighed, squinting back at me.

I looked out the window. A custodian was slapping a dripping paintbrush over a shoddy, spray-painted anatomy lesson.

After the bell work was done, Mr. Stewart began lecturing. I probably would have been interested, might have even listened, except a headache started and my eyes were so sandy dry I could strike matches off them. I wished I'd taken another migraine pill at lunch, like Janie had told me to.

I let my eyes close, but I couldn't drift off. Michael's presence behind me, poised like a scalpel, kept me awake.

The bell finally rang. Kids shoved their things in bags and headed out to last period. I stood up. Grabbed my notebook.

Michael slid up beside me like a friend. "Don't worry." His voice was soft. "I'll think of a way to take care of your problem, too."

"Jason. Stay a minute, will you?" Mr. Stewart frowned at us.

"See you after practice." Michael sauntered out the door.

Like I was going to wait around for him.

I walked up to Mr. Stewart, keeping my eyes down.

"Look at me, Jason."

Any other teacher would have to wait for hell to freeze first. Any other teacher would've let me go on through the door without scrutinizing my face or the note too closely.

I looked at him, cut my eyes away fast.

"Here"—he held out some papers—"these are the notes from the three days you missed." I reached out to take them, but he didn't let go.

"Damn it, Jason."

The curse caused my eyes to flit back to his face. He was staring at my hand. He grabbed my wrist, turning the palm up.

The notes spilled onto the floor.

I yanked my hand away.

"What the—" I bit off the curse that rose when he'd grabbed me.

"I'm supposed to believe you fell out of a truck?"

My chin snapped up and out. "Yes."

"And yet your palms don't have a mark on them. Your arms don't have a scratch. But your face looks like you went a few rounds with a prizefighter."

I shrugged. My eyes dared him.

"Jason." His tone caught my eyes again—like bugs flying into a web. "I know."

I shook my head. "What?"

"You didn't fall out of a truck."

"Yes. I did."

He sighed, stooped, and picked up the pages. He turned and handed them to me. "You don't have to do this. You can let me help you. There's help to be had. Ways to get out—"

I must've laughed, because he stopped talking. He took off his glasses and pinched the bridge of his nose like his eyes hurt. "Take a chance, son." His voice was soft. "Let me help."

The only thing worse than a bully is an ignorant do-gooder. I walked to the door.

He followed like a kid sister. "I'm not the only one who knows, Jason. I'm ashamed to say, I didn't notice like I should have, until your friend came to talk to me. We're worried—"

I whirled on him, hands bunched. "Who? What the hell are you talking about?"

　　　　　　　　　　　　　　　ASH PARSONS

Was it Michael or Cyndra? Or someone else?

"I have to report this. I have to call the police—"

"Don't do me any favors. You'll make it worse."

"Jason, it can't get worse."

My arms drew in. If he said another word, I'd hit him.

He saw it. Wasn't completely ignorant of my past, then. Wise teacher.

I walked down the hall.

Mr. Stewart didn't follow.

I went to study hall and sat, staring at nothing. When the last bell rang, I walked through the interior of the school toward the old gym. I would get the money out of the glove and leave before Michael or the others could find me. I figured I wouldn't run into anyone because of football and cheer practice.

The hell with it. With them. Cyndra and Michael. With Mr. Stewart's heart-in-the-right-place. With love and concern or game playing. Whatever it was. The hell with it all.

No one was around, and the money was still in the glove. I shoved it into my pocket and walked back into the afternoon sunshine.

"Hi." Cyndra stood beside the door.

I waited.

She stepped closer. A hand fluttered near my face. "Sorry." Like she had anything to do with it.

Maybe she did.

"I'm fine." I shook out a cigarette and lit it, facing the security camera, thinking it'd be a relief to be sent to in-school suspension.

"Did you get my note?"

"You mean the one-sentence one? Yeah." I hoped I didn't sound like I felt.

"I can explain." She took a step closer. Her hand landed on my arm.

I took a step back, still feeling the heat of her touch. "You don't owe me anything."

Thinking of the money she'd paid me in her room, thinking of her taking me to Michael's bed.

"Look, I do stupid stuff sometimes. I don't know why. I . . ." Her voice trailed off, palm scrubbing her thigh. "It was like revenge. You know?"

"What—sleeping with me or doing it in his bed?"

"Both."

Smoke plumed out of my mouth. "Glad to be of service."

"But it wasn't just that. I mean, it was more than that."

"Whatever you say, princess."

Her perfect eyebrows lowered. She made a little grunt of annoyance.

I touched her shoulder; let my hand rub her hot skin. "It's okay. You had your reasons. It's not like I didn't get anything out of it."

She knocked my hand off. "I wasn't just using you."

I shrugged. "Sure."

"I wasn't."

"I heard you. You weren't *just* using me. Using me, sure. But not *just* using me."

She let out a breath like I'd punched her.

I nodded and took the last drag, squinting like I was really thinking about it. And I guess a part of me was.

A tear slid down her cheek. "He scares me sometimes." The last word added, like she wanted to believe it wasn't all the time. "He used to make me feel safe. He's not always like this. I thought he'd protect me. Somehow."

Sometimes. Always. Somehow. I sighed. Didn't know what to say. Because I wanted to believe it. Knowing even if it was true, it wouldn't be enough. Because it still hurt.

She was studying me—must've seen it wheeling in my eyes, because she reached out again. Touched my arm. "I didn't mean to hurt you. Please believe me."

"Why should I?" Her hand fell off my arm when I pitched the cigarette butt into the parking lot.

Her voice was small. "Because I like you."

I tried to ignore the stupid skip my heart gave. Closed my eyes instead of looking into hers.

"I like you, too," I said, surprising myself. "It's okay." Meaning it this time.

She stepped into me. Laid her arms gently over my shoulders—like we were at some dippy junior high dance. I put my hands on her waist.

"It hurts to look at you," she said, frowning at my face.

Her eyes were an ocean.

I smiled. "It hurts to look at you, too."

She grinned and pushed her body against me. "Well, that's a pain I can do something about."

Her kiss was deep but gentle. The way everything should be.

CHAPTER TWENTY

I confronted Michael privately after his football practice let out. I wanted to beat the living crap out of him, but I wanted the money more. So I told him if he mentioned anything about our parking lot conversation, or my dad, or if he talked to Mr. Stewart again, it was over and he could face his reckoning alone. Which he might be doing anyway. I was making no promises.

It was like truce talks after a battle. He denied talking to Mr. Stewart. Said it was maybe someone else in class or at school, and had I ever thought about that possibility? I left it alone. As long as my message got through.

Cyndra had given me the clothes she'd bought, and I put them in the locker room of the old gym. I changed Friday morning before joining them in the parking lot. No one asked where I'd been all week, and no one mentioned the bruises. The weekend came and went and nothing happened. I spent most of it playing video games at Clay's.

On Monday, Nico and Spud were waiting for me as I crossed the athletic field. Nico shifted his knit cap, olive green today. He thumbed his nose, a gap-tooth smile spreading.

"We found out who's dealing."

His face, the irrepressible, impish grin, told me I knew who it was.

"Dude. Everyone *thinks* it's you. But it's not." Spud held up his hands like he meant to stop a presumed cutting denial. "We know that." Rotating a hand at the three of us. The privileged circle of knowledge.

I shook out a cigarette. Lit it. Waited.

"It's Cyndra."

Smoke gouged my throat.

"What?"

"It's true," he said. "She's dealing to everyone, but real sly. Hiding behind you, saying she's getting it *from* you. Ain't that something?"

She liked me. She wasn't *just* using me.

Slurry filled my chest. Ice cold and rigid. It didn't take a genius to tell whom she was really dealing for.

Something buzzed in my ears and under my heart, like a fuse, disbelief and numbness sparking, devouring only to detonate.

I thanked Nico and Spud. Let them throw one-arm hugs on me. Slapped hands.

Then I went to the parking lot.

Cyndra was in her car, laughing with Samantha and Monique, waiting for Michael to arrive. Since I hadn't gone to the old gym to change, I must have beaten him to school.

I rapped a knuckle on her window. She took one look at my face and climbed out.

"What is it?" She touched my arm. I didn't say anything, just turned and walked away. She followed.

I went to the old gym. For privacy. For time. To get away

Still Waters

from the bite in the air that seared my lungs with cold.

On the track that looped the court, I turned on her.

"You're dealing for Michael." Not a question. "Why are you saying it's for me?" Making myself stop from asking the next question, the question underneath. *What are you doing with me?*

"I never say it's for you." She reached out. "I just don't say it *isn't* for you."

I shook her off. "Big difference in results."

She shook her head, fast and tight. "You don't understand. I'm scared."

My heartbeat sped. The slurry in my heart sludged into my veins. For the first time, I looked at her. Really looked.

There were smudges under her eyes. Sleepless circles, drawn over with makeup. Her lips were chapped—the queen of lip gloss. Like she'd been chewing on them. Little webs of strain tensed the muscles of her face.

"Is he hurting you?"

"Michael? No. No!" She grabbed my forearms. "I wanted to help him. He told me everything—about Cesare. But something's not right. He's hiding something."

Air huffed through my nose. "Just one thing?" Feeling it, how everything with him was this ocean of lies. Of ego. Of control. Manipulation.

Her hands dropped. She stepped away from me. "He's not like that."

I closed my eyes. Took a deep breath. Pushed it out slowly, through my nose. Because now I knew, what I hadn't been able to ask. Where I stood with her.

"What do you think it is, then?" I asked.

Her head shook again. That minimalist move. Almost unconscious. "Maybe I'm wrong."

The silence stood between us. My hands itched, wanted to reach out and stroke the hair feathering her temple.

I crossed my arms over my chest. "He's the one I should be talking to, then."

She didn't say anything. Chewed her lip instead of looking at me.

I left her standing there.

As I crossed the parking lot, the bell sounded. Michael wasn't at his car, so I went inside, to his homeroom. He wasn't there, either.

I went to my homeroom.

Michael was waiting by the door. "Come on," he said, taking my arm and propelling me toward the bathroom.

I shook off his hand, but followed him inside. Michael checked the stalls to make sure we had privacy. He spoke before I could.

"I'm dealing for Cesare," he said. "Cyndra's helping me. But everyone thinks it's you."

My teeth ground tight. "Why are you telling me this now?"

Michael's hand went up to the blade of muscle alongside his neck. He squeezed and pulled, trying to shift an invisible creature. "You were eventually going to find out. I thought it would be better if I told you myself." Knowing that I'd already heard.

Cyndra. Giving him the heads-up. She'd probably texted him as soon as I left her. A muscle jumped in my jaw, something telling it to bite. "We're done."

I turned to the door.

Michael lunged in front of me. Blocked the door, hands up like I was a car skidding across ice.

"Wait! Why should this change anything? It's exactly what everyone has been thinking anyway. Ever since you started hanging out with us. Ever since you started showing up at our parties in new clothes."

"Think I don't know that? Move."

"Stop and think. You're not dealing. I don't want you to deal—"

"Good."

"It's perfect. Classic misdirection. Everyone thinks it's you. But it's not. You won't get in trouble, you won't get caught, because you're not actually *doing* anything. Meanwhile, they'll never even think to check me. Or Cyndra. It's perfect. It helps me, but it doesn't hurt you."

"How do you know what hurts me?"

A smirk curled his lips, but he was smart enough to keep his mouth shut.

"What if you get caught?" My fist pressed his chest.

A wide smile split his face. "I won't."

"If you do? I'm sure you'd take the weight for everyone, right? For me?"

He tried to shrug, but pressed against the door, it looked more like a small struggle than a gesture of nonchalance. "If I get caught—*if*—I can handle it. And no one else will get involved."

Like he wouldn't throw me under the bus if it came to it.

"I told you. I can get away with murder," Michael said.

Using the expression, although it was literally what he'd proposed.

I let my fist drop. Because he was right. It didn't change a damn thing. It was what everyone thought, and nothing would change that. And it didn't even matter if it did. I was already implicated. So the only real question was: Would Michael get caught?

I told myself it didn't matter what people thought. That it didn't matter what Michael did or didn't do. That it didn't make a difference what Cyndra did, either. And what would happen if I quit now? It sure as hell wouldn't be safer. If Michael wanted to run his little schemes, he could do it just as easily without me. At least if I kept working for him I could keep an eye on him.

It was too late. I was already involved.

What could I do to protect myself and Janie? The answer was simple. Help Michael get away with it. Help him get out of his jam. Think of all the angles. Cover them.

Exactly what Michael wanted.

"Fine." A smile tugged my mouth. "Hey, thanks for telling me." In honeyed tones of fake gratitude.

Michael had done what he always did. Tried to get in front of the situation. Take control, by "breaking" the news to me.

So he could either think I'd bought it, which I wasn't a good enough actor to sell, or I could call him on it. So he knew I wasn't a clueless idiot.

Either way. He was right.

Nothing had changed. I'd keep taking his money, and he knew it.

And Cyndra had shown me precisely where I stood.

CHAPTER TWENTY-ONE

he rest of the week and half of the next one went by quickly, feeling like a curve in the track. I kept my eyes open and my mouth shut.

Michael acted different—like he knew something. Like he'd gotten the upper hand, maybe with Cesare. Maybe with someone else. It put me on edge, but the money kept coming, and all I had to do was hang out.

It was safe enough. I'd see it coming—whatever it was that put that oil-slick grin on Michael's face.

And it was too easy to keep going. I'd walk Janie to the bus, then walk to Clay's, and then to school, where I'd change clothes. Breakfast in the parking lot with Michael and his gang. Break in the courtyard, lunch outside at the picnic tables (except one day when it rained and we displaced the drama nerds inside), and afternoons of mostly free time.

Rinse. Repeat.

It was weird. Weird because I got used to it so fast.

Janie got me some greasy bruise-ointment from the

Asian grocery. By the end of the week, they'd faded to yellow-brown and my ribs felt good enough with the brace on that I went to help Jonesy.

More money. Every bit got us closer.

I even fell into a routine with Cyndra. At break she'd sit with Michael, playing with his fingers, threading hers into them or holding them near her mouth.

But at lunch she'd sit close to me, leg alongside mine, leaning against my arm. Sometimes she'd show up in the hall after my first period, and we'd cut class, ducking into the back of the library to talk or going to the dugout to make out. Another thing I told myself I was in control of. Or that it didn't matter, because she was there, and she wanted me, and I needed that something she gave me.

Told myself she felt the same way. Made it sound simple. We each needed something from the other, no more than that. Even though the ache in my chest when she'd walk away called me a liar.

If anyone else knew that Cyndra had won the bet, they never said anything. But Monique had backed off, and so did the others.

Cyndra was like two people: one, this sexy, pouty bitch-princess who taunted you, shot her hips when she walked, and let her eyes burn. And the other was the girl I knew. The one I started to think of as mine. The one with the laugh so loud it sounded like a shout. The one who, when we were really talking, would change, her face shifting, like she was letting a pose fall away. She could transition between the bitch-princess armor and the real girl so quickly the slingshot force of it would send your brain leaking out your ears.

After a while I got used to that, too.

Although I never really got used to the fact that she had to change in the first place.

Michael didn't seem to notice or care about me and Cyndra, and he didn't mention Cesare. But sometimes I saw the slick grin slide off, and the scared kid would reappear in his eyes. Just for a moment. But after he'd show, I started to notice that Michael would do something mean. Like play Beast off Dwight. Or throw out down-to-size remarks.

Clay said Michael was exerting dominance to make himself feel powerful. Making the others twitch when he yanked their strings.

Crap like that was always happening. Stupid, sometimes ugly, always on the edges of the day. Underneath everything, like the buzz of a busted speaker when only certain notes are hit.

I didn't think about it much. It was like the smooth part of the roller coaster or the clicking ascent. Nothing much going on right now, but you don't for a minute think it's over.

So I wasn't surprised when Michael stopped me at break one day. We slapped hands as he slid in close.

"I need you for a job tonight. I'll pick you up in the parking lot at seven."

"Fine." An extra fifty for the expanding roll in the coffee can.

Michael stood beside me, looking out at the others.

"I've figured it out, by the way," he murmured, as if this was a regular conversation between two normal people. His voice was soft, indiscernible if you weren't standing right next to him. "I told you I would."

"Yeah?"

"Yeah." He smiled at me, turning, hiding even his lips from the rest of them. "I've figured out how we can do it."

"Do what?"

Even though I had a feeling I knew.

"Kill your dad, of course."

"You've got enough on your plate," I said, thinking of Cesare.

"It goes *with* that."

The girls walked by, slowly. Cyndra blew a kiss. I couldn't tell who it was for.

"I'll tell you tonight." Michael picked up his backpack.

I shrugged. "Fine. Where'll we be going?" The bell rang across the courtyard. People picked up their bags and started hustling in.

"What do you care? Anywhere's better than here."

The story of my life.

I went to the old gym after school. The punching bag looked lonely, and I was feeling healed enough to take a few test swipes at it.

After an easy workout, I went home and caught Janie, told her about the job. She called Clay and told him she'd be spending the night.

"Be careful," Janie said as we walked to Clay's together. "Remember: You don't have to do anything you don't want to. Just because you took his money doesn't mean you have to take his shit."

"That's catchy. Wanna put it to music?"

She walloped my arm.

"I'm serious, Jason."

"All right, all right."

"We have enough money now to survive for a few months. Any extra is gravy."

"Never enough gravy." Sometimes I had to pull out the can and look at the cash curled inside, wrapped in rubber bands like a cocoon. Had to look, just to be sure that it was still there. Each time, before I opened the can, it was like there was a hole in my stomach.

I was starting to have nightmares about it. Because for the first time since we came up with The Plan, it actually seemed within reach. It made my stomach knot. I'd look at the roll, and I'd think of deposits for electricity, water, or an apartment. I'd see clothes and pots and pans and bus fares. Groceries and medicine. I was even starting to see the tuition for cosmetology school, which Janie had said would be a good skill for her to have. All these things, all these possibilities, rolled inside a coffee can stuffed down an air-conditioning vent.

It was making me sick. Because I had no safer place to keep it.

"We have enough. To make a start. A good one. It's not entirely what we had in mind, but we could go now."

"We need more. We need all of it."

Janie stopped walking, so I did, too. "Seriously, maybe we should just go, Jason."

She put a hand on my forearm. "Let's not wait for your birthday—not wait for the guardianship, or to be eligible for food stamps or housing, or any of it. We have the money. We can just go."

Her hands lifted, palms up and flat, like a bird. Or like she was praying, seeking blessings from the sky.

"Won't work." I shook my head. Crossed my arms, pressing fists into my sides. "We need the government assistance."

Couldn't look in her depthless eyes.

Because I was thinking about Cyndra. Holding her, feeling the softness of her and the long taper of her ribs as she pressed into me. Her arms tight across my shoulders, squeezing with all her strength, like she's trying to tell me something. The shadows in her eyes and the tiny flecks of gold you only see when you are a breath away.

Janie's hands closed. "We have enough to last until your birthday. That's what I'm saying. We could go now, and get the assistance later."

"When the money runs out."

"Maybe."

She waited for me to look at her.

I did, and it felt like something was being pulled from me. From my wrists and my chest, drawing it out in one long tug. Would Cyndra even care? I pictured her fingers lacing with Michael's and somehow knew the answer.

"Jason," Janie's voice cracked. "I'm sorry. It was just an idea."

"Yeah. But you're right. Why not go? There's no good reason."

"We don't have to choose now. It's enough just to think about it."

"Sure. We'll give it a few more days."

"Okay."

So it was decided then. And we both knew it.

We walked another block in silence and stood on the corner. Janie would have to walk a few more blocks by herself. I'd head back to school.

"Be careful," Janie said.

"Hey, I'm off to a good start. He's not picking me up at home."

"Stop playing." Her dark eyes grabbed me, wouldn't let my gaze slide away. "Don't do anything stupid. Don't let him get to you. If it's that bad, walk away. Don't come home and—"

The pain in her voice ripped at me.

"Janie, I promise."

She sniffed and swiped her eyes. "Good." She hugged me quick, like she was stealing it. "We're so close."

. . .

I walked to school and waited in the parking lot.

I didn't have to wait long. The vintage Mustang prowled into the lot. Michael was the only one in the car. He put the window down.

"Time to make yourself useful."

CHAPTER TWENTY-TWO

e drove to a long stretch of empty road. Michael pulled to one side of the two-lane, and turned the engine off. The feeble twilight made colors hard to see, even the cherry red of the Mustang's hood.

"Wanna make out?" Michael asked, the same old joke.

"You're not my type."

Michael laughed. "What, you think your girlfriend would object?"

I shrugged, unsure as always how to act when he mentioned Cyndra.

Michael turned on some music—heavy, screaming stuff. We waited on the darkening road. Finally he spoke.

"There'll be others here soon. I just wanted to be early. To talk to you about it. You know where we are?"

I knew the road by reputation, but not experience.

"Drag Race Road."

"Right. And everyone will be here soon. People come from different schools, not just Mercer, and there's always a bunch of races. You may even want to try your luck."

"What would I drive?"

He smiled. "There's plenty of cars to be had." He squinted out the window. I rubbed a fist on my leg, remembering Janie.

"Nah," I said.

"You wouldn't get caught."

"Sorry. Sure hope that wasn't the job."

"We're here to meet Trent."

Headlights glinted in the distance of the straightaway. Michael gave me a glacial smile. "Trent is a security guard at a swank development full of doctors' offices. I'm paying him to be somewhere else so we can break in, steal some drugs, and trash it."

"The drugs'll square you with Cesare?"

Not a bad idea. You had to hand it to him.

"That, and one other job he has for me after. Two little jobs, and I'm in the clear. But that's not the only reason I'm doing the doctors' offices." He pumped a fist in the air, like an overenthused coach. "For the team, son."

I thought about Michael's cold, empty house. How Clay called him a puppet master. Michael called himself a user. He wasn't interested in teams.

"What's the second job?" I asked.

He shrugged. "Who knows? One thing at a time."

Headlights threw our shadows across the windshield as a car pulled in behind us. Michael opened his door, so I followed. We walked to the back of the car and stood in the glare.

The lights went out as the car door groaned open. Trent

strutted up, wearing a navy blue security uniform. He held out his hand. "Michael. Jason."

We shook and stood in the dark, blinking away the after-images that floated on our retinas.

"It looks like tomorrow will work."

"It's definitely on, then?" Michael's voice was cool, but his hands fisted in his pockets.

Trent nodded. "My partner is out on leave. His wife just had a baby. And we're already spread thin because Earl was busted on the drug screen. So, yeah, Thursday it's just me and one other guy on the whole shift, and we won't be patrolling together."

"Tomorrow." Michael's voice was firm.

"You got my money?"

I tried to pretend I didn't sound just like that when I said it.

Michael handed over a fat envelope. "Half now, half after."

Trent didn't count it, just slipped the envelope into his pocket. He nodded at me. "You looking forward to losing your cherry like him?"

I stared him down.

Trent laughed like he was my chummy uncle. "Who am I kidding? Won't be your first time at the dance."

I crossed my arms and leaned against the trunk. Two cars appeared down the road.

"It's set, then," Michael said. Dismissing him.

Another pair of headlights appeared.

"Tomorrow." Trent shook Michael's hand and walked

back to his car. The door protested as he closed it. He turned the car around and drove away.

The second car pulled in behind us where Trent's car had been.

I turned to Michael. "I'm not coming along on your little adventure."

Michael waved his hand, like he was shooing a fly. "Later. We'll talk about it later. Along with my idea for your problem."

My dad.

Of course, I had already decided. I *would* go, provided the circumstances and price were right. But coming out of the corner fighting gave me leverage to get more. Because if I didn't go, what use would Michael make of my absence? If I was with him, I could control it. Could control the way it would roll. Make Michael think he had me and squeeze him for just enough extra money that Janie's acceleration of The Plan could work.

Game the gamer. I had to stifle the smile, picturing his face as he arrived at school to find me gone. Disappeared with Janie, leaving him holding the bag.

Monique and another girl got out of the car that had parked behind us.

"Are we the first?" Monique called. "I can't believe we got here first." She walked up to us so fast, what little curves she had jiggled.

"No, Mona." Michael sounded bored. "*We're* first."

"You don't count," Monique said. "You're always here first."

More cars parked. People started leaving their head-lights on while music competed from different windows. Hoods were propped open so passersby could ogle the goods.

Cyndra arrived, wearing a tank top and low-slung jeans. Her long legs flickered the glare of the headlights as she runway-walked up to us. She kissed Michael and pressed into his side.

Mona sat on the trunk next to me, letting her leg touch mine. I didn't move away.

The others arrived. LaShonda and T-Man fighting about which rapper was playing on the radio. Dwight and Mike-Lite started talking trash about the cars. Michael gestured for us to follow him.

"Come on."

Dwight, Mike-Lite, T-Man, and Beast came with us. We wandered down the road, looking at the various engines, talking about which ones were the best. There were only a few real racers. Most people were there to drink and hook up.

We kept moving past the cars and people, walking down into the blackness.

Michael stopped. The others ranged around him, listen-ing.

"Tomorrow night."

Dwight cursed and grinned.

"All in," Michael continued. "No opt outs."

Beast's eyes shifted around the circle.

"Security's been taken care of." Michael crossed his

arms over his chest and took a wide stance. "There's nothing to worry about, even for you, Beast."

The guys laughed. Beast looked like someone had squirted lemon juice in his eyes.

"I don't know," he murmured. "What about security cameras?"

"We'll be wearing masks, and we won't be driving one of our cars. We'll wreck the place and get the drugs."

"We should just get the drugs and go," Mike-Lite said. "Get in and out quick and not leave any evidence behind."

"Evidence? Look who's been watching crime TV." Michael's hand swept, palm up, at Mike-Lite, like he was on a game show. "Evidence." He spat the word, a dismissal. "Are we referring to broken glass, here? You planning on touching it after you bust it? Or, uh, no"—Michael glanced at T-Man, who laughed ahead of the joke—"you're gonna write our names with the paint?"

Michael dropped the taunts and made a blade of his hand. "We trash it. It'll confuse things, make them wonder what we were after. Plus, it shields the guard if it looks like vandals broke in."

Mike-Lite spread his own feet and tipped his head at Beast. "But something could go wrong," he said. "This one's too much," he said to Michael. "How can you be sure it won't go wrong?"

Michael leaned forward, casual as a viper. "Because I paid the guard. Because I know the building inside out. And because of him." He pointed at me. "Ice has all the angles covered, so you daisies don't have to worry about a thing."

All eyes shifted to me. Michael raised an eyebrow.

I nodded once.

Dwight popped his knuckles, glaring at me. "I don't need his green light."

"Go without me, then."

"Dwight, shut up." Michael's eyes bored into him.

"Why are we supposed to be impressed by him again?" Dwight sneered. "I don't give a damn about him."

"Sitting this one out, Dwight? That's a win in my book," I said.

Michael popped a fist against Dwight's chest. "I said shut up." His eyes slid around the circle.

Beast looked uncertain, lips moving like he wanted to say something. Mike-Lite's weight shifted from foot to foot.

"We don't need him," Dwight told the group, looking at me like I was a leech bloated on their blood.

Michael turned to Dwight. "No. It's you we don't need. Shut your damn mouth."

Dwight opened his mouth. Closed it again. A red flush spread in his cheeks.

Michael pivoted and stalked away.

"I can't wait." T-Man followed—pacing with sharp, arrested movements. Michael smiled at him, like a teacher when you've given the right answer.

Dwight fell in behind Michael, a kicked dog, eager and cringing. He glared at me.

Beast and T-Man walked in the road, ignoring the yells and revving engines. T-Man walked with his arms out— like if a car came at him he'd show it who was boss.

Tires screeched. Two sets of headlights hurtled down

the road. T-Man jumped out of the way at the last possible moment.

We walked behind the parked cars and through clusters of people until we were back at Michael's car.

I glanced around at the scene. Similar to the party, except scattered down the edges of the dark country road. People drinking, dancing, making out. Same as ever.

I sat on the hood of Michael's car.

Two cars started revving their engines, shuddering where they stood. All noise, no performance.

Cyndra perched on the hood next to me. A can was pressed into my hand. Cyndra smiled and tipped her beer up to her lips.

The can was warm. I popped the top and drank.

Michael slid a hand up Cyndra's leg. "Cyn, Ice and I are going to talk."

Cyndra stuck out her lower lip and arched her back so her shirt strained. "Can't I come?"

Michael smiled and spanked the side of her thigh. "Try not to get into too much trouble." Not deigning to answer her question. Reprimanding her with a tease.

It flickered in her eyes. The rebuff, making her mask of confidence slip. Maybe she didn't know where she stood, either. It didn't make me feel better.

We got in his car. Cyndra slid off the hood and walked over to stand with Monique. Inside the car, the revving engines dimmed to a dull thrum. Michael palmed me a fifty and popped the top on a beer.

"Here's why you should definitely, absolutely, take part

when we go," he began, without preamble. He then spent the next ten minutes talking. Taking long pulls on the can. Explaining what I already knew—about how he figured it all out and it would be safe. Trent being on the inside. About how we'd all be wearing masks, and he'd have a beater car that couldn't be traced.

I just looked out the window into the darkness of the woods.

He talked about the money he'd pay me to come along. Six hundred dollars, half up front, half after. He said I was worth it because I inspired confidence in the others.

My fingers dug into my leg.

He talked about destroying things. Seeing things break, shattering glass, throwing paint. He talked about it like it was the part I'd like the most.

And then he wrapped it up. Put a bow on it.

"This office, they do minor surgical procedures there. They have drugs, and like you said, that's the first half of how I'll square it with Cesare. But they have *all kinds* of drugs. More than I need. And that's the best part of the whole damn thing." He stopped talking and waited for me to look at him.

"That's how we do it."

He looked like a kid who'd just gotten a pony for his birthday.

I waited.

Michael continued. "It's perfect. We take all we can get and save some for us to use to do it. Then we slip them to your dad. In a drink. A beer. He drinks it, passes out.

Maybe we've even given him enough to kill him right there. But if not, we finish him off with an injection, or we pour more down his throat."

It would work. I could already imagine it, but not in the beer. My dad always started with beer, finished with whiskey. I'd wait until a fifth was getting low, then put the drugs in. He'd swallow right from the bottle, all in one swig. It'd probably be enough to kill him.

My father, sprawled on the sling-back sofa, the bottle loose in his grip. But not passed out. Not this time.

I rubbed my forehead. "What about an autopsy?"

"Who's going to do one? He's just an ex-con. No one will care. And so what if they do?"

"They'll find the drug."

"That's the beauty of it. As long as we get rid of the beer bottle, who's to say he didn't accidentally overdose? He's a known user. We just leave some out. Stage the scene."

He drummed the steering wheel.

I shook my head. "Overdosing is a good idea, but not what you're talking about."

"Don't forget who you're talking to, Ice." He smiled, a coach encouraging a star player. "I know about your dad's prison term. Drug dealing."

"Then you know it wasn't for any prescription drugs."

"So? He can't move up in the world? And like I said, we leave some lying around—"

"That'll trace it all back to the offices."

He waited for me to catch up. "Exactly. The break-in. It's perfect. A nice, neat package for the cops."

"It won't go down like that. We'll get caught."

"No, we won't."

"It's too complicated. Something will go wrong."

"It's simple."

I shook my head, wishing it actually *was* simple. "It won't work."

"You're afraid? It's *easy* to doctor a drink. You don't even have to confront him. We just have to get some into him. Enough to knock him out, or something close. It doesn't take much if you get the right stuff. Isn't that right?"

Something then. Glinting in his eyes, like acknowledgment. An inside joke in a glance. The ozone scent of lightning in the air.

The skin on the back of my neck prickled, and for an instant, it was like I could glimpse something, shifting and dark, growing bigger.

"Monique," I began. Trying to think back. To where Michael had been during the party when she'd drugged me.

His hand cut the air, like the look I gave him was beneath his comment. "Monique simply illustrates my point. It would be easy, and it wouldn't take much."

Was that all there was? Suspicion littered my thoughts. I shook my head. "No. I'm not doing it."

Because if anyone was killing my dad, it was me. And I didn't need a power-hungry accomplice for my part of The Plan. I couldn't trust Michael, never could. I sure as hell wasn't committing murder with him.

Michael's storm-dark eyes lightened. A slow smile edged across his face. "Oh well. If you change your mind . . . It's entirely up to you, isn't it."

Not a question.

"What about the rest of it? You coming along, or is it your last day?"

"I'm in if you agree to my conditions."

Michael smiled, that crooked shark's smile.

"It'll take eight hundred, not six. And you leave your gun at home. Robbery and vandalism are a hell of a way off from armed robbery. If it goes wrong, we ditch. Leave everything behind. And I say if it's going wrong. I make that call."

Michael nodded. "Fine. And of course, no guns. I'm paying the man precisely so we don't need them. So, yes. All reasonable requests. Half up front, half after, though."

I nodded.

"I haven't even told you the best part. Well, the best part for only you, since we're not doing your dad." Michael cut me a poisonous smile.

"When we get the drugs, we'll be helping Cyndra with her stepdad. One of the drugs we'll get, Depo-Provera. It's birth control, but it's also used to chemically castrate sexual offenders. Usually given by injection, but I'll let her in on my drug-his-beer idea. He'll never know it's happening. So we'll be helping her, too."

The people in the road yelled and shoved. Hard to tell if it was the start of a fight or just playing.

"Birth control? This guy's an obstetrician?" I asked.

"I told you. It's a suite of offices."

He couldn't have it both ways. Either Cyndra had her stepdad exactly where she wanted him, or she was a victim.

When I thought she was a victim, he'd told me she was

in control. Now he said she was a victim, so I'd believe we were helping her.

"Why do you want me to care about it? I've already said I'll come," I said.

Michael's eyes shot between my face and the play-fight in the road. "No reason. I just thought you would."

"I don't."

He shrugged. "Whatever you say." He popped his door open, climbed out of the car without waiting.

We walked back into the crowd.

I told myself not to watch Cyndra as she sat down next to Michael. Curled around his back, chin resting on his shoulder. The perfect girlfriend pose for the perfect boy-friend.

I sat on another hood and slapped hands when they were presented. One thought I couldn't stop, needle-dragging in my mind.

It would all be over soon. Janie and me, leaving all this crap behind.

I told myself I couldn't wait.

Cyndra glanced at me. My heart shuddered.

Monique was watching me, hip cocked. Ray-Ray and Mike-Lite were standing just like they did every time they were together in a crowd: Mike-Lite wrapped over and around her shoulders. Her head rested against him. All of them doing what they always do, oblivious.

Maybe they'd miss me. Maybe she would, too.

Cyndra saw me watching her. A little smile hovered on her mouth, telling me she liked the way I looked at her.

She said something to Michael and slid off the car, walking down the road a ways before slipping between two cars and into the dark woods at the edge of the road.

She didn't have to look back to know that I would follow.

I drained my beer and waited a minute before walking around behind the cars, slipping into the dark after her.

She was waiting for me just a few feet into the trees. Her hand floated toward my face, like the day in the food court, moving slow, like sudden movement might make me attack or take off.

She stroked my cheek, then stepped into me, nuzzling her forehead against my neck. "Let's go somewhere, Jason."

Hot needles stung my eyes. I wanted to unwrap my arms from around my sides and hold her, pull her tight and feel her hug me back. I wanted to be out of the dark on the side of the road, standing in front of a headlight, everyone watching, everyone knowing.

That I was worth it.

I took a step back.

Her hand stayed in the air for a moment before it dropped. "My car's this way."

We walked to it, passing behind Michael and the rest of them. She drove us through the city and over the river. Winding our way down deserted streets to where the water lapped the shore.

I didn't mention the plan to break into the doctors' offices or ask her if she would really want that drug for her stepfather. Because I wanted something from her that was just for me. That didn't have Michael, or his games, or Cesare, or drugs, or anything else.

Just us.

After, she drove me to the edge of Lincoln Green. Gave me a goodnight kiss. I tried to pretend we weren't counting down to the last one she'd ever give me.

I walked to Clay's house and let myself in with the hidden key. Spent the night on the sofa, staring up at the featureless ceiling, telling myself it was good that it was almost over.

Chapter Twenty-Three

n the walk to the bus stop the next morning, I told Janie and Clay about the doctors' offices. Gave all the reasons why I would be going along.

"I don't know." Janie scuffed the heels of her shoes as she walked.

"Yeah," Clay agreed. "It sounds risky."

"Inside job, though," I said. "I was at the meeting with Trent. Easy money."

"No such thing. Besides, haven't you made a lot already?" Clay shook hair out of his eyes. "Maybe it's time to start hedging your bets."

"Jason, we already have enough for—" Janie started.

I cut cold eyes at her, warning her not to say any more. Not to mention how we were going to start The Plan early.

"—for now," Janie finished.

I'd find a better time to tell Clay. When Janie and I knew more. Like where we were going and how we were going to get there. All the questions he would ask.

"Can always use more. Especially that much more." I shoved Clay slightly, bumping him sideways into Janie.

"It'll be fine. I can handle it, and if it goes wrong, all goes to hell, or if the zombie apocalypse comes, I'll ditch them."

"And come back for us," Janie said, a slight smile quirking her mouth.

"Even if I have to fight a zombie horde, uphill through the snow—"

"Both ways," Clay added.

"Who ignores the laws of topography like that?" I asked. "Uphill both ways? Impossible."

"Don't care. That's what it'll be. It's the zombie apocalypse. The world as you know it has ceased to exist." Clay's voice, like a self-important teacher.

"Can zombies fly in this world? Just wondering what other rules you're changing."

Clay clapped a hand to his head. "Why did I never think of that? Flying zombies!" He mimed holding a fat cigar between two fingers, then pretended to put it between his teeth.

"Someone take this down." He made a frame with his hands. "Flying zombies. Genius! Cupcake, get that hotshot director on the horn." He waved at Janie like she was his secretary.

"Cupcake?" She laughed and shoved him sideways into me.

"Damn. Flying zombies. It's like I'm printing money here," Clay said.

I went to push him against Janie, but he leapt back, and I stumbled into her instead. She shoved me hard, then took off running after Clay.

I chased them, making guttural zombie noises.

At Janie's stop we settled down, but were still laughing and shoving each other lightly.

"All right, you win," Janie finally said to me. "Easy money. But remember your promise."

I put a fist over my heart. "Uphill both ways."

Janie's bus ground to a stop. She got on. I watched through the windows as she found a seat next to that kid Hunter. He put an arm around her.

I showed my teeth and waved.

Hunter winced and waved back. Took his arm off her as the bus shuddered forward.

Clay and I walked to school. Stopped at the far edge of the parking lot. Clay squinted at the cluster of showroom-shiny cars where Michael and the others waited.

"In all the movies, in all the books and shows, when the zombie apocalypse comes, the humans turn out to be worse than the zombies," he said. "Always."

I followed his eyes, watched Michael's group churning between the cars like flies over meat. I nodded. Clay left, walking to the building.

I crossed to Michael and leaned against his car. The others stood around, like always, although there was an undercurrent of tension. Nods and intense eye contact, everyone watching each other and pretending they weren't.

The impending break-in hovered behind smiles and glances.

Dwight glared at me from T-Man's car. He stayed back, a distant moon circling the planet that held him.

Like Michael's magnetism had reversed and now forced him back.

Cyndra arrived and smiled at me before kissing Michael and standing under his arm.

Something rose in my throat, burning and sour. I mumbled about the bathroom, slapped hands with Michael, and left.

The first bell toned as I hit the bathroom door. I leaned over a sink, gripped the scarred porcelain in both hands. A couple of stupid freshmen eyed me as they edged out.

My eyes closed. I pushed deep lungfuls out my nose, forced the choking mass in my throat back down.

Behind me, the door creaked. I opened my eyes as the lights went out.

The door groaned as it was shoved shut.

I turned, fists clenched, listening to another person breathe. Waiting.

My first thought, stupid as it was, was that it was Cesare, that Michael had played me for a fool, had set me up to take the fall for dealing drugs, because Michael had dealt the man's drugs but had kept the man's money.

All while saying it was me. Which anyone in the school would confirm.

But I was at school. And Cesare would never come for me or anyone here. A flashlight beam swung into my eyes.

I lifted my arm. The flashlight winked off, and whoever it was tackled me. We fell against the wall. My head glanced off the cinder blocks. He put a hand on my throat.

I grabbed the arm that held me as a point of reference. Jacked a punch into his unprotected side.

The grip on my throat loosened.

I held his shoulder and punched again, white dot after-images from the flashlight floating before my eyes.

Our breaths sawed the air. He grunted as I grabbed at his head.

Three things bloomed in my mind with the rapid perfection of a time-lapse flower. The arm was covered in leather, but at the shoulder was scratchy wool. The head was buzz-cut.

A letterman's jacket. A big guy with buzz-cut hair. A grudge to settle.

I laughed. One hand held the back of his head. With my other, I made a fist and punched the guy in the face. Felt the scrape of his teeth against my knuckles.

Dwight crumpled toward me.

I shot an elbow at his face. Chunked against his cheek-bone. He hit the floor with a groan.

I walked, hand out in the dark, to the light switch. Flipped it.

Dwight shifted up, propping his shoulders against the wall nearest him. Swiped a hand across the blood and spit smearing his chin.

"Thanks," he said.

I reached for the door.

"Don't go yet. I haven't even started." He shifted against the wall again. Touched his cheekbone gingerly. "Is it bruising already?"

I flexed the hand that had punched him.

"You did exactly what I wanted. Busted lip and all," Dwight said.

"What the hell are you talking about?"

"I wanted you to hit me. There's not a mark on you, except your knuckles. From when you jumped me. Do you honestly think I'm that bad a fighter that I couldn't even hit you once?"

He smiled, gap-wide at the corners of his mouth. "This is what I'll tell the principal: I went to the bathroom. And you jumped me."

"So what? I'll tell them you jumped me first. Worst case, we're both suspended."

Dwight squeezed his lip to get more blood up. "Wait. You haven't heard the whole thing." He giggled like he was performing how funny it was for me. "See, I'll tell the principal that I followed you to the bathroom because I was angry and wanted to confront you. About how you make Cyndra deal for you. *Then* you jumped me."

I forced my fist open.

"Those cameras in the hall?" His voice like a teacher trying to lead you to the answer. "They got both of us walking in here. No one else. So you can't say it wasn't you who did it." He gestured to his face.

"What do you want?"

"Let me enjoy this for a minute." He got up and checked his face in the mirror. "Yes. This is so much better than hitting you. Although I'll eventually get to that."

"We'll see."

Dwight flashed a self-satisfied grin. "You're not worried about the principal? The cops?"

I shrugged. "Again. Say what you want. I'll deny it. Cyndra won't back your play."

"You're probably right. But that won't matter when they check your locker."

Cold stroked up my spine.

Dwight laughed. "Look at your face!"

"What do you want?"

He stepped forward. "I want you to quit. Yeah, I know about Michael thinking he needs you. And I know you're not really his friend."

Unlike him. He didn't have to say it. Wounded pride and resentment at being shoved aside pulsated from his eyes.

"Quit." He grabbed the edges of his athlete's jacket, resettling it on his shoulders. "Or I go to the principal, and it ends with the drugs in your locker and your arrest."

He curled a hand on the door handle. "You have until lunch. I'm going to the nurse now. For my timeline. But don't worry. I won't rat. Not yet, anyway. Maybe never. Either way. You're out. It's up to you if it's in handcuffs."

The door scraped the tile as he left.

My fist rammed the closed door. I turned and slammed my back against it. Scrubbed my hands over my face.

If I quit, I'd be out eight hundred dollars. I could take that, but would Dwight really stop there? What would happen to the drugs he'd planted in my locker? What if there was a random search today or the police received an "anonymous" tip?

And what about Clay? Dwight wasn't so stupid he wouldn't remember my pre-Michael friend. If I didn't cave, Dwight could try the same ploy on Clay's locker. Or worse.

My shoulders bunched.

I went into the hall. Didn't go to my locker, although every part of my brain screamed that I should. *Go, pull out the drugs, flush them. Can't make the obvious play. It's what Dwight would expect. Maybe even want. Too many people around, anyway.*

I made myself turn away from the hall where my locker stood. Made myself walk to my first class instead.

The bell dismissing homeroom toned. Kids swarmed into the hall. I let the crowd carry me past the nurse's office.

Glimpsed Dwight in there, a cold pack held to his lip.

In English I sat at an empty desk. The teacher pretended not to notice that I had no book, paper, or pencil. I looked out the window the whole time. My mind like a rat in a maze.

The best move would be to go. Get Janie out of school somehow and take off, like we planned. But it was still too early in the day to go home to get our money. And we could really use the extra eight hundred. I couldn't just leave without telling Clay. And Cyndra . . .

I could pretend to quit. Tell Dwight to ditch the drugs or I'd rejoin. Watch him do it, but from a distance. Once they're gone, squirt superglue into the lock, and Clay's lock, then go tell Michael. Get Dwight exiled permanently. Hang around tonight, long enough to get the money.

Then leave.

Leaving Clay unprotected.

Too much trouble for an assured revenge from Dwight. I should just stop like he wanted. It was all ending anyway.

But I already knew it wasn't safe. Winning might not be enough for Dwight. He'd liked the handcuff idea.

At break I waited for Cyndra by the courtyard door. Watched out the window as Dwight edged closer to Michael. Dwight's eyes cut around the space, looking for me.

"Jason," Cyndra called as she walked up. She gave me a perfect, heart-stopping smile.

I took her elbow, pulled her away from the windows.

"Listen," I said.

She turned her face to me, and her expression stopped the words in my mouth. It was tight. Frozen and tense, but aiming at relaxed. Fake.

Paranoia slicked into my brain. And a question I wasn't ready to learn the answer to: Did she already know? Was she in on it somehow?

Was she playing me?

I couldn't keep it off my face.

She bit her lip, and her eyes glimmered. Was something forcing her? The strain was naked on her face. She didn't want to do it.

"What is it, Jason?" Her voice mouse-small.

"Has Michael told you about the drug for your stepfather?" For some reason, this question bled to the front of my brain. Instinct, like a razor against my throat.

"No. What drug?" Cyndra's emerald eyes slid away, like she was worried about us being overheard.

"You're lying to me."

She chewed on her chapped lip. "Yes." The word just air.

"Why?"

"Michael told me already, but he said if you told me, I should pretend I didn't know."

"Why?"

"Because it would make you feel good to tell me. That's all. That's not bad, right? It's a good plan. I think that stuff could work. And it's nice he's thinking of me, and you—if you wanted to tell me."

Contortions of thought. All jutting elbows and knotted flesh.

"Don't lie to me," I said. "Ever."

"I can't." She shifted, tightening her arms over her books. "I couldn't. You saw." She flashed a smile, open this time. "It was stupid to try. Even if it was a white lie."

"Do you know anything about my locker?"

Her eyebrows creased together. "No. What?"

A pure gaze. Unwavering.

"Nothing. I'll tell you later." Because what could she do? She'd go to Michael. And his constant lies, his feel-good manipulations, made me want to keep him out.

I sent her into the courtyard and drifted toward the front of the school—and my locker. Still didn't go to it, though. Some instinct kept me moving, floating right by.

In my next class I thought about it. At lunch I'd have to choose or have the choice made for me. The skin on my back lifted and tightened.

Then it hit me. A choice, something to get me out of the corner. I needed an ally.

I didn't wait for the bell. Stood and walked out of class. Jogged down the hall, up the stairs, taking them two at a time.

Mr. Stewart. He'd offered to help me. Well, here was his chance. I'd tell him drugs had been planted in my locker. I'd get him to go with me to the principal. I'd turn the tables on Dwight.

Save myself and maybe get him to be the one wearing handcuffs. Stay around long enough for the heist tonight, even set up Michael to take a fall after.

Why not?

At Mr. Stewart's door, I drew up short. A young guy was locking the door, holding a lunch bag in his other hand.

"Where's Mr. Stewart?"

He frowned at me and pocketed the key. "He's at an in-service."

Like I'd know what that was. "When will he be back?" I asked, but already knew the answer.

"Tomorrow."

Of course.

I kicked the lockers. The substitute jumped. "Hey," he said, faintly.

I turned and pressed my back against the cool metal. Tipped my head back and closed my eyes. Forced my breathing to slow.

The substitute edged away.

So that was it. I'd go to lunch, pull Michael aside, then

quit. Get Dwight to remove the drugs. Glue the locks. Warn Clay and keep an eye on our backs until late enough in the day to get Janie, get the money, and run.

It was the best I could do.

I opened my eyes and stared up at the ceiling. Large tiles with zigzag scar patterns hung in a grid. My eyes tracked them, circled the gray bubble of a security camera cover. Tracked farther down the hall. Circled another bubble.

Then I had it.

Dwight may have backed me into a corner, but he'd left a weapon there. And now I knew it.

CHAPTER TWENTY-FOUR

utside at the lunch tables, Michael listened to Beast tell a story. Indulgence on his face like a mask of formerly withheld parental approval. Beast was flushed, happiness spreading color up his neck.

Dwight rolled his shoulders as I walked up.

"I need to talk," I said to Michael.

Beast froze, midsentence. Disappointment staining his face.

Michael stood to walk with me. I turned to Dwight. "You should hear this, too."

Dwight's expression changed as his brain caught up with the implications. His eyes daggered threats.

The three of us walked out, away from the building, stopping on the other side of a short stand of rangy pines.

"Dwight planted drugs in my locker. He jumped me in the bathroom this morning so I'd bruise him up. He says if I don't leave the group, he'll tell the principal I jumped him and about the drugs."

Michael's eyes widened, then narrowed. He turned on Dwight.

Dwight shook his head. "No. That's not what happened. He did jump me." He opened a hand at Michael. "He won't be happy until he's taken my place completely."

Michael knocked Dwight's hand aside. "Your place isn't big enough to hold him."

Dwight drew back as if he'd been slapped. He jabbed a finger at me. "You've just signed your arrest warrant. You think I'll stop now?"

"Something you said this morning stuck with me. Funny how something can be so obvious, you don't think of it, or even notice," I said.

Dwight shook his head.

"Go ahead and report me, Dwight. You just knew I'd go to my locker, right? Well, I haven't. Those security cameras you talked about? Yeah, they got us going into the bathroom. Bet they also got you going into my locker."

Dwight's jaw worked. A muscle flexed in his cheek.

Michael slapped my hand, then clasped it. He turned on Dwight. "This is what historians would call a rout. Right, Ice?"

Fierce joy surged into my veins, like power. Raw, bloody, and blazing hellfire. "I'm not going tonight if he is," I said to Michael. "We can't trust him."

My fists throbbed.

"Ice, he's not going to be anywhere near me." Michael turned sharp eyes on Dwight. "Don't speak to me. Don't come near me or any of the others. You're out."

We left him there. Watching as we walked back to the tables—and the group he was no longer a part of.

The drugs were still in my locker. As long as I didn't go there, I'd be fine.

And if Dwight came after me or Clay, I could handle it.

As lunch ended, Michael gestured for us to stay as other groups of kids jostled their way inside. Michael turned and stared pointedly at Dwight, still lingering in the background.

Dwight flinched like acid had been thrown in his face, but he hunched into himself and went inside.

"Dwight's out," Michael told the small group that remained huddled around the picnic table. "Ice, I'll pick you up at the old gym at eleven. The rest of you talk to Cyndra—you'll all be at my house by midnight. Where we'll wait until the guard calls. Questions?"

T-Man shook his head with the certainty of a fighter cracking his knuckles. Beast's eyes were wide-round like all he had were questions, but he didn't know where to begin.

"Good," Michael said. We filed inside as the tardy bell toned.

After school Clay had an academic club meeting, so I went home and got Janie. We grabbed dinner at the closest burger joint, and I walked her to Clay's as the sky got dark.

At the door, she squeezed my hand. "Stay safe. This is it, right?"

"Yeah. Be thinking about where you want that bus to take us." Trying not to think of Cyndra, of her smile, holding her, the soft pressure of her body against mine.

Janie squeezed me in a hug. "Florida?" Her voice lifted at the end like a balloon bobbing on a string.

She let me go before I could get uncomfortable.

It made me happy, though, in between the jagged pieces. Picturing Janie there. Sunshine and oranges and one of those stupid hats that the tourists all wear. Hell, maybe she'd relax enough to grow out her nails instead of chewing on them all the time.

"Okay," I said. "I haven't said anything to Clay yet."

She nodded. "I'll let you tell him. When you're ready."

I watched until she was inside, then I walked back to school. Once there, I slipped into the old gym and changed into a pair of black jeans, a black T-shirt, and the hoodie. I lay down and threw an arm over my eyes.

. . .

Banging on the gym door woke me. I went out to Michael's car. He drove silently, weaving past the gatehouse and up into the hills. We parked and then walked through his empty house. Michael didn't call out to see if his mom or dad were home, didn't creep in because it was so late and we might wake someone. Because he already knew they weren't there.

Because they were always anywhere he wasn't. Almost as if they knew he was dangerous—or just plain didn't like him.

Cyndra, Beast, T-Man, and LaShonda sat in the downstairs bar, scattered around the room-long sofas, waiting. Energy and nerves for the night yet to come were charging the air and making everyone laugh a little too loud.

Mike-Lite and Ray-Ray weren't there. And unless she was in the bathroom, Monique was missing, too. I cocked an eyebrow at Michael. "Three more down?" Couldn't help the taunting note that edged into my voice.

He shrugged and brushed his palms together twice—like he was knocking dirt off. "We won't even notice they're gone."

Ray-Ray and Mike-Lite had each other; exile wouldn't hurt them. And as for Monique, always so eager to please, needing to be a part of things—that was about fear. The same fear that kept her away tonight.

Just as well.

Finally, Michael's phone went off. He glanced at it and nodded.

"Yeah," T-Man said, drawing it out. "Let's have some fun." LaShonda kissed him like he'd invented adrenaline.

The web of tension around Michael's eyes eased. He held out a hand. T-Man slapped it.

We climbed the stairs and walked out to the four-car garage. Michael pressed a paddle, turning on a light and opening one of the bays. A battered black cargo van was incongruously parked next to a Lexus. The sliding door squealed as it opened.

Beast climbed in and settled on the floor. T-Man and LaShonda scooted to the back. Cyndra got in last. Michael gestured to the front seat, so I climbed in.

"Where'd you get the car?" LaShonda asked.

Michael started the engine and slowly pulled forward. "Bought it in cash. No registry. Got it off an illegal at the farmer's market. It's completely untraceable."

I wondered how many people had seen him drive it up here—or if the security guard would remember it.

The black van eased down the driveway. Michael stopped at the Mustang to reach in and press the garage remote clipped to his visor.

At the road, the engine squealed when he turned. Michael's hands drummed the wheel, eyes manic, mouth a hard line.

We drove down into the city.

CHAPTER TWENTY-FIVE

We approached a medical conclave—sort of like a suburb of doctors' and dentists' offices, surrounded by dried, clear-cut scrubland. Each office had its own lot and driveway. They almost looked like houses in a subdivision, developed and built by the same soulless company.

Michael piloted us down the winding street. I knew we were at the right one when he tracked it with his eyes, head swiveling as we slowly drove past.

"No one's around. No night cleaning crews. No security guards, no one," Michael said. He pulled into the driveway, and then drove around back and parked by a short delivery ramp.

"Here." He handed out black hoods. I pulled the stretchy fabric over my head. There were only eyeholes. I glanced behind me. LaShonda was making a face, like she didn't want to muss her hair or makeup. She pulled the hood on, though.

Even though he was already wearing his hood, you could tell T-Man was smiling under the tight fabric. Beast looked like a hulking executioner in a Bugs Bunny cartoon. Except his eyes were scared, not mean.

I couldn't stop the laugh that choked out.

Michael's eyes shot to me. Misinterpreted my laugh as excitement. He reached out and cuffed my arm. "Atta boy." The mask muffled his voice a little. "Get in the spirit of the thing."

"Don't touch me."

Beast glanced between us. His scared eyes crinkled in confusion.

T-Man scooted up, elbows on the backs of our seats. "Easy, Ice," he said. "Easy." Like he thought it was nerves.

"Let's get it over with," I said, feeling the skin of my neck drawing tight, even as adrenaline jangled in my veins.

Cyndra locked eyes with me.

"Fine," Michael said. "We'll go in there." He nodded at the delivery door. "LaShonda, you're the lookout on the front door. Cyndra, you're back door. T-Man, Beast, you're wrecking. Rip it up."

Michael gestured to the back of the van, where a canvas tarp was folded. "Get whatever you need."

Beast flipped the tarp off a few hatchets, picks, a crowbar, even a chain saw. There were cans of spray paint and a couple buckets of red paint.

Michael turned to me. "Ice, you find the surgical suite and dispensary. Grab all the drugs you can find." He rummaged in the duffel and brought out a black backpack. Handed it to me.

"Ready?" his eyes swept the group huddled in the van. "All in. Trash the bastard."

The back doors of the van opened with a shriek like a woman being stabbed. Michael and I piled out, slamming the doors behind us.

We hustled up to the back door. It was unlocked. I guessed we had Trent to thank for that. T-Man tore through first, smashing tinted camera bubbles as he ran down the hall. LaShonda followed, disappearing through a swinging door into the front waiting room. I shouldered the backpack and started opening doors.

All the doors on the right were little examining rooms like the one where Beast was already working. I hurried to each in turn, double-checking that they were empty.

I found some cabinets and drawers in the hallway. Pried them open with the crowbar and found some samples in little blister packs. Shoved all of it into the bag.

There was another private office complete with a massive desk. I didn't even go in. After a janitor's closet and another, lesser office, I found it.

The surgical suite.

Large silver lights hung in the middle of the space. There was a table for a patient to lie on and gleaming stainless steel trays on wheels. Suspended from the ceiling was a flat-screen monitor. A microscope under a cover stood to one side. There was a double sink with foot pedals, rolling cabinets. IV carts, tubes, sterile drapes. A portable X-ray machine. A defibrillator cart.

You could almost smell the money.

I went over to the rolling cabinets first. Immediately, I found vials of liquid and bottles of pills—some names I recognized from commercials or the street, sedatives, paralytics, antianxiety medicine, painkillers.

I pulled out more drawers, found more. They all went into the bag.

The crashes in the hall doubled. I went back to the door and glanced out. T-Man was ripping the framed art from the walls. He smashed the glass, picked up a hammer, and darted into the waiting room. As the door swung, I caught a glimpse of him taking aim at a television mounted on the wall.

Michael shoved me aside, barreling into the surgical suite. He kicked over the stainless steel rolling trays and jumped on them, warping them.

"What are you waiting for?" he yelled. He climbed onto the surgical table and yanked at the lights.

They fell with a crash. Their cords dangled.

Michael jumped off the table and ripped the monitor from its mount. He swung a mini-sledgehammer at the microscope. He shrieked at the empty room as he wrecked it. He didn't even see me leave.

I walked into the hall. There were holes in the Sheetrock all the way down to where Cyndra kept watch.

I went to the front office. It was completely trashed, the counter broken and dangling from the wall in two pieces. Papers strewn on the floor. Broken glass from the reception window glittered across the carpet.

The waiting room was equally destroyed. Fish lay gasping on the ground, their aquarium glass, water, and gravel spilled across the sofa and floor. LaShonda ignored them, watching out the front windows.

My lungs squeezed.

T-Man lugged paint cans in through the back door, pushing past Cyndra.

I went back and forth, first helping Beast wreck the bathrooms, then helping T-Man slop paint onto the furniture, floors, and walls.

LaShonda's scream pierced the sound of shattering porcelain. "Someone's coming!"

I dropped the paint and ran up to the waiting room. My heels skidded on wet gravel and dead fish. I fell against the chair next to LaShonda.

Outside, headlights threaded through the medical park. The car passed under a streetlamp, and the crest on the door was briefly illuminated.

T-Man scooted around Michael and stood next to LaShonda. He caressed the back of her hooded head. "It's okay, baby."

Paranoia gnawed on my synapses. I went to the front door into the office, gave it a tug to make sure it was locked. My eyes snagged on the writing on the glass. The words were backward—meant to be read as you walked up to the door from the parking lot, not as you stood inside looking out.

"Stay calm," Michael was telling the others. "He'll drive away, whoever he is."

My eyes tracked the words from right to left: **Beautiful**

You Cosmetic Surgery and Dermatology Associates.
There were three doctors in the practice. Dr. Singh Patel, Dr. Sam Reaves, and Dr. Michael Springfield.

My brain felt like it was twisting, warping in my skull.

Dr. Michael Springfield, who named his only son after himself. Who was never home in his mountaintop mansion.

Plastic surgeons wouldn't keep birth control medication in their offices. Cyndra and her stepdad had nothing to do with this. Michael had lied about all of it. Hadn't said it was his own father's practice we were planning to rob.

Did it matter?

I stalked to the window, glaring at Michael as the car got closer. It turned onto our street.

"We're bailing," I told him. "Now. Everyone, go to the van."

The security guard's car drew closer.

"Relax. It's a rent-a-cop." Michael didn't even glance at me. "Maybe even Trent."

"T-Man, LaShonda, Beast. Go to the van. Get Cyndra to start it," I said. They scuttled out of the room.

"I'm not done here, Ice." Michael turned cold eyes to me. His hand went to his waistband.

The security car turned into the office parking lot. Headlights swept the plate glass.

Michael and I dove for the floor.

The car parked and the driver's door opened. The security guard passed in front of his car's headlights, making them flicker in the window.

He was too tall to be Trent.

Michael swung the gun toward the door. I crouched like a racer, weight braced on my fingertips.

"What are you doing?" I hissed. "Let's go!"

I eased around the bank of chairs toward the hall and the back door.

The security guard stopped at the door and gave it a tug. He turned on a flashlight and aimed it inside.

Crouched behind the row of chairs, Michael kept the gun trained on the door.

The flashlight glinted off the shattered glass of the television.

"What the—" The guard's voice was muffled. He fumbled at his belt, pulled out keys.

A percussive blast ripped through the room. A second shot answered it. The door shattered. The security guard fell backward with a scream.

"Time to go," Michael said. His eyes gleamed with jittery triumph. He lowered the gun and whirled.

We sprinted down the hall and crashed through the back door.

Outside, the van waited with Cyndra at the wheel.

Michael and I leapt in. He pulled the sliding door closed, straining against the acceleration as Cyndra spun the steering wheel.

She steadied the van, heading toward the driveway back to the main road.

"No!" Michael handed me the gun and wrenched the steering wheel hard. The tires screeched. The van skidded in a circle.

I fell against the door, half expecting it to shoot open.

Michael pointed out the windshield. "Over the scrub. They'll be looking for us on the roads."

Cyndra nodded and turned toward the curb. She took it too fast, bottoming out on the concrete.

"That way." Michael pointed. "Head toward the radio tower. Turn the lights off. Don't worry, it's safe. I used to walk out here when I was a kid."

Cyndra hit the switch. The lights went dark. The van bounced and lurched over the scrub.

The moon was bright enough to show a little of the ghost landscape outside the windshield.

I gripped the gun as the van lurched over hummocks and washouts.

After a few moments, Michael pointed again. Cyndra adjusted course, and the road suddenly smoothed to the whisper-jar of a dirt road.

"Access road for the tower," Michael explained, shooting bright, junkie-with-a-fix eyes to the rest of us. He turned back to Cyndra. "Turn on the lights. Punch it."

The lights blazed as Cyndra floored the accelerator. Pebbles pinged the side of the van.

I ejected the gun clip. Popped the slide and palmed the bullet in the barrel.

LaShonda watched with saucer eyes. T-Man nodded like he knew the first thing about guns.

We wound down the hill. The tires bit and spit rocks. At the base of the hill, a gate hung open where the pavement started.

Cyndra slowed and followed Michael's directions. Everyone pulled their hoods and gloves off.

I kept my gloves on. Held the gun, clip, and bullet.

Michael directed Cyndra to a box store off the main road that bisected town. Parked in the lot were T-Man's Lexus and Cyndra's silver Mercedes.

T-Man whooped and held a hand out to Michael.

A worm, edged with razors, burrowed into my chest.

The cars were here. He'd brought the gun.

The lie about helping Cyndra, all to get me to be invested, somehow. When it was his own father's practice he'd targeted all along. As if suspicion somehow *wouldn't* focus on him, or his friends.

Or me.

The well-executed escape. Almost like he'd planned everything. Even getting interrupted. All so he could save us and get his adrenaline fix. Hero worship, adulation, and brain buzz in one great needle.

Me, the perfect fall guy.

And even though Michael didn't know about it, now Janie and I couldn't leave. Or if we did, it'd be a whole other proposition. Because it was one thing to leave town as nobodies. Something else entirely for me to disappear as a suspect in a crime.

And I never saw it coming. Idiot.

"Okay, Cyndra, you'll take Beast and follow me in your car." Michael turned to me. "Ice, you go with T-Man and LaShonda. I'm going to ditch the van and meet you back at my house."

I shook my head. "This is where I get off."

"What?" Cyndra's voice reduced by the acid in mine.

I threw the clip at Michael. Then the gun. And the bullet.

"Fuck off, you psychotic bastard." I got out of the car and then took off the gloves, shoving them in my pocket with the hood.

"Wait." Michael jumped out and ran up behind me.

I whirled, hands up. "You going to shoot me, Michael? Is that next? What the hell was that?"

"Shut up," he hissed. "Keep your voice down."

"Does your great plan involve me getting arrested for your little stunt tonight? Because I fail to see how that helps you with Cesare."

Although, I could see how my arrest would help Michael, just not with Cesare. I was his safety if the cops figured it out. A get-out-of-jail-free card. The kid with the record pulling the heaviest weight.

"Calm down, Ice. No one's getting arrested for anything. We got away clean."

I bit off a curse at his idea of clean.

"You know what? I don't care. I'm done," I said.

"Finish the job, and you can be done."

"Screw you. I'm done now."

Michael crossed his arms high on his chest. "Go ahead. Ditch. Don't get the rest of your pay."

Rage arced through me like a lightning strike.

Michael saw it and stepped back. Then he took another step back. "They were blanks, Ice. Blanks. No one got hurt. No one ever gets hurt."

The shattering glass. The fallen guard. Blanks my ass.

He got back in the van. After a moment, Cyndra and the others got out. Michael screeched the tires as he drove the van away.

Beast, LaShonda, and T-Man got in T-Man's car and trailed the van out of the lot. Cyndra leaned against her car, watching me.

After a few minutes, pulled like she was magnetic north, I went to her. She held out a roll of bills. "He said to give you this."

Her crimson-tipped fingers hung there, holding the money.

The razor-worm writhed in my gut. I took the money.

"I'm to drive you where you want."

I got in the car and turned down her unspoken invitation. "Take me to the school."

CHAPTER TWENTY-SIX

hat night I slept on the mats in the old gym. Mostly because I didn't want to talk to Clay or Janie. Didn't want to explain what had happened at the offices. Because that would lead to Janie getting upset that we couldn't leave yet, and then me having to explain to Clay about Florida. And I was too tired to have that conversation now.

I needed to think. About the offices, and leaving with Janie. And something, tugging at my mind like an unraveling thread: Michael had planned it all.

Part of me expected a cop to show up. Was waiting for the blare of a siren, remembering the shots, the shattering glass, and the security guard. I was the perfect fall guy, after all.

Another reason not to go to Clay's.

I texted Clay—asked him to tell Janie that I was okay and that I'd meet her at home after school the next day. Thanked him for taking care of her.

It was cold enough that I went into the locker room and pulled on extra layers before huddling on the frigid mats.

The gun, the shot, Michael's eyes—shining at the turn of events. How he couldn't have been happier, or more unsurprised. T-Man playing right into Michael's "save." Michael's claim that the bullets were blanks. And Cyndra, the magician's assistant.

I didn't sleep.

Friday morning, the first tone sounded. I didn't move. Just waited there.

I knew. Through the tones that buzzed across campus after each class and at lunch.

It wasn't over.

Just like I knew Michael would come to find me.

When the first lunch tone went off, I folded up the mats. Shored them behind the heavy bag. Then I went into the locker room and stripped off the extra layers of hoodie and shirts. Like shucking skin.

Came back out in one of my old shirts and thrift-store jeans. Walked back out to the heavy bag, taping my hands. Pulled on the gloves and began working the bag.

Didn't stop when the door behind me groaned and then banged.

Michael edged into my peripheral vision. He watched as I put my shoulder behind a short jab, experimenting with flowing into the bag. Trying to deliver the most power in a tight move.

I stopped after three more hits. Waited for him.

"I thought you'd be here. Not the best idea, skipping class. If the cops come sniffing around, they might find that unusual."

I shot a vertical fist into the bag. Then popped out two more.

"The second job's tonight," he said. "I can pick you up here or—"

"I'm not going anywhere with you." I stood beside the bag, gloves up.

Michael frowned. "I'm sorry about last night. It got a little crazy. Trent said it was just dumb chance that the other guy showed up. But it's okay. We're safe."

"What about the guard you shot?"

"I told you. Blanks."

"Blanks don't shatter glass."

"That was the guard's shot." He started stretching, twisting at the waist, loosening his back. "But it doesn't matter. It's not even in the paper yet. Shows the priority the cops are giving it."

He made a fist. Thumped it into the bag. "Tonight. Late. Around three in the morning."

"Stop talking. I don't want to know any more." I squared off in front of the bag.

"I'll pay you a hundred just to listen. And I'll pay you a grand to come." He dug out two bills. Laid them across the top of the bag, threading them under the chains.

I pulled a glove open with my teeth. "You have ten minutes."

He took fifteen.

It was the second job for Cesare. He was quick to say that robbing his father's practice had been for Cesare, too. That he did need the drugs to get to this point. To get Cesare to trust him. To see that he could do it. This one was personal. And a promise, straight from the man's mouth, that this one would be the last. Would wipe the slate clean, and even set Michael ahead.

It was a robbery. Someone who'd pissed off Cesare more than Michael had. Someone who needed a lesson, and that lesson was going to come due at their strip club.

When Michael said that, my head rocked back, and for a moment I thought it was my dad. That somehow my dad had gotten into a pissing contest with Cesare. That in a strange, small-world way, it would be my dad we were knocking over.

But the hit was too late at night. And the strip club was out of town, just over the river. A few rungs down from even the jet-trash airport strip club where my dad ran his sorry little kingdom.

My father had nothing to do with it, and neither would I. I wouldn't be going anywhere with Michael, and certainly not to a strip joint in the sticks, complete with its own jumped-up security and rackets.

And I wasn't fool enough to trust Michael again. That this would be all. That he didn't have some other little adventure up his sleeve.

And there was Florida, which I sure as hell wouldn't be telling him about.

"You have to come," he said, ignoring my refusal. "You inspire confidence in the others. Of course, they're all little adrenaline junkies now." He smiled like a proud parent. "And I'll pay you a grand. Big money, for little risk. Then we're clear. Completely clear of everything, and it doesn't have to end. It can be just the start."

His eyes glinted like he was holding Cyndra out to me. Like he sensed the radar of my heart looking for her, missing her when she was gone.

I threw the gloves aside. Drove a fist into the canvas.

Michael placed himself behind the bag, steadying it. I punched again. Visualizing my punch going through the bag and into him.

"Good," he grunted. "But correct me if I'm wrong, here. It doesn't matter how much you train or how good you hit. You're outmatched. With your dad, I mean." His eyes were innocent-wide, like how could he have been talking about anything else?

My shoulders knotted. I threw another punch, pushing against the tightness.

"Out of your class," Michael continued. "It's why lightweights don't fight heavyweights. Not that you're a *lightweight*. I don't mean that as an insult."

I bit through the tape that bound my knuckles. Tore it off. "The answer is no."

"I didn't hand over all the drugs. To Cesare." Michael went on, as if I hadn't said anything. "I could give you what I saved. I don't have to help you, with your dad. I could give the drugs to you, and you could do it. It'd be like a tip. The money and the drugs."

"No. It's too dangerous." I looked in his eyes, letting him read the accusation there. The gun. His adrenaline high. His addiction to risk. That every word he said was suspect.

And that although I may be outmatched, at least I understood that much. And it was enough to keep me from doing anything else.

You can't be outmatched if you don't play the game.

His voice cut. "So, what? You go back to your pathetic burnout life? No one will talk to you. Cyndra won't even look at you."

He didn't know me if he didn't realize I already knew that.

And I knew enough not to open my mouth about leaving town with Janie.

Michael lunged and shoved the bag out. I slid back before it could slam into me.

"Everything I'm offering. More money than you've ever had. Solving your problem with your dad. It's all worth it."

"No."

Michael's mouth pressed into a cancerous smile. "Then I hope he beats you to death." His eyes shone, not with the manic glow, but with something else.

I wondered if anyone ever said no to him. If he ever didn't get exactly what he wanted.

Of course it had happened before. It was why he'd targeted his dad's office. Reciprocity for not giving enough. For making Michael invisible in his own home.

I shrugged. "I guess I'll take my chances."

Michael's eyes narrowed. "Because *that's* the risk you'd rather take."

I didn't say anything. Just held his eyes as he stalked out from behind the bag and left the gym.

CHAPTER TWENTY-SEVEN

fter he left, I started running around the court. My feet hit the boards, the dull thudding sounding like a drum in my brain, saying the same thing: *Over. Over. Over.*

I'd be fine.

More importantly, Janie would be fine. It was getting more dangerous to stay than to leave, no matter what the police thought. If they even had anything to connect me to the doctors' offices. So we'd get on that bus. We'd start our plan—

I couldn't go along with the job. It was too risky.

A thousand dollars. I told myself I wasn't thinking about it.

My fists flew at the heavy bag.

The bell tones buzzed through the rest of the day as I waited for the time to pass so I could go home when my father would be gone. Janie and I would pack. I'd have to tell her to leave her happy endings behind—we'd need to carry whatever we were taking with us. We could get a library card when we got there. Then I'd go say good-bye to Clay. Warn him to watch his back.

I thought of Cyndra. Kept punching.

Over. Over. Over.

I wanted to find her and say good-bye.

Could I trust her if I did? Not to say anything to Michael? I knew better, despite the stubborn hope that I was wrong.

In the locker room, the hot water pelted over me. After I got dressed I headed home. The sky was darkening, the early fall sunset fading in the sky before the football team finished practice.

On the walk home, everything looked different. Darker, leached of color somehow. Like the slate-gray sky had sucked everything dry.

I closed the army jacket, fighting a shiver at the bite in the air.

It was too early for him to be home, but when I opened the door there he stood—leaning against the wall.

Janie sat in the center of the swayback sofa. Tear tracks streaked her face. My heart hammered.

"There he is. The big man." My father flowed forward. "Here." He held out a fifty. Waved it. "Go on, take it. Your friend gave it to me for you. Nice kid. Too young to be going to strip clubs, but hey—what do I care, right? And we had an interesting talk."

My heart stopped.

Michael hadn't meant what he'd said. He was pissed, sure, but he wouldn't do this.

I shouldn't be surprised. I shouldn't feel betrayed.

My father looked over his massive shoulders theatrically, first one, then the other.

"Now. Where do you keep big money like this? When you have a secret stash. When you've been working a little angle all your own. Where do you keep it? Inside a book? Taped to the back of a drawer?"

Janie sobbed.

The coffee can sat beside her on the sofa.

"Hmm?" My father's ice-blue eyes burned into me. He followed my glance. Pointed at the can. "There? Inside the coffee can? Stuffed down the air vent, right, Janie?"

He patted the lump in his pocket. "Nice little bank. Smart, too. I don't think I ever would have found it if I hadn't known it was waiting to be found. Even then, Janie had to show me."

Janie sobbed and looked away from me. There was a red mark across her cheekbone.

"Know what else your friend Dwight said?" My father laid heavy hands on my shoulders, thumbs stretching across the back of my neck.

Dwight. My biceps knotted with rigid pressure. Seething blood coursed into my heart as bands of rage constricted my chest.

Dwight was back in his rightful place. Maybe he'd never been anywhere else.

"He said there's an opportunity for you to get more. Isn't that cute? An *opportunity*." The stress on the word sounded amused. "But Dwight says you don't want to go. Now is that any way to behave toward *opportunity*? No! Of course not. So you're going. Come on home with those nice, nice profits for me. Clean and easy.

"But it does make me wonder," he continued. "Why

haven't I put you on the rolls before? If you have *opportunity* with that little puke, why not with me? Like tonight. You're doing that for me."

His hand slid along my shoulder and tightened, catching a nerve and making my eyes water. My stomach clenched.

"You're going tonight, understand?" His hand closed so hard I gasped and had to take a side step to ease the pressure.

He let go of my shoulder and grabbed my arm, twisting it. "You understand?"

"Yes."

He shoved me away.

"Good." He turned and walked into the kitchen. "Someone will pick you up here late tonight. So don't go anywhere. And don't get any ideas, because Jane will be waiting with me for you to come back."

Janie jumped off the sofa and ran upstairs, slamming our bedroom door behind her.

I picked up my bag. Climbed the steps with weighted feet.

Janie grabbed my hand when I walked into the room.

"I'm sorry!" She swiped at her eyes. "He made me. He came in, barged in—then he, he—"

I lay down on the bed and draped a rigid arm across my eyes.

"I know," I told her.

It didn't feel as bad as you'd think. Losing everything. It's not like I had much beyond some stupid plan. I tried to tell myself it had never been real.

Ash Parsons

Dwight. Had Michael sent him, or had Dwight come on his own, seeking revenge? The end result was the same.

My vision blurred. I closed my eyes. Bile rose in my throat.

The fat wad of cash in his pocket.

Food, bills, medicine. Freedom.

The Plan.

I lunged for the trash can. Retched until it made my ribs sore, water leaking out from under my eyelids.

Janie rubbed my back. "Take a deep breath. It'll be okay. We'll figure out something."

I wiped my sleeve across my mouth and put the can down.

"Shut up." I knocked her hands away. "Don't touch me."

Chapter Twenty-Eight

e didn't talk about the money, or Florida, again. For a long time, we didn't talk about anything. I sat on the floor, back pressed into the corner. Shudders ran down my arms. The rage pulsed white-hot through my head, shaking in clenched fists that ached to hit something, someone, anything.

And on the heels of the anger, so close that you couldn't feel the transition, this burning coil. A molten knot of shame and realization.

There was no move to make. There was nowhere to go but along.

My jaw clenched, teeth pressing tight like I could get something between them. This is what it was to be truly trapped. No plan. No money. No dream of someday. And on his radar. With his notice, the inevitable end. A concrete wall at the end of the road.

Because even if I got through this night, this dangerous strip-joint robbery, in one piece and not under any suspicion or inevitable arrest, it would still never be enough. There'd be the next, and the next. No matter if Michael decided he was through with me, my dad never would be. Now that he could see the potential—the money I could bring him.

I was trapped for the rest of my life. And maybe that wouldn't be too long.

I leaned forward, then slammed my shoulders back against the corner. Shifted until they were squared against one wall.

Made myself a promise. If we got through it, when the night was fully behind us, I would beat the hell out of them both. Dwight and Michael.

It made me feel better, until I thought of Janie, waiting with my dad.

The rage winked out. A shift in my mind, like watching a fan, and suddenly it seemed the blades were turning in the opposite direction.

My revenge wasn't what was important. Getting through this night. Coming home to keep Janie safe was.

She came and sat on the foot of my bed. We waited. For three a.m., when Michael would pick me up for the job.

Finally, after hours, Janie spoke.

"What are we going to do?"

"Get through it, I guess." I got up from the floor and scrubbed my hands over my face. "Keep our heads down. Keep our powder dry."

I couldn't stop the bitter laugh.

Jane eased closer, so tentative that the springs barely sagged with her movement. "I'm so sorry. I'm so sorry about the can. About all of it."

I didn't have to say it. That he would have had to kill me before I would have shown him where it was. And she didn't have to say that I had a death wish or that we could start over. Or that everything was going to be okay.

I sat next to her. She sighed, and the breath coming out stuttered in little puffs, like she was about to cry.

"I don't know what we should do," she said in a tiny voice. "What if you get caught? Or get hurt?"

"You're going to be fine, Janie."

"I'm not worried about me!"

Her eyes were so dark I could see myself in them. I wrapped an arm around her. "I love you."

She tucked her head on my shoulder and hugged me like she thought she'd never see me again.

"I love you, too. Please be careful, Jason."

"I will. If you get the chance, take it. Run to Clay's." I hugged her back.

"I'll text you if I do," she said. We both knew it was a forlorn hope. "Should you call him now?" she asked.

I sighed. "What would be the point?"

We waited.

The clump of my father's steel-toed boots came up the stairs and knocked the door open.

"Your ride is here." Knife-blade eyebrows lowered in a glare.

I put on my work boots while my dad watched. Nodded good-bye to Janie and walked down the stairs and out the door.

On the front stoop I paused and shook out a cigarette.

Michael's cherry Mustang idled by the curb. Michael stood beside it on the passenger side, hands in his pockets, a small, knowing smile hovering on his mouth. His clothes were dark.

His eyes flicked over my ripped jeans and stretched-out shirt. "No time to go change, sad to say," he called. "Not that you would, right? Wearing your clapped-out clothes is the only screw-you move you've got left."

I crossed the dirt and stood in front of him. Waited.

He crossed his arms high on his chest. "I guess you're in now, huh? It's for the best. You'll see. I know you won't believe me, but I really didn't have anything to do with it. Dwight crossed a line, man, and he knows it. And when we're done, if you want to break him, whale on him till he's raw meat, no one will blame you, and no one will stop you."

Like they could.

"But even though he was wrong"—he held up his hands in a now-let's-not-be-hasty position—"it's for the best. And you look fine, so you obviously handled your dad. For now." He edged closer, dropped his voice. "My offer still stands. Tonight, after it's over, let's take care of him, and you'll never have to worry again."

I glared at him.

Michael took a step back.

"You're right. I don't believe you," I said. The smile on his face tightened. "And, yeah, I'm in tonight. Not because you convinced me, or hired me, or any lame-ass reason you could dream up that you thought I'd go for. But because you forced it. That's your control. Force instead of manipulation. Just so you get what you want."

His eyes crinkled at the edges, though no smile crooked his mouth. "You suppose God cares if people love or fear Him? As long as they're obedient?"

Smoke plumed out my mouth. "Tell me what I'm doing. And after it's over, stay the hell away from me."

Michael smiled like I had agreed to come to my own party. He dug in a pocket and handed over five crisp hundreds. "Be yourself. The badass we all know and love." His eyes had that manic light—like he had tilted the table and everything was spinning his way.

We got in the car and drove away from Lincoln Green.

"The others are meeting us there," Michael said as we accelerated onto the highway. "Dwight, too. We need him. And he was only too happy to be loved again." He glanced at me like he thought I'd act surprised or argue or make some pointless threat.

When I didn't speak he kept talking.

"Cesare says the safe and security computer will be in the same room. He says if we can get in and get into that room right at four thirty—that's when the video server backs up—if we can get in there on time, we can get the money *and* destroy the video footage."

"That's a load of bullshit. There's no way we're disrupting the video feed. Unless we go in with masks on, we're getting ID'd."

Michael shifted lanes. He shook his head. "Let me worry about that. The cameras might get us going in, but so what?

Cesare says there's a blind spot to the left of the bar—
there's a little recess there. That's where we do it. We go
in as customers—we come out as victims. Scared kids who
took off running when the rival gang came to call. That's
the story. Simple."

"You're taking a lot on faith."

Michael smiled. "No, I'm taking a lot on *greed*. Cesare
wants this, which means I do, too. And to get out from under his thumb, I have to get out clean. It's all good."

"You can believe any story you want. You still have to
deal with witnesses."

"Kid. You ever hear of a good lawyer?" Michael wove
between cars. "These witnesses you're worried about.
Drunks. Strippers. Gang members. Unreliable in the ex-
treme. We'll be fine."

It didn't matter if he was right or not. And it didn't matter if we got away with it in the long term. I had short-term
worries.

Janie. My dad. The security at the club.

We drove onto the bridge.

"This'll be fun," Michael said.

The Mustang wove through an alley lined with gasoline
stations and convenience stores. Took off down a twisting
county road into the darkness of a country night for miles.
Until we arrived at the roadhouse, a clapboard, squat
building. Red neon curled on the gray-painted exterior:
Raunch.

A different crappy van was parked by a Dumpster beside the building. Other beater cars parked on the edge of

the lot or near the door. Thumping music blared from inside the club.

Michael parked near the van. We got out and walked over. T-Man slid the door open and we climbed in.

Cyndra sat in the driver's seat, Dwight in passenger seat. He gave me a self-satisfied grin.

Even though I knew he would be there, I had to stop myself from grabbing his head with one hand and driving the other into his nose.

Cyndra wore the sparkly dress from the party. Next to her, Dwight wore a collared shirt and khaki pants, like a frat guy. In the back of the van were the others. LaShonda had on a shirt thin as a whisper. T-Man and Beast wore crisp shirts and tailored jeans.

They looked like a bunch of rich kids. An inviting combination for the doorman.

Michael passed around a flask. "Dwight explained it all, right? We're just kids out to have fun. Follow my lead. You know what to do when it starts."

Nods and some grins.

Dwight gave LaShonda an empty backpack. She rolled it up and shoved it in her bulky purse.

We climbed out. Cyndra came beside me.

My hands itched to grab her. To ask what she knew about any of it. About Dwight telling my father.

Michael looped an arm over her shoulders and pulled her under his chin.

"Showtime." He stumbled suddenly, leaning on her for support. A loud, drunken laugh cawed out of his mouth.

On cue, the others took it up. Babbling, stumbling, slapping shoulders and hands. A weaving pack of drunk high school kids, out for a good time.

Dwight smiled at me and took a pull from the flask. He fell in behind Michael and Cyndra. Bending over, he waggled his fingers along the bottom edge of her dress. An obscene gesture just for me.

I ignored him. Choked off the molten rage with a promise.

We walked to the door.

CHAPTER TWENTY-NINE

 rope-muscled bouncer stopped us. He was bald and tall, and stupid, because he wore gauges in his ears that were big enough to be easily grasped in a fight. Which told me that for all the out-of-town-rough-element atmosphere, there really wasn't much trouble calling if he controlled the door.

"Hold up," the bouncer said. He squinted at T-Man and Dwight standing behind Michael. Eyes tracked up to Beast, hulking behind us all. "Go home, kids. You can't come in here."

"It's my birthday." Michael slurred his words.

"Happy birthday. Now go."

Michael let go of Cyndra, held up a hand. "Hang on. I think we can come to an orangemet. Uh—arrangement." He dug in a pocket, spilling twenties on the ground. He teetered as he collected the money. Didn't count, just shoved it at the bouncer.

"That's for me and my friends." He swayed, smiling. Swiveling owl eyes to the rest of us.

The bouncer flicked the bills into a neat stack and pocketed it in one slick move.

"That buys you one hour. If the cops come, you go out the kitchen." He stepped back, holding the door open.

"Thank you, my good man." Michael sloppily swept through. I let Beast go in before me. I glanced back at the cars in the lot, did a quick count. Noted their placement relative to the doors and the road.

Inside the club, music punched my ears.

On the stage, a girl twirled around a pole as red lights pulsed. A bar curved around the stage, where five men sat and watched her with the empty gazes of habitual drunks. Almost like they weren't looking at anything at all.

Beast was already at the stage, pulling up a chair, eyes transfixed on the girl.

Music throbbed in time with the lights. To the left was a bar. I walked around it and found the others already sprawled in the recessed space Cesare had described.

"Ice!" Michael yelled over the thumping music. He whapped a hand on the seat beside him.

I threaded around the small cocktail table and chairs. Sat down next to him.

"See? Just like he said." Michael nodded up at the camera bubbles on the ceiling.

"Impossible to tell if we're on it or not," I yelled over the music.

Michael shook his head. "We're clear." He checked his watch. "Just don't get comfortable."

"I never do."

I glanced around again. Apart from the girl onstage and her paltry audience, there was a burly bartender and a waitress. Two doors in the opposite corner. One hung with beaded fringe, the other painted black like the walls.

The beaded one led backstage, no doubt. Private dance room, maybe, or a row of cheap mirrors and a bathroom. The black door led to the office. Where the safe was. And the security computer.

The bartender was another security type. Thickset with blunt fingers. The kind of guy you imagined would start panting after climbing a flight of stairs.

So all we had to worry about was everything we couldn't see. How many girls in the back? How many workers in the kitchen? Who sat in the office? How many guns under the bar or tucked into waistbands?

Who was it, exactly, we were about to fuck with?

The waitress sauntered over to us. One of the guys at the stage tried to flag her down, but she'd already made us as the better tippers.

"What can I get you?" She licked her teeth at Michael.

Cyndra tracked her body in one glance. Dismissed her just as quickly.

The waitress's eyes narrowed.

"We want a bottle of Jack." Michael dug more bills out of his pocket. "And some shot glasses."

"I can pour the shots, honey. You don't need the bottle."

"We want the bottle." Michael's voice hardened. "You can carry a shot to my friend at the stage, if that makes you happy." He pointed at Beast, still slack-jawed and sitting near the pole.

"We're not allowed to sell the bottle."

Michael waved at her in a run-along gesture. "Go get the bartender. Let me talk to someone in charge."

The bartender came over. Michael murmured in his ear and slapped bills in his palm.

The waitress came back, laid out some shot glasses and the unopened bottle of whiskey.

Everyone did shots.

I left mine on the table.

The waitress touched my bicep. "You want a dance, handsome?"

Something in Cyndra's face made the waitress smile and move closer to me. "I'll give you a dance if you want."

Another person for sale.

"No thanks." I picked up my shot glass.

The waitress pouted and turned to T-Man.

The music crescendoed. The girl onstage picked up her clothes and sway-walked off. Fog blew down from the ceiling as a new song started. A redhead, maroon-dark hair almost black in the dim light, stalked out.

The burst-balloon scent of chemical fog wafted over the tables.

The redhead attacked the pole like it could fight back. She looped around it, swung upside down.

"I want a dance!" Michael yelled over the music. "It's my birthday!"

The waitress smiled at him and edged away from T-Man.

"Not you." Michael tipped his head at the stage. "Her."

The redhead righted herself, slid around the pole.

"She's dancing," the waitress said.

Michael snapped his fingers, an intentionally rude dismissal. "Go get her."

The waitress stalked away and spoke to the bartender. He waved the bouncer over. Michael smiled at them when they looked at us. Waved another bill in the air.

The bouncer nodded and spoke to the waitress. She slammed her tray down on the bar. Stomped onto the stage, where the redhead froze in surprise.

The waitress spoke, gesturing to our corner.

Michael held up a bill for the redhead to see. She smiled, collected her dollars slowly, and came over. The waitress stayed on the stage and started to dance.

"I'm Blaze." The redhead tossed burgundy hair over a shoulder.

"Michael," he said. "It's my birthday."

Blaze nodded. "You want a special present?"

"Indeed I do." Michael held out the money. Then leaned back, legs splayed, holding the whiskey bottle by the neck. A drunken grin spread across his face.

Blaze tucked the money away and stepped into the space between Michael's legs. She started undulating, slow-twitching her hips and shoulders in time with the music.

Michael reached his free hand out.

Blaze leaned back, took his hand away. "No touching, Birthday Boy."

Michael just smiled. Reached out and caressed her again.

"No touching," Blaze began, moving to stand away

from him. Michael's hand shot out and fisted her long hair. Yanked her down. She fell across his lap, jostling into Dwight.

"Hey!" I stood and took one of Blaze's arms to help her up.

"Let go!" Blaze screamed. The thumping music didn't come close to covering it. She kicked out, foot connecting with Cyndra's leg.

Cyndra yelled and grabbed her calf. The bouncer rushed over from his place by the door.

Michael shoved Blaze away as I pulled her up. She fell against me, knocking me back against the side of the bar.

"What the—" she yelled, pulling her arm away and shoving me hard. I held my hands up. The bouncer barreled in, grabbed Michael's collar.

"You're out, kid."

Michael didn't fight, just sat there, laughing. A dead weight as the bouncer hauled on him.

"She kicked me," Cyndra yelled.

"Let go of him!" Dwight pressed in between Michael and the bouncer. They shoved each other.

"Cole!" the bouncer shouted. The bartender came around the bar, closing in on Dwight.

"You dick!" Blaze yelled at Michael. She picked a glass off the bar to hurl at his head. I pushed her arm up and back, twisting the glass out of her hand. Corralled her back with the force of the block. Opened my hands out at my sides.

Blaze's eyes cut between the fighters and me. I turned aside slightly, put Blaze and the bar to my back.

The bartender took a swing at Dwight. Michael jumped up, his drunken-kid act disintegrating in a burst of clear-headed movement. He swung the whiskey bottle at the bartender's head. It connected with a loud clunk but didn't shatter.

The bartender fell in an unconscious heap. Michael swung on the bouncer. The bottle bashed his arm. The bouncer stumbled back, grabbing at the waistband of his pants.

T-Man tackled him, slamming him against the bar.

The bouncer screamed and fell to the ground grabbing at his back.

T-Man snatched a gun out of the bouncer's waistband. Swung it between the bouncer and the unconscious bartender.

Michael pulled his gun out and fired a shot into the ceiling. Plaster and wood chips showered down.

The music thumped and roared, but everyone froze.

Michael hurled the whiskey bottle at the stage. The waitress ducked as it exploded against the cinder block wall behind her.

Michael twitched the gun at the men seated beside the stage. "Get out," he shouted.

They spilled out of their seats and dashed to the door. The waitress scooped up her clothes from the stage and followed.

Beast hurried to the door after them, knocking over a chair on the way. He locked the door after the last one left. Stood looking out the spy hole into the parking lot.

ASH PARSONS

Dwight fished a gun off the unconscious bartender and gave it to LaShonda. She held it gingerly, like it would go off if she squeezed too hard. She ran to the kitchen. A moment later she reappeared, shook her head to show the room was empty, and disappeared behind the beaded curtain. The music cut off with a squawk.

She came back. "Anyone back there left when the gun went off. I locked the outside door."

She moved to the black door and tried the knob. It was locked.

Blaze stood beside me, statue still.

"Dwight." Michael gestured at the bouncer, rolling on the floor and clutching his back.

Dwight yanked the front of the bouncer's shirt, pulling him half up. "We need the key and the combination."

"What?" the bouncer gasped.

Dwight backhanded him. The crack of it echoed in the silent room.

The bouncer sobbed and began fumbling at his pocket. Dwight held a finger in his face. "Ah-ah. Hold it." Dwight dug in the pocket. Brought out a ring of keys. He handed it to the bouncer.

"Which one?"

The bouncer fumbled, held up a single key. Dwight gave it to Cyndra and turned back to the bouncer. "Now. The combination to the safe." He looped a finger into an ear gauge and yanked down.

The bouncer shouted, putting a hand to his ear.

"It's not like it's your money," Dwight said. He ripped

the gauge out. The bouncer screamed and clapped his hands to his torn ear.

"Twenty, seven, three, thirty-one, nineteen, four!" he screamed the numbers.

Dwight stood up. He pulled the backpack out of LaShonda's purse. Then he strode across to where she stood by the black door. Taking the gun back from her, he fitted the key, and disappeared inside, gun drawn like a cop storming a room.

LaShonda followed him inside.

Michael smiled at me. He kept his gun pointed at the men on the floor. "See? You haven't even had to *do* anything."

Cyndra stood and moved a little closer. "It's working." Her voice was disbelieving. "It's going to be all right."

After a moment, LaShonda came out from the office. She ran to us. "No one else is here. And I trashed it. Just like you said. Dwight's unloading the safe."

Michael tipped his head at me.

I ignored him. Let my eyes flick around the empty club instead.

Dwight came out carrying the now-bulky backpack. He crossed the club and gave the pack to Michael.

"Nearly done here," Michael said.

On the floor, the bartender moaned as he regained consciousness.

"T-Man, LaShonda, go out the kitchen. Get the van started."

They left. Michael moved closer to the stage.

Dwight walked into the alcove. Waited near the bartender and bouncer, gun drawn.

"See, Jason?" Michael asked, flicking the gun at me, or Blaze beside me. "Almost done."

On the floor, the bouncer curled, grabbing at his ankle. He pulled up the cuff of his pants leg. A second gun was strapped there.

"Get down!" I screamed. I twisted and lifted Blaze onto the bar. Pushed her over.

Shots boomed through the room. I ducked beneath the front of the bar.

The acrid tang of gunpowder mingled with the fading scent of club fog.

A groan and the crash of something big falling near the door behind me.

"Jason!" Cyndra screamed. I edged forward, around the corner of the bar where she crouched.

Cyndra's eyes wavered between me and the bouncer lying facedown on the floor. A dark stain spread from his torso. His gun lay on the floor beside his hand.

Dwight stared at the motionless bouncer. He didn't blink. The gun in his hand started to shake.

The bartender rolled and grabbed the bouncer's gun. Lifting his shoulders off the floor, he aimed at Michael.

Michael shot first, and the bartender's shot went wide. Cyndra screamed and fell sideways.

Something clawed my throat as I lunged for her. I pulled her to me, trying to twist her away from the next shot. She hissed as my hand gripped her upper arm.

Another shot rang out. The bartender howled and dropped the gun, clutching at his thigh. Red-black blood spurted between his fingers.

Michael lowered his gun and kicked the bartender's away. "Blaze?" he yelled. "Have you called the cops yet?"

Silence from the other side of the bar.

Cyndra's arm was bloody, but not serious. The bullet had either grazed her, or passed right through—close enough to the surface to avoid bone and artery.

I pulled my T-shirt off and ripped it. Tied a strip around her arm and helped her up off the floor.

Michael nodded. "Put her in my car."

"I'm all right," Cyndra said.

"That's my girl," Michael said.

My arm around her, we wove through tables and the swinging kitchen door into the grease-splattered kitchen. Kicked open the back door and helped her into Michael's car.

In the distance, sirens howled.

T-Man and LaShonda watched me from the van. Their eyes were saucers.

"Have to get the keys," I told her. "Be right back."

I shivered and glanced at the gray-lit sky. Dawn was coming.

I shut the car door and ran back to the kitchen. As I opened the entrance, Dwight stumbled out. Michael pushed him forcefully toward the van. Dwight moved like a panicked sleepwalker—disoriented and unsure what was real.

Michael tucked the gun into his back waistband with one hand. The other held the backpack loosely.

Instinct made me grab the backpack. I hoisted it on my bare shoulder.

Michael's lips twitched like he knew what I was doing and was trying not to smile about it.

"We got to GO!" T-Man yelled from the van. He grabbed Dwight's arm and hauled him inside.

"Where's Beast?" I asked Michael.

"Not coming." He ran to his car.

"What?" Cyndra called from the passenger's seat. "We can't leave him!"

"Wait—just wait," I told Michael. "I'll get him. And if you leave without me, you'll lose this." I settled the backpack on both shoulders. Backed up, pivoting on my heel.

Inside, the building was silent. I ran through the kitchen.

Beast lay against the front door. His massive arms clutched over his wide stomach, a bloodstain widening beneath.

"Beast, come on." I helped him sit up. Dragged his arm over my shoulder and pulled him to his feet.

"Michael shot me," Beast panted as we staggered into the kitchen. "He said our guns weren't even loaded. Blanks."

"Shut up. Help me, will you?"

"Why'd he shoot me?" Beast sounded more mystified than hurt. As if he couldn't process it—couldn't believe that Michael had done it.

Needles prickled along my skin. The user and the used.

Beast fell suddenly, swerving onto me so hard that he knocked me to the ground. The air rushed out of my lungs. Beast propped himself up against the stove, groaning.

My ears rang from when my head hit the floor. I rose on my hands and knees. "Come on. Get up." We struggled to our feet and staggered to the door. Beast wheezed.

I kicked the door open and hauled Beast out beside the Dumpster.

The van was gone.

So was the Mustang.

CHAPTER THIRTY

or some reason, part of me was surprised. I stood there, swiveling my head around like a lost kid at a carnival, certain that Mom was just ahead, right there where I left her, and that she'd be right back for me.

I let Beast down, easing him against the wall until he was lying on the ramp.

I resettled the backpack against my bare skin.

"Knew it," Beast said. "You should've left me, too."

"Shut up."

I scanned the parking lot, empty except for a few cars, knowing she wasn't going to circle back.

"Seriously." He kept talking even though you could tell it hurt. "Leave. I'm dead meat anyway." He stopped, took a few deep breaths.

A siren screamed closer.

Getting caught wouldn't be that bad. I wouldn't have to worry about my father. I could just go to a juvie detention center—and that would be a piece of cake. But I couldn't do that to Janie.

"Sorry, Beast," I said, easing toward the scrubland behind the club.

He started coughing, slid backward until he lay flat. Then didn't move.

My foot was already on the curb. I stopped, watching him.

"Beast?"

He didn't answer. I stepped back from the curb, huddling close to the Dumpster.

"Beast!"

I took a step closer.

A cop car screamed into view, its siren echoing off the building. In just a minute, they'd find Beast. He'd get help soon.

Predawn light seeped slowly into the sky.

Janie.

I took off into the woods.

Knee-high grass whipped my legs. The crackle of dead leaves and the stomping of my feet felt like percussion blasts announcing where I was.

I waited for a shout behind me, for a warning shot. I waited for a bullet to catch me between the shoulders, knocking me to the ground and stopping my heart.

Nothing happened, except more sirens gathered in the stillness of the morning.

I came to a large creek. Splashed through the water, slipping on algae and cruddy sediment. The backpack grew heavier, pulling me off balance as I stumbled up the bank.

The sky grew lighter.

I ran more, fast as I could, an all-out sprint—against pursuers and more, against the sun.

I doubled back to the road, heading in a giant arc toward the stop-signed intersection and the gas stations there.

They weren't open. I circled around back. I didn't know what I was looking for. A car. A bicycle. A motorcycle. Something.

Behind the row of gas stations was a clear-cut hill, dotted with rectangles.

A trailer park.

My legs trembled, but I forced them to sprint again, dashing for the trailers. The backpack full of money bounced against my back. The straps chafed my bare shoulders.

My lungs burned, gasping in the chill air. I took deep breaths and slowed to a walk. Making my way up the row of angle-parked metal houses, looking for the most likely one. The last thing I needed was to set off a car alarm or invite more gunshots.

Found one. The one. The only one worth trying.

The faded Chevy Caprice looked defeated, faded Dead Head stickers studding the back window and bumper. The trailer behind it was equally beat up. There were paint cans, a stagnant dish for a dog, the wafting odor of dog crap from behind a little wooden fence, a torn ladybug banner that said **Summer!**, and rusted wind chimes. I bet the inside of the car would smell like pot.

I felt under the wheel wells, letting my fingers sweep the mud spatter. Duckwalked across the front bumper, feeling under the edge again, legs trembling with the effort.

Still Waters

Under the back bumper, tucked over the muffler, my fingers closed around the flat box. I pulled out the magnetic key-hide box. Unlocked the car and threw the backpack in. I fell into the seat. Didn't smell pot but did smell rancid fast food. Grease-stained, brightly colored bags littered the car floor.

I cranked the engine and backed out.

No one made a peep. The dog didn't even bark.

I drove onto the street, trying to remember the route Michael had taken, searching for any familiar sign or road number. I kept driving and saw a sign for the major thruway that bisected the city.

"Yes," I hissed. Floored the accelerator and chugged onto the highway.

Sunlight gleamed on the hood.

Once over the bridge, I threaded through other cars, slowing only when I saw how fast I was going.

I exited the Mercer High School ramp and wove onto Dean, racing past the building supply store and fast-food joints.

"Come on. Come on."

I tried not to think about my dad's threat. Tried not to think about his buddies. If he'd hurt Janie or let them hurt her.

Tried not to think about what was going to happen when I got there.

I had the backpack. It would be enough.

The tires squealed as I took the last corner too fast. I laid tread, black marks weaving behind me as I yanked the wheel over. I cut the engine, grabbed the backpack, and bailed. Ran across the dirt yard and was at the top of the porch in one leap.

The door opened before I touched it.

My breath and heart competed with each other to see which could go faster.

My father smiled from inside the door, welcoming me with a sweep of his hand. "Jason. Just in time."

A trickle of sweat stung my eyes. The backpack dangled by my leg. I hovered on the doorstep, unable to move, unable to make myself go inside.

"Come in." My father took a step closer, and I could smell the beer and cigarettes lifting from the pores of his skin. "We've been expecting you."

Janie.

I stepped forward. Made myself take another step. Walked over the threshold and past my father and the door. My eyes searched for Janie.

Fell on Cyndra and Michael instead, seated together at one end of the couch.

Janie hugged herself at the other end.

"I was just talking to your friends." My father closed the door behind me.

CHAPTER THIRTY-ONE

y lungs heaved. My father blocked the door, weight balanced between the balls of his feet, standing with his arms slightly out. Not a good sign. That stance can flow in any direction and the hands even faster.

I glanced at his eyes. They had that look, that murderous, psychopathic glint. If anyone in Michael's crew ever saw it, they'd never call me Ice again.

"Michael?" I eased toward him and the sofa, legs weak from running and adrenaline. Cyndra's eyes were red-rimmed, her face splotchy. The bandage on her arm was stained slightly. Her eyes darted around the room. Kept snagging on Michael, watching him like he was nitroglycerin.

She was terrified of him. Of where she was and what was going to happen next.

Michael glared at me. Half-smile in a pissed-off hover over his lips. Shaking his head like *The nerve of you.*

Standing over Janie, almost looking protective, was a tattooed member of my father's group. The only other person there.

Janie didn't look up.

"What's going on?" I asked Michael, stopping between him and my father.

"Thought you'd be smarter than to come here, after what you pulled." Michael's voice was detached, musing like he was interested in the mental processes of an insect.

"What?" I asked.

I heard the creak of the floor. My father hit the back of my head with his open palm, hard enough to be both a warning and an omen.

I cursed and slid back, rubbing my head. I tossed the backpack on the floor at his feet. "Here, you two fight over it."

My father had the backpack in his hand before Michael could even speak. He threw it to the tattooed man.

"This all you got?" my dad asked. "'Cause Michael says you have a whole lot more."

"I should've done it without him," Michael interrupted, gesturing to the backpack as he stood. "I had to leave a second one behind when your idiot son started shooting up the place."

What was he doing? My eyes ricocheted between them. This wasn't about helping me with my father.

Wasn't even about the thrill of getting away with murder.

This was something else.

"Shut up," my father said to Michael. "Whiny little shit. Your boy Dwight said you needed him."

"We're square after this, though. Right? We're square now." Michael eased closer to my father.

It bolt-shot through my mind.

"Sure. We'll be square." Laughing to underscore the sarcasm.

There was no Cesare.

The realization shifted, a tangle of razor-edged hooks. Snarled and suddenly shaken free, scalpel barbs piercing into my mind and lungs.

The knowledge stabbed, twisted, and lodged there.

There was no Cesare.

Because my father *was* Cesare.

Everything Michael had said had been about my father. Michael's day spent drinking and gambling with his step-brother after dropping Cyndra and her mom off for their trip.

My dad's shift. The airport strip club.

It had all started there.

Drugs, debt, and Michael's inflated opinion of himself had deepened it. Everything had happened like he'd said.

It just hadn't happened with the antagonist he'd painted.

Same story, different villain.

And now a different ending. Because it had *never been about* squaring with Cesare. Never been about getting free, or getting away, or wiping the slate clean.

He wanted to blow the slate away.

So he had hired me. Paid me money he owed to my dad, because while Michael may be a narcissistic sociopath, he could still see one clear thing about my father. The one clear thing even I always knew.

Only one of us was getting out alive.

My father or Michael.

My father or me.

Because with my father, it would never be over. He'd latch on and keep paying it out, feeding Michael drugs, running him credit on races or fights—whatever it would take to keep the golden boy in his debt.

Small-time, but not stupid.

And Michael knew it.

This whole elaborate setup, from hiring me to going on this insane strip-club robbery, all of it had been about one thing.

Getting Michael in the right place.

In exactly the right position to be able to do it.

To kill my father and get away with it.

Hell, he'd even tried to take a shortcut, by getting me to do it with him earlier. And I'd turned him down and forced him to continue building this scene.

He'd bought my friendship, but it was really about setting up his alibi. It would go like he'd said it would that day in the school parking lot. That we were friends, that my father beat the hell out of me. And Michael had to kill my dad—to save me.

He'd had Cyndra show up at my house before the party, knowing it would cause a fight with my dad when he saw her car. Then everyone else had seen my face at the party afterward. And the next morning, dropping me off at school, Michael had paid to see my back. He'd played me like a violin. I'd gone off, in a self-destructive haze, and had provoked the confrontation when I'd gotten home.

Which had led to even better, undeniable proof. Absences and worse bruises.

Mr. Stewart was worried about me. A friend had told him they were worried about me, too.

Michael.

All of it set up the believable backstory. Framed the justifiable homicide—in defense of another.

Even tonight, the club and the bouncer and Dwight. It could all be explained away by saying my father had made us do it, while holding Janie captive. It showed how dangerous he was. And we didn't know what else to do.

Now all Michael had to do was cause my death. Get my dad to go for it.

Would Michael stop it in time? Save my life at the last minute? Or did I have to die now, too? And Janie with me.

What about Cyndra?

She huddled on the sofa, tear-streaked face taut with fear.

Something ripped in my chest. The space between my lungs tore and constricted.

My father stepped closer, hand up, knuckle ridge bowing out as he showed me his fist. "Where's the second bag?" he asked. "I know you didn't leave it."

"He's the one with money, not me." I pointed at Michael.

Why didn't I say it? Say *It's a setup* or *He's got a gun. He's just waiting for the right moment to kill you.*

Can't you smell the trap?

I know what's going to happen. It feels like a poorly rehearsed play that the high school admin makes the whole school attend so they can justify having drama class.

And I have to play my part. Have to say the right lines.

Only the right move will get Janie out alive, and Cyndra with her.

I was wrong before. *This* is what it feels like to be trapped.

My stomach roiled beneath my trip-hammering heart.

Michael stood up, jabbing a finger at me. His eyes glimmered, an imitation of my dad's psycho look.

Maybe it wasn't an imitation. He'd arranged it all. Even shooting Beast at the club tonight. Everything to get to this precise moment.

"Wasn't I your friend, Jason? Where's the shit?" Michael asked.

"You're full of it," I said.

My father growled and seized my shoulders, yanking me up and shoving me against the wall. He shifted one hand to my throat, the other hand pointed to the backpack.

"That all you got? Is *that*"—he pressed into my throat, cutting off the air—"all *you* got?"

I brought up a knee. He blocked it, but the shift of attention loosened the hand on my throat. I jabbed stiff fingers at his eyes and tore his thumb off my neck, twisting away.

He cursed, rubbing his eyes and blinking.

The back door was behind me.

Janie was on the sofa.

"Janie—"

A hand came down on her shoulder, tattoo of a squid wrapped around his wrist and hand, tentacles fat, green, and glistening.

I stood, shaking, my body screaming at me to get out, to get away, to run and never come back this time.

Looked at Michael. He shrugged. I couldn't see any emotion in his eyes other than anticipation. No regret. No reassurance.

No way out.

I was bait on his hook. That was the use he had for me.

The only thing I'd done right was keep Clay out of it.

My stomach churned, an engine blade whipping sludge. The sour tang of acid rose in my mouth.

Cyndra didn't meet my eyes. Tears coursed down her face. She hugged herself like if she didn't, she'd come apart.

My shoulders slumped. This was it, then. Whatever Michael wanted it to be. Because if I said anything, it wouldn't matter. My father would still come for me, wouldn't believe anything I said, wouldn't stop now.

My father cursed, then laughed. It raised the hairs on my arms.

"Run, little boy. Why don't you run?"

I glanced at Michael. Wondered if there was anything I could say that would change what was about to happen.

Michael's eyes were reptile flat.

The only thing I could change was how I'd feel when it was over. If I lived.

I threw myself across the room at the man with the tattooed hand. Punched him in the gut, brought my knee up in his groin. Grabbed the back of his head and slammed his face on my piston knee.

He fell, groaning. I grabbed Janie, pushed her at the front door. "Run!"

The tattooed hand grabbed my ankle, yanked hard enough to make me stumble. I kicked out.

My father was there ahead of us, of course, the confined space and tattooed hand ruining our chance. My father caught Janie by the hair and yanked her backward. She fell, clutching at her scalp and screaming.

"Let her go!" I grabbed the corpse-white hand snared in her hair, trying to ease the tearing.

He shoved her away. Caught my wrist instead and whipped it to the side, pulling my arm straight and exposing my ribs. He punched, then kneed my ribs, the ones that were newly healed, and maybe not as well healed as I'd thought.

I collapsed. He didn't let go of my arm, but twisted it up behind my back, driving his weight on my shoulder until the joint screamed and so did I, scrabbling on the ground like a beetle having its legs torn off.

My arm came out of the shoulder socket with a wet crack.

I screamed, almost drowning Janie's yell as she tried to tackle my father from behind.

She was so slight, and he so big, that she barely swayed him. He let go of my ruined arm and flipped her off his back one-handed.

I rolled onto my side, clutching my shoulder. Got my knees under me, then my feet. Stood swaying.

Adrenaline sewage-dumped into my veins.

The man with the tattooed hand lifted Janie off the floor, hands not taking care what parts of her they grabbed as he hauled her up.

My father strolled toward me, calm as you imagine Death would be.

"So, Jason," he said, giving a sideways smile and a this-one's-for-you nod to Michael, "where's the bag?" He pulled a long face, a comedian going for a laugh. "Outside?" The fang-grooves over his canine teeth reappeared.

My foot edged along the wall. I couldn't stop myself from backing up. Couldn't stop my eyes from darting to Janie, twisting in the tattooed hand's grasp.

I let go of my shrieking shoulder, cocking the fist of my good arm.

"He's a lying piece of shit who wants to watch you beat me to death," I told him. "And then he'll kill you."

My father started laughing, cutting too-round, ain't-that-something eyes to his audience.

Michael laughed, too. If I saw a moment of appraisal in my father's eyes, it didn't last. He saw what everyone saw: prom king, golden boy, someone with a future assured, a future they wouldn't risk.

Right assessment, wrong conclusion.

My father turned back to me, massive hands flexing like he was preparing to bench a weight.

"He has the van." I gestured to the backpack. "And that's all there was."

My father smiled and nodded like he thought as much. Took a step closer.

My foot wedged in the corner. No more room to back away. No way out.

"Now, Jason. Time to give it up." My father fired a huge hand out, batted my injured shoulder with a quick pop before I could dodge.

I gasped, twisted, and realized too late that was what he wanted. He grabbed my shoulders and drove me to the ground. I tasted blood.

And since he wasn't thinking about the school, or the truant officer, or the social worker, or anything else, he punched me in the face.

My nose snapped. Blood gushed out my nostrils, flowed over my lips and into my mouth. I brought my hands up, tried to jab or claw him, tried to remember myself.

As someone who fought back.

He punched me in the stomach, ramming his fist into my solar plexus again and again until I couldn't tense around it.

His thick fingers gripped my neck. Cut the blood off and put me out in seconds.

I struggled awake, through pain, through layers of mental cotton that smothered my thudding heartbeats.

My eyes opened.

He smiled down at me. His fingers rested on my throat.

"Where is it, Jason?" He lifted a knee, settled it on my dislocated shoulder. "Where?"

Pain sparks flared behind my eyes.

I strained against the weight on my shrieking shoulder, gagging on blood from my broken nose.

His fingers clenched around my windpipe. Something in my throat broke with a wishbone snick. His grip eased off, letting me grab wisps of oxygen.

"Talk."

I reached my good arm up. Scratched his hand. Gouged

his arm and neck, straining for his eyes or his nose, just out of my grasp. I made his arm run with blood, but he didn't move, didn't flinch, just kept squeezing and easing off his grip, giving me a few sips of air. Squeezing and easing.

I passed out.

Came to moments later, my arms flopping by my sides. Heard my sister sobbing.

Wanted to tell her I was sorry. For getting into Michael's car that day. For taking his money. For thinking I could stay in control of any of it.

I wanted to tell her she'd be all right without me, if only so I could believe the lie.

Don't watch this, Janie. Close your eyes.

Telescoping haze constricted my vision. My chest filled with lava that burned through my heart and dripped chunks of impotent fury onto my roiling stomach.

Black, churning waters pulled at my heels. Filled my lungs and spread into my throat.

"You'll kill him before he'll tell you." Michael's voice, close by.

My father's admiration was grudging. "He's a tough little shit."

"He's what you made him." Michael watched my face with murderous avidity.

Watching for the moment of death.

I reached out to him, my hand stretching, something I couldn't control even though I knew it wouldn't change anything.

"You're killing him." Michael's tone was conversational.

My father merely grunted acknowledgment. I blinked, refocusing. Was there a chance he would stop in time?

My heart skittered, stopping and starting like a stalled engine. My vision narrowed, Michael's face, the fang-grooves over my father's mouth.

"Wait," Michael said.

My father eased off, slapped my cheeks. Over his shoulder, Michael grinned at me. A gun appeared in his hand. Michael showed it to me, feigning surprise at finding it there. He held the gun before his stomach, so the man with the tattooed hand couldn't see it.

My father didn't look back at him. His fingers pressed into my throat. My fingers clawed over his arms, seeking a crack, a lever, a switch to turn off the crushing mechanism of his grip.

"Oh my God, stop. It's the worst thing I've ever seen," Michael said, and then laughed. He screwed a silencer on the gun barrel.

My father and the man with the tattooed hand laughed with him.

I blinked tears from my eyes, felt like my lungs were struggling to connect to the air through my skin, through my fingertips, through my tear ducts.

My clawed hands slid on my father's arms. A surge of adrenaline arced over my veins. My body bucked, struggling to dislodge him, bringing my hands that much closer to his eyes, fighting for the final breath.

The constricted muscles of my neck flexed against the granite of my father's grip.

Vision blurring, I saw Michael step slightly back. "Oh my God, somebody do something. Stop or I'll shoot."

My father kept smiling until he heard the click of the hammer being pulled back. He turned.

The gun was so close you could barely see the suppressed muzzle flash. The bullet tore through my father's head and plummeted out, taking blood, brain, and skull with it.

He fell to the side, following the trajectory of his mutilated brain and the bullet, collapsing on the floor next to me.

His hands fell off my neck. I sucked in air, couldn't breathe for coughing.

"Holy—" the man with the tattooed hand screamed, clutching at Janie.

She kicked away from him, slithering onto the floor.

Michael whirled and pointed the gun at the tattooed man.

"Wait! I could—" The bullet drove his body against the wall. He slid down, leaving a bloody smear.

I fought to a sitting position, gasping. Struggling to send oxygen everywhere that needed it at once: heart, lungs, brain, arms, legs.

Cool air rushed in, flowed into me like energy, but not enough.

"Janie." My voice was a grating whisper. She crawled to me.

"He was going to kill you." Janie's voice was tiny, like it was hiding under a table.

My hand bumped her arm.

"And . . ." Michael drew a hand down over his face. "Scene." He pulled his cell phone out and dialed 911.

My lungs heaved.

"We need help! People are dead, shot, my girlfriend has been shot, and my friend can't breathe. We need an ambulance!" Michael's high-pitched voice cracked. "Yes. We're at 233B, Lincoln Green. Please hurry. My girlfriend . . . the blood—" He hung up. Threw the phone down.

My air wasn't coming right. I swayed as I sat, struggling to find the oxygen, still feeling fingers around my neck, still feeling the constriction of my esophagus.

"Most satisfying." Michael scratched his head like a sleeper awakening. "You, sir, were excellent," he said to me. "Going back for Beast. Just like I knew you would. You're a predictable performer, and we love you for it." He leaned over Janie.

Janie shivered, shrank into herself.

"You've got the scene straight, Janie? I saved your brother. That's what happened here. I can keep all of us out of jail, even Jason, but you've got to back me up. I mean, no love lost, right? And I *did* save him. I'm the hero now."

Janie didn't move, didn't agree. Did nothing.

Cyndra watched me try to breathe, not moving from where she was nailed to the couch. Like Michael would kill her next.

"You, too, Cyndra," he said. "Stick to the script."

Cyndra nodded, a battlefield surrender. Her horror-wide eyes showing that now she saw him. Truly saw him.

"Hmmm." Michael frowned at her as he stood, stretched. Cocked his head, listening for sirens. "Won't be long, now. Do I trust you all? To sell the story?" He held up the gun, aimed it at Cyndra for a moment, then Janie.

I blinked black spots out of my eyes.

Michael crouched in front of me.

"Jason. You thought I was going to let him kill you." His smile was clean. Real. Like there was a chance I'd believe him now.

As if he wasn't going to kill us all before the cops came. He'd say it had been my father or the tattooed man. He'd take the gun from my father's waistband, shoot us, then put it back in my father's hand. Or near it.

Rage gathered behind the lodged screams in my throat. My eyes burned, though no tears came.

My eyes found the gun in Michael's hand. Gauged the distance of the reach.

He tracked my glance. The perfect smile returned. "You gonna go for it? Do it, Ice. You'll never get there in time."

My shoulders and head shuddered with each crushed breath.

Michael held the gun out, sighted down the barrel at me. "God, what a rush." He whipped the gun to the side and mimed taking the shot. "It's official. Nothing compares."

"You won. It's over." My voice was a wisp. I slumped against the wall. My eyes fluttered, gauged his grip on the gun.

I sat, fish-gasping. Let my arms fall to the floor on either side of me like they were dead weights.

Michael watched me struggle for air as sirens gathered in the distance.

"Not quite yet. Soon, though." He rolled his head and shoulders, like a fighter warming up. "Like I said. There are users and the used. You can't transcend, only accept."

The gun floated between me and Janie.

He *was* going to kill us. The knowledge was inevitable poison burning under my skin, working its way to the surface. Blood-sweat pinpricking each pore.

Michael turned slightly away from where I slumped. The sirens grew louder.

I lunged for the gun in his hand. My arm pushed toward it through tar-thick air. I fell against Janie's side as my numb hand knocked against the metal, sending it clattering onto the floor.

Maybe he was right and it was too late, after all.

Michael spun back to me as I fell across Janie's knees, pathetically intent on the gun. A sleepwalker trying to thread a needle.

One move and he'd get to it before me.

I reached, knowing I was dead. Hating the defeat in my mouth. I reached, waiting for him to get it before me. Waiting for the silencer-muffled puncture of the final shot.

Behind us, Cyndra shrieked.

Michael pitched forward beside me as she tackled his legs.

He kicked at her, stomping, leveraging off her toward the gun.

My fingers brushed Janie's arm as she grabbed Michael's

wrist and pulled it away from the gun. Screaming as his fingers tore at her.

I seized the gun. Brought it down to his eyes.

Fired.

The bullet slammed into the bridge of his nose, drill-pulping metal and bone into his brain.

Michael lay there, staring up at me. The muscle tension in his straining neck let go.

The gun in my hand felt different. The pads of my fingers thickened somehow, desensitized. Like Halloween-creature fingertips had been glued on. The layer between me and the bullet in his head.

I collapsed on the floor, feeling the gun fall out of my hand.

Janie fumbled for it, threw it across the room toward the front door. She sobbed and pushed her fingers into my hair as I lay struggling for air.

"Hold on." She rocked slightly, fingers rolling over a lock of my hair. "Just hold on. Just hold on."

A new mantra for me.

The sirens stopped in front of the unit.

Cyndra knelt, wiping blood from her mouth. She crawled toward the front door.

"Hold on." Janie's tears fell on my face. Her hands in my hair shook.

"Help! Help us! We're unarmed!" Cyndra called outside.

Police screamed to each other.

The air grew cold and thick, harder to take in the little sips I was getting. Cyndra lay on the floor. Screaming police told everyone to get down. Janie tented her body over mine until an officer ordered her away. They cleared the room, aiming two-handed as they checked the corners for danger. They picked up Michael's gun, and then an officer knelt at my side.

My lungs struggled, my throat clamping like a weak straw under too much suction. I couldn't make myself breathe slower.

Phased out. Came back to urgent voices and pressure on my chest.

My fist connected with someone. Hands grabbed my arms, pushed me down. Restraints fastened around my wrists. My dislocated shoulder ground against the backboard. I tried to yell. Nothing came out.

"It's his larynx. We need to intubate."

A piece of curved metal pressed into my mouth and down my throat. The EMT pulled the metal out, leaving a tube jammed down my throat and hanging out my mouth.

Nausea pinpricks bloomed in my cheeks, my heart shuddering like it was submerged in freezing water.

Another EMT attached an air bag and started squeezing.

Tears slid out my eyes and ran into my hair. The forced air filled my lungs, left, pushed in again.

My trapped hand grasped the shirt of the EMT. He glanced down at me. His small, round-frame glasses reflected the sunlight from the window.

"It's okay." His voice was calm and deep. "I've got you." He squeezed the air bag again. "I've got you."

I couldn't let go of his shirt.

Janie crouched by my head, gnawing her fingertips. Distant eyes, transfixed by some internal collapse.

By the door, Cyndra hugged herself, sobbing. A cop listened to her torrent of words. A second EMT was examining her arm.

I felt it all running away, flowing out of me into the floor, into the air. Into the spaces between. Looked down on it all, the huddled people, the white-shirted paramedics working over me.

My fist, clenched on a shirt.

The world swam away, pulling with confident strokes that it was on to better things without me.

CHAPTER THIRTY-TWO

ime is strange. It doesn't always help. Or heal. Sometimes it just passes.

A stay in a hospital, doctor visits, a move to a group home and lessons with homebound teachers. Meetings with a judge, a court-ordered counselor and advocate, calls and visits from your best friend where neither of you says much. Weekly visits with your little sister. They're just things that happen. To fill the time. That mark the passing days.

It doesn't do any good to fight against it. Like I did in the hospital, demanding to see Janie. Worrying about her. Her eyes sucking in the darkness. Seeing inside and hating what she found there.

Self-hatred, a coil of knotted bone. Paralyzed, cement gathering in your core.

And when I finally did see her, that first time after. How she edged into the hospital room, arms clamped tight across herself, like she was made of air, or like if she opened up, dark-winged birds would burst from her chest, scattering what was left of her.

How we barely talked. Just watched it in each other's eyes.

The muffled explosion of the gun, the heat of the barrel, and the kick. The impact of the bullet.

His face. Empty eyes looking up at me. Bone and blood and brain spatter. Blood glossing from the hole.

Fingers on my throat. Trapped, struggling. Powerless.

The images strobing behind my eyes. Cool air drying the sweat on my face, my heart dog-paddling in oil-slicked waters.

That was in the hospital, before I learned to keep my head below the surface. Before I learned to bury myself, sinking into the nowhere blackout.

I made myself forget. Held it down, deep inside. Built a dam to keep it there. Slept to keep it away, took the pills to help me sleep. Wouldn't let my mind drift unsupervised.

I pushed it all down. Held myself under, cushioned by the empty water. Insulated from the noise, from the buffeting chop. Submerged beneath it all.

Beast and the bartender had stayed in the hospital longer than me, but both made it through.

The bouncer had died. And the tattooed man. And Michael.

My father.

I let it all wash over and past me.

Same thing in the courtroom. I sometimes saw the others on the way in: LaShonda and T-Man, Dwight, Ray-Ray, and Mike-Lite. Blaze and the waitress, who both spoke up for me. The words would flow by, and what I did or said was irrelevant.

Clay, a constant presence. Just being there. So much meaning in that action. Not telling me *I'm here*. Showing me instead.

And Janie. She's in a foster home now, a good one, get that. Her eyes are starting to look outward. And she's seeing a counselor, just like me. Although she thinks it's actually helping her. "Talk to them, Jason," she says. "Talk to them."

Maybe they tell her to say that.

So much of healing is belief in the cure.

But I don't. So I have nothing to say.

And if I wake up sweating, his face hovering above me, fingers squeezing my throat, or if Michael stands in the corner, watching me, blood and brain oozing from his mangled face . . .

It's just a moment.

It's just a dream.

It doesn't mean anything.

And nothing will change it.

Some things get to me, though. Stab through the cushioning waters. Make it hard to breathe. Like Cyndra's phone calls.

They started about a week after I got to the group home. I was handed the phone. I listened and could only hear her breath. She doesn't talk, and neither do I. She keeps calling. Sometimes I can hear her crying. I have nothing, so I always hang up. But not before listening for a little and thinking of her.

Not thinking. Remembering. This sudden image, vivid,

the feel of her body against me and how maybe she really did care for me. And how it wasn't enough.

Could never be enough. Because Michael was right about her. Not that she was a user, not that she wanted power. But how she wanted saving. Maybe that's what she saw in me. How I wanted to save her. And never could.

Maybe she thinks she loves me. I loved her. But none of it matters anymore.

Just like me. Useless. Empty. And with no future. No dream revenge for another day.

And not strong enough to reject it. Or accept anything else.

That catches my breath, because I think of Celia in eighth grade, Cyndra, and before them, Janie, and something the counselor said. How I wanted to save them—and hide from myself. How I take responsibility to feel it as power. When what I need to do is realize what I can and cannot do.

That I can't just get better. That I have to "work" on myself.

Sometimes feeling moments come, thinking about Cyndra or Janie or all the mistakes that led me here—to this group home. It isn't a juvenile detention center, but it's only one step off. A halfway house. And that's right, isn't it? That's right. Halfway there, wherever there is, struggling to keep from either sinking or surfacing.

Halfway under.

After a while, Clay stopped letting me pretend that everything was okay. Started calling BS on all the ways it wasn't. Trying to draw me out, to make something better. Shining his light into all the dark places.

Calling me a robot.

I told him I was on his page now. A pacifist. Calm.

"That's not pacifism, that's self-annihilation," he said. "That's not who you are."

I shrugged and saw the hope slowly die in his eyes. The hope that he'd found the right combination to make the locker spring open.

I kept it shut tight. Locked down.

So time went, and I went with it. After another month they said everything was over. After Christmas, with a sorry little tree strewn with loose-tossed tinsel and paper ornaments. And after Danny, the special-needs kid who's only here, let's face it, because he's so damn special no one will have him, sang "Jingle Bells" a million times. And we all opened our cheap-wrapped presents, and Danny laughed and laughed, hugging himself and rocking when he saw the stupid robot dog he wanted.

After the turkey dinner and dressing on plastic plates, nicer and better than any Christmas meal I'd ever had. After me and Danny got picked up by Janie and her foster mom and went to their church for the music and candle service. All of us in this row, trying to look like we knew what to do. Danny next to me, whispering about the windows, the organ, the handbell choir, the candles with their little paper collars, and *When do we light the candles, Jason? When?*

After all that. And after Mr. Lance and Ms. Jay—the

group home "mother" and "father"—asked if Danny could swap into my room because he was having "personality conflicts" with Alex. Which was a bunch of bull because Danny wouldn't conflict with a flea, but whatever.

And after the New Year's party—soda out of plastic cups and Chex Mix—where nothing much happened except Alex kept hassling Danny about wanting to watch the crystal ball drop, changing the channels just to see him get upset.

And after the homebound teacher came and collected the schoolwork, and after the judge met with me and my advocate again.

It was finally official.

All of it was over, cleared—done with. Even though people were dead. And the bartender was out on disability, and Beast's dad was still talking about a civil suit. It was over.

Over.

And they said I should go back to regular school.

So I went back. Climbed onto the bus in front of the house. Told myself to ignore the stares. Figured if people avoided me before, they'll sure as hell avoid me now. Now that I've . . . now that he's dead.

Him. What they knew of him. King of the school. Mr. Popular Super Jock.

What they know of me. Iceman. Psycho.

Killer.

His supposed friend.

But it was all right. It was all right. All morning, eyes

followed me like crap magnets—and I didn't even wonder, much, what everyone knew. Or thought they knew. What everyone had heard about it all. About how it happened.

I avoided them. Head on desk, empty gaze out the window. It hadn't even been half a day. But I was already looking at it as time. Doing time. Waiting it out. Thinking the rest of the semester would be like this. Empty eyes to hostile faces.

Letting time pass, and me insulated from it all.

Clay stayed with me, through the day, through the stares and murmurs. Meeting me at break, between classes.

Then Beast found us. Fell into step beside me as we walked into the lunchroom. Slapped hands like we were friends. Followed me through the line, then to a table. The other kids got up and left.

Beast and Clay stayed.

We didn't talk during lunch. Just ate. Looked at the table. Or out the window. Or stared into nothing. Behind me, some kids hissed and taunted. It started out low, and as nothing happened, gained in volume and nerve.

I didn't care, didn't respond. Beast turned and glared, asked if they had a problem.

I could have told him that wouldn't work. You have to back it up. You can't just put on a show.

Clay, sitting across from me, locked eyes with one of them.

The voices rose. Something bounced off my back and rolled under my feet. A small orange.

Clay slammed his tray flat on the table with a tremendous

bang. The remnants of his lunch scattered. He stood, holding the edges of the tray in a tight-knuckled grip.

"You don't know jack, so shut your damn mouth." He hauled the tray sideways in one hand, holding it like a sword—or a rock. Then he hurled it, a gorgeous, spinning plane—like skipping a stone, or throwing a Frisbee.

It clocked a guy. Knocked him off his seat. His friends brayed with laughter.

The guy stood, holding his nose. He glared at Clay.

Clay held his gaze. His hands flexed near my tray.

The guy dropped his eyes. Said something about getting out of there before coach came over and handed out detentions. His friends laughed at him but followed as he left.

Clay sat back down.

Conversations around us started up again.

"Who the hell are you?" I asked Clay.

Clay picked up the trash that had spilled off his tray. Finally looked at me and said, "I'm still a pacifist." Then he shrugged. "Sometimes you have to take a stand for something."

"I thought 'violence begets violence.'"

"So you have been listening." His lips quirked up in a half-smile. He gestured at the now-empty table behind me. "Who knows where that started? And it's not over now. They'll take the part I added, take it down the road, put it off onto someone else."

Beast's massive head bobbed in agreement.

Clay's eyes linked on mine and pulled. "But it had to

pass. Had to flow past you. Enough." He paused, waiting for my eyes to meet his again. "Enough."

Sometimes that's the best you can do. Blunt the impact by accepting it. Or take a stand and deflect it. Hope it loses force as it ricochets past.

And I wasn't deep enough to weigh the cost. To know which choice was best. Always just watching out for myself or Janie. But even I recognized Clay's truth, and mine, meshed together, like that snake that eats its own tail.

Violence begets violence.

And sometimes violence is the only way to stop it.

I nodded at Clay, trying to thank him. And wanting to argue with his choice. The choice I always would have taken before. Not knowing if I was sad or happy that he saw what I saw now.

The bell rang.

"See you tomorrow, man," Beast said. Grabbed my tray with his and carted it to the trash.

Clay fell into step beside me as I walked out of the cafeteria. "See you after class." He started to walk away. Stopped to help a freshman pick up a wash of papers that spilled across the floor.

I joined him, grabbing up pages, straightening them and handing them to the kid. "Hey, thanks," he mumbled, and didn't look at either of us, cheeks pink with embarrassment.

"No problem. Pass it on," Clay said, rolling his eyes at the hokey sound of it.

Something shifted in my chest.

I lifted my eyes and watched as the other kids filed past, and for the first time, really didn't care what they thought.

Kept my head up on the walk to class. Met Mr. Stewart's eyes and didn't look down once.

After school I went where I knew she'd be waiting for me.

CHAPTER THIRTY-THREE

he old gym was dim and cold, February rain spattering on the vaulted roof. Cyndra stood by the heavy bag, tucked slightly behind it like it could put an arm around her.

"I heard you were back," she said. Stating the obvious, because it was the easiest.

My lips felt glued. Looking at her was enough.

"You want to go somewhere? We don't have to do anything but talk," she said, and I knew what she was offering. Everything but what I wanted the most.

Pain razored my heart, black-red knowledge welling up from the gash.

"No," I said. Not trying to hurt her, but wanting to cauterize it.

Her eyes glimmered. She blinked it back and dredged up more courage. "Why wouldn't you talk to me?"

The phone calls, the silence on the line. The stupid stutter my nowhere heart would give at the sound of her breath.

"I was waiting for you," I said.

She moved closer, looking like she wanted to touch me, hugging herself instead.

"I'm sorry," she said. "I know I hurt you."

"You saved my life." Met her eyes as I said it.

Cyndra tilted her head. "Does that mean you can forgive me? For not—" She couldn't say it. Couldn't say what we both knew.

That she hadn't loved me enough.

I'd been wondering if I could. If I could let go of the edge of pain. What had been real. If she was as trapped as I used to be. What it would even mean: my forgiveness.

What she was really asking.

I sighed.

"Yes," I told her.

Her smile went nova. She stepped in, reaching her arms up.

I took her wrists and pushed her away, gently.

"I can't."

"Why?"

"Because nothing feels real anymore. Or important. And I don't know what's left."

I didn't say *of me*.

"I know what's important," she said. "I was confused and so scared. But I wanted you. I *want* you."

"If I could believe you." I didn't say more.

What she had to offer wasn't enough.

Guilt is not a substitute for love.

She didn't hear the meaning of my words, only heard the *if*. Saw the chance. She smiled at me, that sweet, perfect smile.

"You *can* believe me." She stepped in again.

I backed away.

Could I let go of the numbness? It would be like un-clenching your fist from the blade of a knife. You don't feel how deep the cut is until you let go. But the wound can't close until you do.

Feeling and numbness. What it takes to choose between them.

"Listen." Cyndra's emerald eyes searched mine. "Haven't you ever made a mistake?"

The laugh compressed out my mouth.

It seemed like all I ever made were mistakes.

Cyndra's eyes wouldn't let mine go. "Then you know, right? What it feels like. That's how I feel about all of this. That I made a mistake being with him. Maybe not from the beginning, but somewhere after. After me and you."

She opened her hands, little cups of hope. "Haven't you ever held on to one thing? And kept holding, even when things began to go bad? Even when they *were* bad?"

The Plan.

That I was going to do something. That I was going to save Janie. Save myself. That there was something worth fighting for. A purpose.

Revenge.

Cyndra gripped my arms. Her jaw tightened, and her eyes narrowed. Like it took everything she had. Like she was opening herself to a madman with a knife.

"You have to really forgive me. You have to feel that much. There's got to be something. You've got to feel some-thing for me. I know you do."

"You're right."

Her fingers gripped tighter, digging into my upper arms. "It's not small, either. What you feel." Her chin lifted, a fighter, daring me with the target.

"I loved you."

"You *love* me."

Something shifted inside my chest. A small movement. A buoy released and rocketing toward the surface.

"Fight for it," she said.

I'd have to trust her—and something outside of myself. Beyond my control. That she saw something I couldn't. Something in me.

Would that be enough? Or would it cost too much to feel it?

Cyndra loosed her hands, like she saw my choice before I made it. That smile torqued her lips. Her arms lifted to my shoulders. "I'm a fighter. So are you."

I felt my arms going around her. Squeezing her against me, pulling, desperately tight. Something unraveling inside, spooling into the darkness and piercing it there.

Her lips were clean water, and I needed to drown.

. . .

That night, I walked her to the Mercedes, the only car left in the school lot. I needed to get back to the home before curfew—and before I cracked in two from the swelling of my heart.

"I could drive you," Cyndra said, settling into my arms for another hug.

"You and I both know we'd never even get the car started."

ASH PARSONS

She laughed but tipped her head back and studied me. She waited.

"It's been a long day," I said. "I need the walk."

"Okay." Her lips brushed over mine. "I'll pick you up in the morning, though?"

"Definitely."

Berry-flavored kisses, soothing and stinging at the same time. Medicine doing its work.

The walk back to the group home wasn't bad. I wandered down tree-lined streets, past small houses with postage-stamp yards, fences and yappy dogs, wind chimes and rusted grills.

I thought about what Michael had said, that there are two types of people in the world. Feeling his words ping in my head like sonar searching for belief. Hitting on something, a jagged outcropping of truth.

He was right. There are users. There are the used. But sometimes people can be both at once.

And there's more than that. Victims and victors, and how a person can journey from one to the other. Like Janie. How she's so much stronger than I ever knew. Digging deep in that trench. Then climbing out again. And Cyndra. Her courage to face it. To risk pain. Strength that isn't about power, or force, or how hard you can hit. Strength that is resilience. If you can come back, all the way back, from anything.

And then reach out, beyond yourself, to grab on to something bigger.

Like Clay, an activist at heart, all the way down, not just pretty words. How he'd take anything, put up with anything directed at him, but how he was willing to cross that line for me.

How everyone is struggling for something. Trying to keep the balance.

Struggling to find their way back. Doing the best they can with what they've been dealt. Staying in place, doing anything to keep from sinking. To keep from rising.

Until something changes. Like a day at school, a friend at lunch, someone standing up for you.

And the choice to feel. Standing before you.

Realizing what part is yours. What you can and can't do. Who you are. Who you are meant to be.

More than the sum of all your broken parts.

In the group home TV room, Danny was crying, the robot dog in two pieces in his hands.

Alex sprawled on the sofa, flipping channels. His eyes slid to me, assessed the threat level, and slid back to the TV, unimpressed.

Something inside me burst with the silent force of an underwater explosion. The final piece breaking away. The last of the captive water rushed away in a torrent.

My hands curled into fists, fingertips lifting and pressing into the flesh. Thumbs locked in front. Left fist poised for a jab. Right fist cocked for the straight drive.

Fight back. Punch Alex in the gut, then drive an elbow up into his face, knock him back. Knock him flat. He'd fall against the bookshelf, take it with him. Mr. Lance and Ms. Jay would come. Alex would get grounded and lose phone privileges for breaking the dog. I'd get sent to juvie.

ASH PARSONS

And Danny would be scared of me. And nothing would change. Nothing would be saved or solved. Nothing ever is.

But you can't just accept it. You can't just take it, because it will never stop. Just gather and grow, this dark weight in your chest, a sucking wound that eats more of you away. All the pain that you hide, and never let yourself feel. Never let out.

Lies, half-truths, and things you tell yourself to feel better.

It wasn't that bad.

I have a plan.

I can take it.

I'm in control.

Something, anything, to keep from being a victim. To keep from being helpless.

You can lose yourself to it. To the need to be anything other than never enough.

What Clay said. *That's not pacifism, that's self-annihilation—that's not you.*

I will never just stand by. So what choice do I have?

My hands loosened. I opened my fingers wide, stretching out the fist. Letting go of it.

"Danny," I said. "Give it here. Maybe I can fix it."

Alex flicked a glance up at my eyes. So I gave him the smile that Cyndra said wasn't real. To show him how close it was—the choice.

How close it still was.

Alex smirked but looked away.

Danny walked over, holding out the toy. Gave it to me.

It sat in my open hands.

I let my glare press on Alex. Let him feel the weight of its promise.

Alex glanced at me, popping his knuckles. The show he'd have to back up. I held his gaze until he dropped it.

"Come on," I said to Danny, and led him out of the room.

"You ever have a real dog?" Danny asked as we climbed the stairs.

"Nah. Too much trouble."

"Yeah. Too much trouble."

I stopped. Danny bumped into me.

"It might not be too much trouble for you, Danny. Not if you really want one. It's no trouble at all, then."

Danny's smile was wide, like he was letting me in on a secret. "They said *you* were trouble. When you got here."

I laughed. "They did, huh?"

The smile on my face felt like it belonged there.

That was the choice I had to make. How to move on. What part was mine. How to handle every shitty thing that had happened—or ever would. The choice to let it ride in me, like a bullet lodged in bone, poisoning everything. Or let it pass through, leaving a scar, a mutilated tissue-trail. The possibility and the choices after, everything that's left after the violence has passed.

Scars prove that you're still here. That you can move on. Maybe missing a chunk of yourself, but here, goddamn it, surviving.

And who knows? Maybe you heal.

ACKNOWLEDGMENTS

TO BORROW AND ADAPT from the Bard, I were but little grateful if I could say how much. However, I must attempt it, so here goes.

First and foremost, to my editor, Michael Green. This book exists because of your vision and understanding. It takes a truly gallant heart to see light through the darkness, thank you.

Thanks also to the team at Philomel, and assistant editor Brian Geffen, for his many invaluable additions and for calling down the lightning.

Special thanks to Jodi Reamer, whose passion for this book absolutely blows me away. Your intuition is impeccable; particular thanks for helping me find Clay.

There are people who come along and change the course of your life. Chantel Acevedo, Eve Engle, and Rachel Hawkins, you crazy, brilliant, wonderful life-changers! Thanks for the encouragement, wisdom, sanity-preservation, and most of all, love.

Doraine Bennett, Kara Bietz, and Vicky Shecter: When I picture the four of us, we're in a treetop fort and we're kids, and I've known you all my life. Thanks for your contributions and for helping excavate the ending. Our retreats at the Roost are some of my happiest writer days.

I never thought I'd say "my friend from Twitter" and get teary. Carrie Mesrobian, endless gratitude for your eleventh-hour read-through triage when I panicked. Who would have thought live-tweeting crap TV would lead to such a great, fearless friend? You beggar belief, Mesrobian.

A book is nurtured by every patient listener. Therefore, my heartfelt gratitude to: Christopher Parsons, Jeanette Barnes, Kelly Ann Griffiths, Peter Huggins, and Steven Hamrick.

Jennifer Taylor, here it is in writing: We will always be best friends. For life. That's a promise. You amaze, enlighten, and delight me. Thank you.

Since childhood I have been blessed to know Amy Heidish and Kristen Pickle. Amy, thanks for your dedication to your craft. You inspire me. Thanks also for your endless patience with my many questions. I love that we can "talk shop" and have heart-to-hearts in the same breath. Kristen, thanks for always being there for me and my family. What a remarkably generous spirit you possess. LYLAS, both.

Profound thanks to the Highlights Foundation, which granted me a scholarship to attend their amazing workshop at Chautauqua.

My sister, Caroline Banks, is my first reader. The writers know what that means. It's a BFD. You're a dream-protector, a possibility-seer. Thank you, Caroline, for your unfailing belief and enthusiasm. You are the bravest woman I know. I love and admire you beyond my ability to say.

Jack, Gus, and Nick, my boys, I love you so much it makes me catch my breath, every breath.

Bob Parsons, there is no other like you. I continue to learn so much from you, about perseverance, art, life, and love. Thank you so much for your support and for your calls to balance when I lose myself in the work. I can't express how much I appreciate your insights into this story, your encouragement, and your pride. I love you.

This book is dedicated in loving memory to my parents, John and Konny Banks. The jagged geography of loss leaves me speechless here.

"Treasure these moments, they are all too fleeting."—JB